A
Vision
of
Doom

Mycal Bono imagined the city of Ricardo falling.

He saw the framework buckle and twist. He saw the great towers sway and split apart, spilling millions of people into the air as the hard outer crust melded with the soft, organic innards.

In his mind's eye he could see people, rubble and machinery tumble to the earth in a rush.

It had taken a thousand years to create the vast union of Structures that now existed. Mycal Bono had just turned thirty, and now it was his job to destroy it all.

A

Hostage

FOR

Hinterland

ARSEN DARNAY

BALLANTINE BOOKS • NEW YORK

A somewhat different version of this novel was serialized in
Galaxy magazine under the title "Helium." Copyright © 1975
by UPD Publishing Corporation.

Library of Congress Catalog Card Number: 76-13584

ISBN 0-345-25306-X-150

Manufactured in the United States of America

First Edition: December 1976

Cover art by Boris Vallejo

A
Hostage
FOR
Hinterland

1

The Bastions of the Whore

Four kilometers from Ricardo, the horsemen stopped for a rest. While their ponies stretched down to graze, the men stared up at the Acropolis. They were Ecofreaks and far from home, dressed in beaded leather suits and wearing floppy black hats. Their long hair was braided, their faces tanned; but these were not ordinary herdsmen, as evidenced by the ornate ceremonial daggers and the gilded red Crestmore bibles that hung from their belts.

Mutagrass rolled in the breeze behind them. It thinned out ahead as steppe gave way to no man's land—the Desolation, in tribal parlance—a dusty, boulder-strewn ring around the city made by the deadly emanations of gravitron.

Mycal Bono, leader of the group, took off his hat and wiped his forehead with the back of his hand. He closed and opened his eyes to ease the wind sting. Then he threw his head back to see Ricardo's five looming towers. Today the tips were lost in moving clouds; he couldn't see the towers in their entirety. Drilla-glass mirrored the setting sun. A reticulation of dark plastosteel held the glass in place and supported the structures. At this distance, the frame resembled a screen of hexagons.

Bono thought: *Poisonous silver stems. Rooted in the Desolation. Full of humanity.*

He shook his head. He had not seen a structure in years, and the prospect of Ricardo, especially at close proximity, was awesome. Most structures, including those of Ricardo, were at least three thousand meters from root to crown, an unbelievable height. The sway

1

of their towers induced dizziness. The observer felt that the structures leaned threateningly down toward him.

Bono turned away, plagued by a childhood memory. It had come on him early that morning while boarding the large helicopters near Wellhead for the long flight north. The feeling had persisted. The forty-kilometer ride from the staging station hadn't shaken his mood.

His father had taken him to Husten, a mono-tower city. He'd been a small boy then. Panic had gripped him a short way into the Desolation. The gravitron vibrations had tightened about his body like so many invisible claws, and he had screamed and fought until his father had sent him back with a mutant slave. At the time his relatives had teased him, calling him a true tribesman—one who couldn't stand the grav.

Now men rested all around him. Some had dismounted. Some sat and stared at Ricardo's visible parts below the clouds. Talk buzzed.

To his left the heavyset Sonder, physicist of the group, explained the mysteries of gravitron to a youngster they had picked up at the staging station to take the horses back.

"Drums," Sonder was saying. "Drums in the caves below the towers. They generate the stuff. And our helium cools the machines. No helium, Freddy, and *poof!* Down she goes."

Bono imagined Ricardo falling. He saw the framework buckle and twist. He saw the towers sag, split apart, spilling millions of people into the air—the hard outer crust and the soft, organic, mushy innards. In his mind's eye he saw people, rubble, and machinery fall down in a rush. Then he imagined Desolation dust rising like a veil to cover the scene.

It was a vision of the Great Change—the end of the structures. Like many other young Activists, Bono had heard the Older Tack hold forth about it with a Crestmore bible open in his hand. "The structures must be destroyed," Old Tack had thundered with a balled, veined fist shaking the air. "We can't let the Abomination take over Earth again!" And with that, OT had always hit the table with a crash. Old Tack had had a florid face, bushy gray eyebrows, and eyes that flashed. You couldn't help remembering such a man. He left a deep impression, especially on the young.

Old Tack was dead. Like the legendary Moses of the Biblibooks, he had died before his dream was fulfilled. Unlike the legendary Moses, he hadn't even glimpsed the promised land.

Bono's situation was not without irony: the least enthusiastic of the younger Activists stood before Ricardo with a mandate to negotiate the last and decisive helium deal. Bono's assignment amounted to nothing less than the destruction of Union's thirty-nine structures. Would Mycal Bono, the silent doubter, achieve OT's dream?

Bono fell into a brooding contemplation of his role. He felt extremely small and puny—a mote of dust in the vast sweep of history that had created the Union of Structures. A thousand years seemed a very long time against his thirty.

A thousand years, yes, give or take a handful. The last of the so-called Limited Nuclear Wars had been followed by a period of interregnum. The last one had been—which? LNW XII? LNW XIII? Bono never could remember. At the Academy of Action, he had had to memorize the circumstances surrounding each war, but how they all ran into each other in his mind. Well, that didn't matter a great deal. What mattered were the structures.

Bono tried to imagine their genesis: how the ancient city dwellers had invented gravitron, with whose aid vertical cities could be flung into the sky. The ancients had gone straight from a molelike existence in underground bunkers into the heights—in one gigantic leap, as it were. In his mind Bono pictured structures rising out of the rubble, yes, like poisonous stems. Structureman had found an answer to the scarcity of usable

3

land. Remarkable as it seemed, nevertheless it was true—nearly one hundred million people in structures occupied a mere eight hundred square kilometers of ground, all of it along the coasts. Their fusion reactors ran on hydrogen ions that were plentiful in the sea.

What a shock it must have been to the pious tribal elders, it occurred to him. If the ancient tribesmen had been anything like the Older Tack, they must have fallen into paroxysms of rage when the first reports of structures came filtering back to Hinterland. The Technology Beast has risen again! No sooner dead than resurrected. Foul Phoenix. And the old hatred had burst into flame again.

Bono knew himself to be a product of that hatred. A thousand years of hate had caused him to sit here before Ricardo on a pony with a secret locked in his brain. The tribes had waited a thousand years for this opportunity. Now they only needed a small assist, a very small favor from Union. If only Union could be duped! If Union somehow could be persuaded to mix up the poison it would have to swallow—then Technology would be finished.

Or would it? Bono experienced a stir of doubt. Union might be destroyed. But then, for all they knew, Technology might rise up elsewhere—in Europe, in Asia, in Australia. Since LNW XII or XIII, whichever it was, contact with those continents had been lost—more by choice than necessity. Structure-men had the means to travel. But exploration was not their long suit. Life in structures seemed to be an end in itself—or else it destroyed curiosity. Maybe. The men of Union lived too far from the surface of the Earth. They saw it through windows. Always. The horizon did not entice them. Bono guessed that life on other continents must be like life in Hinterland: simple and savage. Structure-man wanted no part of that. If it weren't for helium . . .

Helium.

That noble gas was essential for the gravitron reaction. And the pipeline through which it flowed was like an umbilical cord that bound structure dwellers to the Earth. Against their will, in a sense. Bono suspected that Union would pay no attention to the tribes at all if it weren't for those rich Texahoma wells—or if they could get enough helium out of the air, which they could not. But they *did* need helium. And therefore their missiles ringed North America, aimed inland, a perpetual threat.

Bono shook his head. The problem was all too vast, too much, too improbable. His task seemed overwhelming. He had no confidence in this venture, yet here he was. It seemed wrong, somehow.

Bono sighed and turned to his right.

Sunk deep into his saddle, tiresome old Franco Dart had reached over and now pulled Bono's sleeve. He pointed to a hovering airship some distance from the road. Union airships, held aloft by gravitron, resembled large glistening rods. One blunt, rounded end of the ship faced the horsemen. The ship had picked them up a kilometer or two outside the staging station and had shadowed their approach ever since.

Dart said: "They're filming, Mycal. They film and film. I'll bet you Reston Proctor is watching us. I'll bet he sees us talking."

On Bono's left, Sonder, oblivious to all else, was still lecturing: "No, Freddy, you don't get it. The vibes make the *steel* light. Light as feathers. It's the plasto-steel, not the drilla-glass."

Bono didn't answer Dart. He still mused about his chances of success, that worrisome childhood memory in the background.

Dart peered at Bono with a disapproving look. The chief's hooked nose and forked black beard gave Bono an aggressive air, but Dart saw a dreamy haze in the leader's eyes, a telltale trembling around his lips. Bono had a good face, but he lacked something—that special quality: leadership.

With a measure of pride, Dart recalled how he had opposed Bono's appointment as chief of mission. Dart had protested, oh yes. He had the courage to oppose, no matter his age. His was a voice of wisdom among the brash young men around Jonny Tack.

"Go with him," Tack had said. "Keep your eyes on him."

But Tack had sent him as a senior advisor, without any real authority. That made Dart mourn the passing of the Older Tack. Now, there was a man!

"Mycal," Dart called again. "I said, they're filming us!"

"What? Oh, yes. You've said that before. The Media."

"It's more serious than that. They use the films for intelligence. They study our faces. They build profiles of us. Psychometry."

Bono shrugged. "We can't stop them."

"No, not *that!* But you must be aware of it."

"I am aware. Believe me, Franco, I'm aware."

A group in the rear laughed uproariously at something. The noise startled a flock of black carries. They rose from the long mutagrass, flew low over the ground, then dropped out of sight again.

Dart wondered if the men were laughing at him. He threw them a suspicious look.

"Look, Freddy, imagine a molecule like this, see?" Sonder was becoming animated. "Fifteen in a row? The gravitron vibes come in here, see? And they make these little balls stretch. Got it?"

Bono glanced at Freddy and saw that the lad still hadn't got it. Then he turned to Dart, aware that the old man was unhappy. The younger men all humored Dart, the last surviving member of the old core of Activists.

"What do you think, Franco?" Bono gestured toward Ricardo with his hat. "The bastions of the whore —will they fall this time?"

"All thirty-nine of them, on all the coasts. It is written." Dart slapped the red Crestmore bible hanging on a chain from his belt. " 'Her bastions shall crumble, and from the dust shall rise a new time.' "

"It is written," Bono murmured. He stared up. "Collapse they will," he said without conviction. "Sooner or later. The question is when. This time? Or some other time?"

6

Dart answered: "This is *your* chance, Mycal. It's a good chance. Everything aids you: Jonny's courage, Unsler's senility. You're the man if you want to be. You're the chief of mission."

Bono's close friends thought him quiet, sensitive, curious, and somewhat retiring. Those who knew him less well considered him a sullen, moody man. But unlike other sullen, moody men, he was not forever in the lotus posture praying for deliverance from Technology. He was no zealot. But only Bono knew the degree of his own ambivalence about the Activist cause.

Now he felt the excruciating pain of uncertainty. The gigantic pentastructure up ahead attracted and repelled him in turn. Inwardly he scoffed at the crude negotiating strategy Jonny Tack had dictated. The tribes had waited a thousand years for this moment. Why did they have to implement the plan within a month? Couldn't they get microwelders instead, patiently, piece by piece? No, apparently not. Tack had no patience with long-range strategies. Now! Today! But Jonny's hurry, more than anything else, destroyed Bono's confidence. He despaired of success. Yet, at the same time, he had accepted the job. Why? *Pride,* he told himself. *I can't just disregard the prophesies. If this is the time, if the scheme succeeds, my name will live in history. And yet . . .*

"No, no, the other way about," Sonder said. "The vibes enter the atom like this. In a spiral. They loosen the electronic grip. Yes—like that."

Bono turned to Dart. "All right, Franco. We'll see. We might as well go in there and see what fate holds." He swiveled in his saddle and waved an arm. "Mount up, men," he called. "In the name of Ecology, let's go and do it."

In a moment the horsemen plunged down the side of the rise and coaxed their struggling, reluctant ponies into the vibration-filled Desolation.

The Five Percenter

Rivera French left the communications room of the Bureau of Tribal Affairs and, accompanied by a crew of experts, traveled by jumptube to the West Tower reception hall where, traditionally, BTA received Hinterland delegations come to negotiate.

On the way he turned to a member of his staff. "Have you called the Ambassador?"

The staff man nodded.

"And?"

"They thanked us for the information but said that no one would be present at the reception."

"Did you ask them why? Have they been told to stay away, or is Andros Barney playing games?"

The man said: "They acted very reserved. I couldn't get much out of them."

"Did you talk to the Ambassador personally?"

"Yes. I got the feeling Barney resented my calling. He is used to dealing with you."

"Well, there's a nice start," French said.

They arrived in the reception hall and found a crowd pressed against gold roping that hung in slack curves from silver posts. Media crews stood in readiness with cameras and lights near the double-winged portal. Beside a table in the back, servants polished wineglasses. Huge green banners with the white Ecology symbol in the center hung from the walls and trembled in the flow of ventilation air.

The BTA experts arranged themselves in the center—a clump of yellow robes. French, a middle-sized, sturdy man in a purple robe, walked some steps ahead of them and took up a stance beneath a chandelier. He had long blond hair, carelessly tossed. His face, tanned an orange-brown by the rays of artisun, revealed his tension in a movement of muscles under the skin of his cheeks. He pulled down on his robe so that it wouldn't bunch above the belt and waited.

Seven weeks ago word had come through intelligence channels that the Accommodationist faction of the Ecofreak tribe had been ousted by the Activist minority. BTA had worked five years to prepare for this helium round. That news instantly destroyed five years of work. Union marched into this battle blind. No Activist had held power in Ecofreak since the Helium War of '11. Almost nothing was known about Activist personalities, and French was both curious and anxious.

He blamed himself for the situation. His intelligence apparatus had failed to predict the political shift. The Chief Negotiator had visibly cooled toward French as a consequence—and no wonder.

Proctor expected much from this negotiating round —and so did French. Proctor had formed a revolutionary group immediately after the series of executions that had marked the Dynastic Proclamation four years back. Only recently had Proctor drawn French into the plot. French had joined eagerly, flattered by the distinction. Yet now, as the time drew near, he had failed Proctor. The Secret Agenda depended on Ecofreak participation.

French stood and waited, growing impatient.

Impatience was one of his failings.

Miri always scolded him for it. She said he was like a man who tried to leapfrog over himself. "You're a trinity of impatience," she said. "Impatient in love— you proposed to me an hour after we met. Impatient in eating—you bolt your food as if you *wanted* an ulcer. Impatient to rise—what do you want to be? Unifier?"

French always answered: "I'd do better than Bernie Unsler, girl."

Miri disapproved of his ambition. She came from a high-level family and so could not understand a slum kid's drive for the bigger world. Branco was *way* in the bottom. He'd wanted up, up. Dammit, he wanted to rise, and nothing wrong with that! The top was now ruled by stupid, evil men. You had to rise to right the wrongs.

French had his eyes on the floor of the hall. The emblem of the Unsler family was reproduced on the white tiles—a red flower complete with cup, stem, and a single leaf. Ten years ago, when French had entered service at age twenty, this floor had been covered by Ricardo's ancient symbol, the spiral, depicting the flow of gravitron vibrations. Unsler had gathered the power, both symbolic and real, but now his hands grew slack on the reins and his son, Sidney, waxed strong. French wished Proctor luck with the Secret Agenda. Proctor would be a better ruler than Unsler.

An attendant by the double-winged door, whose eyes had been hefted to a narrow observation slit, now turned and called back: "They're here."

The murmuring crowd fell silent. The doors flew open and the Ecofreaks entered Ricardo in a wedge-shaped formation with Bono at their head. It had to be Bono, as per dispatch. Hoofs clattered on the tiles. The ponies were small, hairy mutants and had frightened eyes. The tribesmen blinked in the floodlights of Media.

The noble tribe of Ecofreak, French reflected. They were the largest and most powerful tribe among the peoples of Hinterland. They always came on horseback, as a matter of principle. At home they used the products of Technology with relish. But when they came before the Enemy, they pretended to be purer than the pure.

The delegation stopped before him and French bowed low beneath the chandelier. The smell of horses brought to mind memories of clandestine Hinterland missions. He watched Bono swing out of the saddle and observed the supple grace of the man, the fierce expression on the face. Bono moved like a herdsman. He probably owned whole countries of silvery land speckled with cattle, white Harvey hare, and the black prairie birds tribesmen called "carry" after carrion. Bono's spurs rang on the tiles as he approached. The Crestmore bible on his belt swung on a tarnished silver chain.

As they shook hands, French observed the face

closely. Bono's narrowed eyes were cool, unfriendly. Bushy brows, hooked nose, a sharply sculptured, forked black beard. Aggression. Yet French also sensed a disturbing shyness in the man. *Shy men are poor negotiators,* went through his mind.

They exchanged traditional greetings under blazing Media lights.

"Welcome, Chief Bono, to Ricardo, the Pearl of Union. May your stay be profitable."

Bono answered: "We come under duress, Mr. French, to protest the threat of your missiles."

"We threaten no one but ask only for that which we need to live."

French led Bono to the waiting BTA experts and introduced them one by one. Then Bono did the same in turn, surreptitiously assessing the young Deputy Assistant, the innocent charm of the man: those curls and locks of blond hair, that cleft in the chin, that small pulpy nose, that dimple in the cheek. His whole look of careless, twinkling bravado disguised a tough and able man. Bono recalled French's history, having read it over again on the flight north.

French was a vegetable smuggler from a notorious slum level in East Tower who, by dint of native abilities and a fortunate marriage to a high-level girl (he'd met her in Branco, which was a kind of artists' haunt, among other things), had been lifted up and educated. In the service of the Bureau of Tribal Affairs, he used his pugnacious skills against the tribes. Some years back he had earned fame among the tribes as a reckless agent. They had called him "Starface," in Hinterland, after a small scar on his forehead that he covered up with makeup when in the field. Now French was chief of intelligence, though he carried the title of Deputy Assistant for Public Affairs.

A shrill neigh made them look up. The ponies had begun to panic in the gravitron vibrations. They reared, screamed, and kicked in all directions. Tribesmen rushed to aid a youngster who fought to control the animals. The crowd laughed at the turbulence. It took a moment to unload the pack animals. Then the

11

youngster leaped into the saddle, gave Bono the raised-fist salute of the tribes, and with a cry drove the horses toward the entrance. They disappeared in a cloud of dust.

French met the last of the tribesmen and recognized him, not by appearance but by name. Franco Dart was a small, old, and wrinkled little man with suspicious eyes. French knew him as one of Old Tack's not-so-brilliant associates. He had been a member of the Ecofreak embassy many years back—a First or Second Secretary—one of the few Activists with a profile in BTA's computers.

French turned to Bono. "Shall we toast your safe arrival?"

Bono gave a stiff little bow. "At your service."

They walked to the table at the back. Their followers came behind them like a comet's tail, while the crowd gaped and savored the traces of rank horse smell left behind by the departed herd.

Against the back of the hall hung circular emblems of all Hinterland tribes: Maoling, Peacefreak, Narodnik, Twin River Compromise, Bluegrass Territory, Planetfriends, Gulfrats, Ecofreak, and others. French pointed them out to Bono, but Bono couldn't see them properly.

Moments before, he had begun to see double. Now murmurs in his stomach signaled the onset of nausea. The clammy feel of cold sweat spread from his armpits and neck over his body. His hands trembled as he took the glass of bubbly wine and his tongue slurred the words as he responded to French's toast.

Waiters brought sandwiches on trays, but Bono shook his head.

French turned to him. "I don't see anyone from the Ecofreak embassy. We notified them of your arrival. Did *you* tell them to stay away?"

Bono nodded. "Barney is not a member of our party. We wouldn't expect him to play a role in these negotiations."

"Then why hasn't he been replaced?"

"He shall be," Bono replied. "In due time."

12

"I must say the sudden change in leadership caught all of us by surprise here."

Bono did not answer. He stared into his half-empty glass and blinked in the characteristic manner of a man with gravitron bends, surprising French.

"Tell me, Chief Bono. Is this your first time in a structure?"

The tribesman nodded.

"In that case you've still got it in front of you."

"The Adjustment?"

French nodded. "But it isn't all that bad. It takes less than a week. By the time of the opening ball, you'll be completely attuned."

"I don't suppose we could skip . . . the opening ball?"

French smiled. "Impossible, Chief. Tradition is tradition. Receptions, balls, rituals. How can we hide a man of your distinction from the curious eyes of the ladies. Some of your countrymen are very gallant."

Bono heard French but could not concentrate on the conversation. He felt an unreasoning rage and longed to give it expression. "I'm a strict constructionist," he said, just to be saying something. "I shun frivolity."

Bono's feelings about the subject were more complex than that, but in the eyes of the blond Deputy Assistant he preferred to seem a conventional Activist.

"A good rule, by and large," French answered. "Let me assure you that Union respects your wishes. But the opening ball is absolutely unavoidable. The tradition goes way back—"

He saw an expression of pain flash across Bono's features.

"Are you starting to feel the effects already?"

Bono's rage grew and grew. Pressure choked him. The feeling was entirely physical. His mind and spirit were benevolently inclined toward French, but something made him want to strike out.

"H-how can you stand it," he brought forth. "Th-this . . . v-vibration." His hand described a circle.

13

Wine spilled. Servants rushed in to wipe up the mess. "Are you p-people mad? When will you l-leave your er-rant ways!"

French looked at him indulgently. "Where would you have us go? Where should we put our millions? The tribes control all the desirable land. Short of atomics, how could we prevail against you? We like the High Culture—we also like compression. We don't force you to live here. But it's to your advantage to maintain Union. You've got no use for helium . . . And neither of us wants the alternative."

He noted a pulse of pain in Bono's face. The man's elbows jerked outward.

"You'll get used to it. In five days you'll be adjusted. You won't even feel the vibes," French added.

Bono was a five-percenter, French thought, *one of the small minority that couldn't take the vibes. Tough sailing lay ahead!*

Bono was preoccupied. His lips trembled as he tried to form words.

"I . . . don't u-understand . . . it. Y-your life span . . . is fifty-five at best. You're deliv—delib-berately . . . deliverately . . ."

"Yes?" French prompted.

". . . k-killing yourselves," Bono completed.

Then he took himself in control. His eyes gained focus. His cheeks stiffened under the beard. He took a step toward the table, but his feet seemed heavy. He placed his glass on the white tablecloth with a studied gesture.

Turning to French, he spoke very slowly. "With your permission, Mr. French, we'll now take our leave. We've had a long flight and an even longer ride."

French bowed. "Of course, Chief. As you wish. Jumptubes are waiting outside. Until you and your associates have learned to operate them, one of my men will guide you by remote control."

14

The Chief Negotiator

The Bureau of Tribal Affairs occupied nearly one quarter of Lebel 125, or Old Top, as it was called. It had been the summit of Central Tower until the end of the seventh century, when helium-cooling had dramatically improved grav-drum performance and two hundred new levels, spacious in the extreme, each with several stories, had been added to the tower. Nevertheless, there clung to Old Top a certain hoary magnificence, a memory of wealth and of rooftop gardens open to the public, from where structure folk had gazed out over the Atlantic or Hinterland through pressure-sealed glass.

BTA's current quarters had been the Lord Mayor's domain, and the Lord Mayor's former office now belonged to Reston Proctor. Wood paneling nearly black with age formed three walls of the spacious room. Slender white columns a meter from the wall held up a vaulted ceiling from which the iridescent colors of an exquisite micromosaic reflected light. The outer side of the office, beyond the columns, was an outjutting terrace shut off by floor-to-ceiling drilla-glass. From that terrace Proctor could look across at West Tower or down at the intertower beltway that linked Center to West like a slack hose of translucent silver and was filled with motion at all times of day and night.

Proctor sat behind his desk. Over its cluttered surface he watched the screen of a visiset that had been rolled in over the heavy red carpet, leaving a trail on the soft fibers. His face was pensive, eyes impassive. He wore the shimmering blue robe of a Big, the sleeves rolled up to the elbows. Proctor was a short, heavy man whose powerful neck, barrel-like torso, massive round head, heavy jowls, and an abnormally large and outjutting chin suggested the legendary rhinoceros.

He sat surrounded by mementoes of his rise to

15

power. Models of missiles on his desk marked his years in Defense. On the walls hung certificates of appointment to ever higher jobs in various parts of the bureaucracy: Defense, Commerce, Public Order, Media, Health. Between these framed and ornamented pieces of scriptoplast under glass, and on little tables strewn about the room were signed photographs of virtually every member of the Unsler clan, including an inordinately large holographic representation of Unsler himself. It hung by itself on a wall behind Proctor's desk. On a golden plaque set into the gilded frame of the picture was an inscription reproduced from the Unifier's hand: "To the best damn administrator who has ever served our noble cause. Bernie."

In the visiscreen tribesmen stepped into upright jumptubes parked in rows outside the reception hall. Proctor watched them.

The flat remorite on his desk lit up; a slip of scripto extruded from its slit. Proctor reached to get it. His secretary had written on it: "Blottingham insists that you brief him (telcall is enough) on your assessment of the delegation."

Proctor crumpled the note in a meaty fist. He held it for a second, thinking of pear-shaped Blottingham, whose power increased as Unsler's declined. Then he threw the slip into the dusto and wrote a note for Mrs. Sedlig: "Call Blottingham and tell him to jump down a shaft. Tell him verbatim." Below he penned a large, bold *P*. Then he stuck the slip into the remorite, leaned back in his thronelike chair, crossed his thick arms across his chest, and turned his attention back to the screen.

But his concentration quickly wandered, his mind exercised by Blottingham's peremptory message.

Well, he thought, *as far as I'm concerned, Unsler can do what he bloody well pleases.* Proctor felt strong for the moment. He would not jump every time Unsler's pear-shaped Staff Chief whistled. The helium round was underway—a poor time to change the Chief Negotiator. *A few more weeks,* he thought. *A few more weeks . . .*

His blunt fingers drummed on his desk as he watched the tribesmen. Terrified. They were terrified. They gripped the waist-high tube rails as the jump-tubes rose above the movebelts. They looked manageable enough, these youngish men. Proctor had hopes that they would deliver the brief interdiction he needed to carry out the plan. Of course, one never knew—

The deep, melodious chime of his tel sounded. French!

He reached for the small-screened tel to his right, punched a button. French came on. Behind him, through the telbooth glass, Proctor saw two BTA staffers talking.

"Just a minute," Proctor rumbled. He reached for the black cube of his intercept. A spiderweb of wires trembled on top of the device. He touched its sides, and the cube turned red.

"Have you got your intercept on?" he asked.

French nodded.

"Very well," Proctor said, "tell me what I already know."

French chuckled and gave his report while Proctor wondered how these men would react to his proposal. After a while he broke in.

"How does Bono strike you?"

"Fanatical, uncomplicated, probably rigid . . . But it's too early to tell, Res. You saw his behavior. He's a five-percenter, and I'd wager he'll have a tough Adjustment. Grav-bends make people act strangely."

Proctor said: "I'm watching him now. He's jerky, all right. His eyes are erratic."

"Another thing, Res. He calls himself a strict constructionist, claims to dislike frivolity—by which I guess he means the social side of things."

Proctor, eyes on the screen, nodded and turned to French. "Our women are the devil's brood? Pollute the tribal blood?"

French smiled. "Now, Res, I don't think I'd go as far as that. That'd be the extreme form of the disease."

Proctor recalled the last Ecofreak delegation. "It would be refreshing—after the debaucheries of '51."

French laughed. "I wouldn't expect high moral tone, if I were you. Tack's followers can't be entirely opposed to mingling. OT is dead, you know. Remember the Grand Alliance?"

Proctor frowned.

The five-year-old episode still reverberated. In 1051 Jonny Tack had come to Ricardo with the helium delegation. A technical advisor, or some such thing. Soon a passionate love affair had bloomed between Regina Unsler and the young man, despite the Crestmore prohibitions against the mingling of tribal and structure seed. It had been an insane, trying time, that. Unsler had seen in this romance a new opportunity for expanding his power. For weeks frantic negotiations were carried out under his orders to form a Grand Alliance between Union and Hinterland by intermarriage. Proctor belonged to the hard-line school. He had opposed the venture even though he had led the negotiations; but fortunately the Accommodation policy, as it came to be called—favored both by Unsler and the Ecofreak council—was scotched by the intervention of the Older Tack.

"Don't remind me," Proctor said to French. "That was one time when I was grateful for the late OT. He made short work of that romance. Now, what about strategy? Did you get any hints?"

In the screen he could see that the tribesmen had reached West Tower's central shaft. The tubes rose quickly with the upthrust traffic, bottom jets ablaze. The tribesmen were afraid. None looked down into the chasm and none looked up. None gaped at the many tubes, the movement of pod-shaped elevators, or at the common people moving up and down on hundreds of slide bars, arms and legs wrapped about the darkish rods. The men stared ahead with rigid expressions, terrified but much too proud to show it.

"Bono revealed nothing," French said. "I haven't polled the staff yet. But I still stand by my predictions. They'll try to wreck us economically. Activists can't have any other strategy. The question is how they came to power. If we could answer that question, we'd know a good deal more. For the moment, the best I can do is speculate; and I predict they'll try for a Very Big as hostage—someone from the Meyer family, say. Then I expect that they'll ask for half of our plasto-steel production, which would mean the end of expansion and the beginning of population control. Unsler could never survive that. But I expect that they'll settle for thirty percent. If, that is. If . . ."

Proctor looked back at the telescreen. "If we make a credible military gesture."

French nodded.

Proctor was silent. How to strike a deal with Activists? Their objective was total destruction—and he couldn't give them that. So he would have to find something they really wanted, something short of total war but more than mere economic damage. Perhaps he'd give them Portla structure in the northwest, a hotbed of Unsler support . . .

He *had* to find a deal. The plot probably leaked like a sieve. The Group couldn't be held together for another five years.

"We must get a better feel for their strategy," he rumbled. "See if you can talk to the Ambassador in a day or two. Barney *must* be unhappy with this bunch. He might play with us."

"*If* they tell him anything. I expect he'll be frozen out. Bono even said as much."

"Barney can't be cut out that easily. And it doesn't hurt to try."

"I'll do it," French said, nodding.

"And you better close the loop with our people in the regions. I don't want any sudden surprises on the other coasts."

French nodded.

"Call personally."

"Will do."

"And let's talk further about this tomorrow morning."

Through the telbooth glass Proctor saw the two BTA staff people conclude their conversation. They waved to each other and passed out of sight. They reminded him of something.

"Rivera," he said. "One more thing. Have you talked with Darby Dickens today?"

French shook his head.

"We lost two more people to flame attacks last night."

"You're kidding."

"I'm serious," Proctor asserted. "Ten deaths in as many weeks. That far exceeds chance."

"Do you think Sidney is deliberately picking on BTA?"

"Of course I do! And I think it's more than that. I think the flames are getting encouragement from Top Level. If this keeps up, I'll have to retaliate. Top Level is pressuring us—through the flames."

"Your popularity?"

Proctor stared into the screen, communicating with his eyes. "That . . . and perhaps other things." French understood. The Secret Agenda. "Be careful," Proctor continued. "Don't move about alone. Always take some men with you on the movebelts, especially at night. I can't afford to lose you now."

A grin lit up French's face; his dimples showed. "I can take care of myself."

Proctor's eyes turned angry. "Balderdash," he growled. French still behaved as if he were a Branco gangster. "Take people with you when you move about. Tell Darby to assign you a guard."

"I'll think about it."

"No, Rivera, do it. The conflict may deepen now that Ecofreak is here. I just insulted Blottingham. He also belongs to that group peripherally."

French nodded, amused and flattered by Proctor's concern. He had been on sixteen Hinterland missions and had come back alive. He was a Branco kid. Sidney's flames might harass the people all over the Acropolis, but they stayed away from Branco. A few noble sadists wouldn't have a chance against him.

"And come see me in the morning," Proctor said. "First thing."

Proctor punched a button, and French became a single fading dot of light in the tiny screen.

Into the Tub

Bono stood before the embassy door and pressed the bell. Faintly from within he could hear soft chimes. The door opened, and he entered a terazzoed lobby followed by his retinue. A curved stairway led up to a second level, where Barney stood tall and grave, dressed in a white robe like a Very Big. His white hair fell down straight, structure style.

Bono walked up the stairs toward Barney. Pressure squeezed his lungs and eyes. Terror gripped his mind. His feet were lead. He had the urge to gasp for air in huge, noisy bursts, but he suppressed it. Barney seemed far away, blurred.

The Ambassador looked down at the approaching Bono. *How young he is! And the delegation—a tableau of inexperience.*

"Welcome, Mycal Bono, welcome to Ricardo."

Bono blinked. Barney was an Accommodationist, a man who, through the years, had lived in structures as Ecofreak's representative. A man you couldn't trust. Nevertheless, Barney looked friendly. His hand was large and warm. Crow's-feet extended like rays from his greenish, solicitous eyes. Behind the Ambassador, reflected in mirrors, Bono saw the embassy staff assembled to receive them.

He nodded to Barney, afraid to speak lest his leaden tongue slur the words.

"I knew your father well," said Barney. "We fought together against Maoling in the war of 1009."

Barney wondered how youngsters like these could have wrested the power from Franklin, Denton, Ruff and the others. Jonny Tack had demanded much in the way of information from the embassy, but he had provided nothing in return since the shift. These youngsters would have to bring him up-to-date, whether they wished to or not. Something very big must have happened back home to vault the tiny splinter minority into the political saddle.

Then, noting the rigid look on Bono's face and surprised that the man clung to his hand, it dawned on Barney what the problem was. *I must be getting insensitive in my old age.*

Simultaneously, he saw Bono's elbows jerk outward, saw the head fly back, saw the chief take in air with a violent gasp. Barney felt a surge of pity for the miserable young man.

"Smith, Duffy!" he commanded sharply over his shoulder. "We have a five-percenter. Get the tub ready."

As the two men ran off, he turned back to Bono. "Relax, son. You'll be all right. We'll take care of you."

He put an arm around Bono's shoulder and, dispensing with ceremony, guided the youth through a corridor formed by the curious embassy staff. He walked slowly, knowing that Bono's feet must feel heavy.

Regardless of his ideology, he thought, *a man's a man; and if he is a five-percenter, he deserves both pity and care. Will he be ready for the ball? Should I seek a postponement?*

They went up a flight of stairs. Bono gasped without restraint now in that imitation of an epileptic fit that gravitron imposed on some. The worst part of it was the embarrassment. Adjustment reduced a man to a pitiful caretaker of a defective biomachine.

Up ahead, in an open corridor, closed off by a wooden rail, Smith and Duffy carried small sacks in hand—red gelatin. They scurried along. Barney heard the rush of water from the bath.

"It'll be all right," he assured Bono again. "A minute or two, and we'll get you relief."

He looked back at the group that had followed, a mixture of staff and delegates. He searched for his secretary. His eyes snagged on Franco Dart. Now there was a familiar face. He nodded to Dart, a plan half forming in his mind.

"Martha," he called, seeing the woman at last, "get me a sedative and a glass of water."

He moved Bono slowly along toward the sound of water.

Bono let himself be led, his terror diminished. He let himself go. Mentally he gave himself over entirely to the care of others. In the bathroom, with water rushing into the tub, Barney told him to undress. He complied and stood naked on cold tiles, shuddering and shivering in fits. Two men stirred a red powder into steaming water. Bono smelled plastosteel and inferred that the red color of the powder came from that. His arms and chest were covered by goose pimples. The sheen of his skin was bluish beneath the tan.

The bathroom door opened a crack. A hand reached in, holding a cup of water, some pills.

"Take these," Barney told him.

Bono obediently swallowed.

"And now into the tub with you," Barney said.

Regina

In the late afternoon, Sidney had jumped off the lip of his North Tower domain and after a long free-fall through North Shaft had landed by parachute in the Pit.

At his insistence Regina had been present. When the riots erupted, her bodyguard formed a ring about her and brought her back to Top Level West, considerably shaken by the episode. She asked Selma, her favorite maid, to call St. Theresa of Carmen on Level 188 Central and ask that Sister Serenita be sent to her at once.

Serenita came, a tall, severe old woman in a huge winged coif and blue robe. They retired to the meditation chamber of Regina's extensive domain, where Regina lay down on the couch and Serenita, seated

beside her, read to her calmly from the Biblibooks until the girl fell asleep.

Selma awakened her some time later. Serenita had
returned to the convent by them, and Regina was momentarily confused. She had dreamed about Serenita,
a confused jumble. The nun had spoken about the
Great Change, whatever that signified; and there had
been some business with a turquoise ring.

Selma was excitable, and her eyes opened wide,
resembling fried eggs. "Mistress," she cried, shaking
Regina, "come quickly. We've spied some tribesmen
near the Desolation. It must be *them!*"

They ran through the chambers of Regina's apartment, then passed through a glass door to spiral stairs
that led up to a rooftop garden covered by many small
domes of drilla-glass. In the west the sun reddened the
horizon, but they had still enough light to see the
clump of horsemen through telescopes. Presently the
tribesmen plunged down the side of a small rise, and
soon they were obscured by dust.

Regina sighed and walked pensively back through
the lush tropical vegetation of her garden, down the
graveled path, to the spiral stairs; she was stirred into
memories of Jonny Tack.

"Roll a visiset into my favorite room," she told
Selma. "I'll watch them on the evening news. Meanwhile I'll take a bath."

"Mistress, Clafto Meyer called while you slept and
said he must speak with you."

Regina frowned and didn't answer.

Mention of Clafto set her brooding, and she still
pouted in her marble bath, lounging in the recessed
oval pool while fountains played all around her.
Mounds of foam lay on the water, and she flicked the
fluffy icebergs toward the cone-mountains of her
deeply tanned knees.

She thought of the abject slavery Sidney imposed
on her by his brotherly violence, of her father's inaccessibility, and of swarthy Clafto, who—chosen as
Sidney's latest favorite—now demanded the use of her
body.

Then, with a rush of reassurance, she remembered

something Serenita had said the other day: "Darling girl, I pray for you daily. I commend you to the Virgin Mother Mary, the Star of the Sea. She has turned her face from me for a long time, sealing her ears to my prayers, but yesterday she smiled. I do believe she has now heard me, and you'll be granted your dearest wish."

In the pool, Regina sighed. Then she rose and water pearled down her body. The scent of her bath oil lay on the air; her chemist had concocted it for her. No other oil in Union had the same lubricity or the same fey smell. She tingled with pleasure all over as she rubbed herself dry. Her nightgown, genuine silk from Maoling, snuggled softly against her flesh. She wormed her feet into half-slippers and they beat on her soles as she walked to her favorite room, a circular cubicle cut off at one end by a full-length, gold-laced mirror. She dropped down on the low divan where she and Jonny had made love, their bodies reflected darkly in the glass. Then she reached for a sugared crisp-strip in a white bowl and activated the visiset Selma had rolled into the room.

Jonny Tack. She remembered him vaguely, alas; five years had wiped away everything except a few broad strokes. He was tall and powerful. He shaved his head except for a spot on top of his skull from which had sprung a long horsetail of hair. Jonny had never smiled. He had been rough, tumultuous in love. His blue eyes always glazed when he lusted for her. Once satisfied, he had always cursed her, calling her a wanton temptress, black of mood and tortured by some kind of guilt. But he always came back after a while.

The news had not yet begun. Regina studied herself in the mirror.

She was aristocratically tall. Her legs were pulled up and half hidden by pillows. The gray-blue gown was cut low between firm breasts and was decorated with yellow stars whose points were long like lights seen through drilla-glass. Her high cheeks now showed a bloom. Her pouting lips were full. Her eyes had the brooding look of one who'd loved and lost. She adjusted her red hair. It now hung down to her shoulders, although ordinarily it would have been piled high to show the swanlike arch of a delicate neck.

I've become a woman since those days, she thought.

She reached for and crunched another sugared crisp-strip between white teeth. In mid-bite she stopped, the strip protruding between her lips. For a second she thought she had seen a tribesman on the visiscreen, but it turned out to be merely a man in a beaded jacket advertising some ethnic eatery. She crunched up the strip and licked her lip with the tip of a pink tongue.

The news came on at last. The word *helium* flashed on and off at the bottom of the screen. She saw pictures of the tribesmen on horseback, in the reception hall under the blaze of chandeliers, and in jumptubes traveling through the Acropolis.

". . . Mycal Bono, Ecofreak's Negotiator, arrived in Ricardo tonight," the commentator announced. "He was met by Rivera French, a high-ranking BTA official. Mr. Bono had no comment for Media. He retired at once to the Ecofreak embassy in East Tower. Observers here expressed surprise at Bono's youth. Concern has been voiced that Union's helium needs will depend on the sagacity and skill of so inexperienced a man, a virtual unknown. Reston Proctor, Union's Chief Negotiator, sees no basis for concern and once more denies persistent rumors that this round of negotiations will be hotly contested. Reliable sources within the bureau, however, privately concede that rough times are ahead. Contingency plans have been dusted off and stand-by air-liquefaction units are reportedly on stream. Proctor himself is reported gloomy about prospects. He feels hemmed in by the Accommodation policy and darkly hints that the worst may happen on this round. Top Level spokesmen refuse to comment at this early stage, and reaffirmed the Unifier's absolute confidence in Proctor . . ."

Regina barely listened. She gazed with fixed concentration at the flashing images of Mycal Bono. His dark, brooding eyes and black, forked beard made her pensive.

I could fall in love with him, she thought. *I like that name*: *Mycal. It's the name of an archangel in Serenita's Biblibooks. He isn't like Jonny, of course, but he seems more . . . sensitive. A little sad, I think.*

". . . In other news . ."

A sealing crew maneuvered a section of plastosteel into a gaping hole of Portla structure. The structure renewal had gone smoothly. In Laystruc four mushtanks had been poisoned, and Media showed emergency supplies brought in by air from Frisco. Several jumpball innovations were shown.

Regina plotted. The opening ball was a week away. She decided to wear a green sheer-gown for the occasion, the one with the coiling snakes all oriented suggestively (their split tongues extended) toward her center. She would spread pink tint across her eyelids and hang her neck with silver bells. She'd daub Volcano behind her ears, across her wrists, in the crook of her arms. Her cosmetician said that Volcano vaporized in body heat and burned like incense in the blood. No other lady in Union could afford the price.

". . . In another spirited display of leadership courage, Sidney Unsler, the Underunifier, today demonstrated the art of parachuting . . ."

Angrily, Regina looked up at the screen.

Sidney stood at the lip of the shaft, a foolish grin on his long face. Torches smoked in his gloved hands. He leaped out over the chasm lip, torches held high and away from his body at an angle. His motion imitated that of a diver.

For a dizzying moment the cameras followed Sidney's spread-eagled freefall through the lighted shaft, an infinite depth down. Then cameras deployed on lower levels picked him up, his torches blazing, a dot that became a man, that flashed by like a bullet. Next they showed the parachute furl out of his backpack pulled by a lead. The striped silk cracked open, and Sidney swung down. Finally, they showed him standing at Pit Level, an idiotic and pained grin on his face.

The collapsed chute could be seen trailing from his harness and on out of the picture.

A Media reporter interviewed Sidney, who prattled about the exhilaration of freefall.

Regina jabbed the visi control and the picture went blank.

They had not shown the deaths and the riot. Sidney had collided with three unsuspecting people in jump-tubes. Two girls had lost control and had fallen with terrible screams to the bottom. His parachute had pulled four children from slide bars around level 70. They too had died. Rioting citizens had erupted from several levels and, crowding the slide bars, had descended to the Pit bent on revenge. Regina had been downbound in a tube, when police had stopped her. Below others had battled to save Sidney's life.

She thought: *How I despise him, how I loathe him!* She slipped her feet into her fluffy half-slippers; they slapped her heels as she strode off to bed. *I must marry into the tribes before Daddy dies and Sidney takes over. Bless him,* she thought, meaning her father. *Bless Accommodation.*

She could imagine how things would be with Sidney in charge.

2

Silcoplast

Tradition decreed a one-week gap between a tribal reception and the opening ball—time enough for the Adjustment, time enough to renew acquaintances, and time enough to get an informal feel for the other side's negotiating position.

In 1056 the Ecofreak delegation kept to itself. Bono was a five-percenter and so spent considerable time in the tub; the delegates were new to their posts and so had no friends in Union. Only Dart, who had had structure experience, even though his last stay in Ricardo went fifteen years back. He had time on his hands, and used it to look at the Acropolis.

He toured Ricardo with a young tribal attaché and found the city much the same as he had left it—physically. The pentastructure was fixed in design and could not be transformed like a tribal settlement. But details had changed. The crowds were thicker and the physical plant seemed poorly maintained—except at higher levels, of course. In Dart's day, Ricardo had been a riot of psychedelic color, music, and sensuality, of which only traces remained.

The mood of the place was subdued somehow, and when he asked his guide the reason why, the youngster ascribed it to rot at the top. "Unsler is old and ailing. His brain is turning to mush. He clings to power but won't exercise it. His aides act for him, and his precious son rages through Ricardo unchecked. Things have really deteriorated since the Proclamation, when Unsler made his son Underunifier. His decree was followed by executions and much mayhem of that sort. Life in the structures is different from life at home. Here everything is integrated. When the chief is sick, everyone sickens."

Dart answered a little huffily: "You don't need to tell me that. I'm an old structure hand myself."

On the day they toured a lower level, Dart saw an urchin selling hand-printed scriptos. Such things, he knew, were illegal; Media controlled all communications. Dart bought a copy of the rag and found it filled with the gruesome escapades of someone called Fink.

The embassy aide explained. "Fink is their name for Sidney Unsler; and it's a mild word, if you ask me. Sidney is a degenerate. He thinks he is the reincarnated person of a mythical hero or god, someone called Julius Caesar. Young up-level nobles, who have formed a cult brotherhood around Sidney, call themselves 'Flames' and call him 'Ignis,' 'fire' in Latin. They all study Latin and use the tongue in secret conversations. They hold initiations and fight duels with short Roman swords and round shields in a room set aside for that purpose in Sidney's domain. All this wouldn't bother a soul, but they also maraud through Ricardo at night—drunk, as a rule. They rape and loot for the sheer hell of it, and the police look the other way, of course. You can imagine Union's future. Sidney takes over when mushbrain dies."

"I take it you don't like the Unslers."

The young man laughed. *"No,* indeed!"

"You should be pleased. A weak Union means a strong tribe."

"I'm an Accommodationist myself," the young man said, suddenly brusque. "It gives me a pain to see the High Culture decay."

Hearing this, Dart canceled the evening excursion they had planned. He did not want to be associated with a vocal Accommodationist—and the entire embassy seemed to be riddled with them. Only one man, Dulsol, the chief of maintenance, appeared sympathetic to the Activist cause.

Dart sat in the embassy's library that evening when Barney approached him and suggested dinner for old times' sake. He left the choice of restaurants to Dart, who recalled a cozy little place on Level 68 North called the House of Eighty-Two Flavors. They went there the following evening.

They dropped down East Shaft, crossed to North by the intertower beltway, and descended to Level 68.

From the tower's central shaft, narrow streets fanned out like rays and fed traffic to Inner Ring, the first circumferential. Sixty-eight was a labor quarter with low ceilings. Parking their tubes in a garage, they entered on foot and found the feeder street deserted. Inner Ring seemed to be blocked by huge inflated bags, one on each side. Through a gap between the bags, people slowly passed into the interior, watched by police in blue uniforms.

Dart pointed to the crowd and asked what the fuss was about.

Barney said: "That's a roundup, Franco. Remember the riot a few days ago? When Media filmed Sidney's jump, they also filmed the riot. Now they're rounding up the participants."

"How? How can they possibly pick individuals out of this mob?"

The people of Union all looked alike to Dart, especially those on lower levels who, deprived of the luxury of artisun, had blue-white faces. They looked like things you might find at home under a rock.

"They condition the police to remember the faces. Recruits sit in front of viewing screens for days on end. Later, their recall is also boosted by a mnemonic drug."

The two men joined the crowd at the rear and shuffled forward as it moved along. Barney towered above the people, a giant in a white robe. Dart saw several people pulled out of the line by police. One older man in the green jump suit of a nutrition-tank attendant protested his innocence with vigor. His fat mate came to his aid swinging a plastic shopping bag. Both were quickly dragged away.

"What'll happen to them?" Dart asked.

Barney turned a thumb toward the reddish netting of the flexoplast.

"Surely you're joking," Dart cried. "They wouldn't execute them for simply taking part in a riot, would they?"

Barney recognized an opening for the attack he had planned. "Where have you been, Franco? Don't tell me you don't know about conditions in Ricardo. Have those youngsters cut you out of the cable traffic?"

That *hurt*—it really hurt. Dart mumbled something.

Barney persisted. "What *is* your function on this delegation, Franco? I've assumed all along that you're the Number Two."

At that point, to Dart's relief, a policeman noticed them and waved. Barney's white robe meant Very Big!

"Look," Dart said, ducking the question. "They're pointing."

They wormed their way through the sluggish crowd and soon were past the barrier, walking along Inner Ring on the stopped movebelt.

Barney didn't repeat his question. It had served its purpose. He already knew Dart's rank.

31

Dart, for his part, mumbled to himself. He *should* be Number Two. He consoled himself with the reflection that even Bono had no real authority; he was merely Jonny's mouthpiece, not a plenipotentiary.

They walked through a desolate neighborhood. Broken furniture and garbage piled beside the movebelt testified to disposal chute clog-ups. Many windows were broken in buildings to either side. Some of the overhead lights were out. Wild, loud, bold-eyed children played in the streets despite the advanced hour. As they strolled, Dart began to speak about the House of Eighty-two Flavors. Charming atmosphere . . . eccentric chef . . . memorable dishes. The shabby neighborhood compelled him to justify his choice.

The place was disappointing. A smell of burned grease hung about little tables covered with an oily, checkered material. Little candles burned in colored glass. Slick gangsters in jump suits lounged idly in the back. How memory deceives!

To Dart's relief Barney didn't seem to mind. He said he rather liked the place. In the filtered light of the candle, he seemed amused. He joked about Dart's adventurous past. Dart was a deep one, he said. Sly but deep. When the girl came, Barney ordered a bottle of wine.

After the second bottle had been drained and food was on the way, Barney looked up at Dart's flushed face. Time to get down to business. He had a date with French for the next evening, and he meant to give him some advance intelligence about Ecofreak's demands. Tack's inexperienced Activists certainly had no idea how you worked a helium round.

Now the time had come to pluck the vain old cock's dry feathers. To hear him tell it, Dart had been the terror of Union, the savior of the tribe.

"Ah, yes," Barney sighed. "Those were the times. But nowadays . . . Tell me, Franco, how do you assess these brash young kids?"

Dart glowed with wine and memories. "With a bit of wise and seasoned advice, they'll do all right," he winked.

"But will they listen?"

32

"It takes a bit of skill and diplomacy," Dart admitted. "Finesse, my dear Andros, finesse."

"I'm pleased to hear you say that, Franco. They need a man like you. Desperately. Your role is extremely important. You provide that link between experience and energetic youth. It's a very responsible and subtle role. I don't envy you the job. We must work hard to save the tribe from foolishness. With you in the inner circle, I'm not so worried about developments."

Dart compressed a smile into a pleased smirk. If Bono only appreciated his role as much as Barney did . . .

Barney continued: "I suppose you've approved the general negotiating plan. I'd feel better if you had. I realize that my own position is somewhat ambiguous, what with my strong ties to the Accommodationists. But Tack hasn't removed me, so I expect that my loyalty is not in question—and I'd like to help. Unfortunately, Bono is having such a hard Adjustment. Time is wasting. By now we should've had one or two informal chats with the fellows from BTA. They must have some early warning as a matter of courtesy, at least about the hostage question. I'm sure you did that sort of thing when you were First Secretary here. In short, Franco, I thought it best to sit down with the only man in charge who's on his feet rather than in a tub"—at these words Barney grinned—"and see what orders you may have for me."

Dart drew himself up in his chair. "As a matter of fact, I agreed to this delightful dinner because I had the same intentions. I did approve the strategy—reluctantly, Andros, very reluctantly. I meant to discuss the matter with you. Privately, of course . . ."

"Of course."

"Chief Bono and I are not entirely—"

"I understand," Barney hastened to say. "Old diplomats like us know the value of discretion."

"The *real* work is done like this," Dart persisted. "Privately."

"My view to a fault."

"Well, Andros, Tack is determined to obtain the

silcoplast parts, you know." Dart watched Barney's face, but Barney gave no reaction.

"The silcoplast parts," he said evenly.

"And to get sufficient leverage, he intends to ask for Sidney as hostage."

"Sidney Unsler as hostage," the Ambassador echoed.

Dart nodded with a gleam in his eye. "Sidney Unsler." *Barney must be surprised, though he doesn't show it,* he thought.

"In addition—that is to say, to add more leverage yet—he'll ask for eight hundred thousand tons of plastosteel," Dart continued.

"Ten times the usual demand," Barney said without intonation. "He must want the silcoplast parts very much. What are they? Zippers? Buttons? Hairpins?"

Dart heard the sarcasm. Once more his eyes lit up. "Some things are so secret only the innermost circle is privy to the information. But I can give you a hint, Ambassador. There's been a breakthrough."

Barney extracted a small coin purse. The cheap article was made of sil. Barney squeezed the flat round object. A slit in its top opened like a mouth. He repeated the motion once or twice more. Then he put the purse away. "Would this have something to do with the Kaysee labs you Activists have been funding all these years?"

"I am silent," Dart pronounced, but his eyes gleamed.

"Why?" Barney probed. "Why do we ask *Union* to give us SP? Maoling is a major producer, and so is Peacefreak. Why don't we get it from them?"

Dart raised his eyebrows. He was enjoying this. "Welded SP? Does Maoling have the clean rooms? Does Peacefreak have molecular microwelders?"

Barney stared into the candle and thought about it. Silcoplast was a common synthetic derived from silicon, cheap to produce, reasonably gravitron-resistant, and much more durable than the hydrocarbon plastics it had replaced. What else? Then suddenly he thought he had it and, reflecting upon it, he *knew* he had it. Sil was also a laboratory curiosity. Low-level energies transmitted through the stuff generated a curious field that inhibited all types of nuclear core reactions. But the inhibiting oscillations were random—had something to do with the crystalline structure of the silicon carbon. Sometimes it worked, sometimes it didn't. Barney decided to test Dart. The little man revealed his every emotion.

"You've learned to control sil oscillations. In effect, you've got a . . . a bomb inhibitor."

"I remain silent," Dart replied, but his eyes flickered.

"Perhaps you're free to tell me this: Why don't we build our own clean rooms, our own molecular welders?"

"That would take years. Jonny has little patience. He wants to act now."

Barney nodded.

A lardy woman brought their food, a circular tray with seven dabs of tankmush, each with a unique flavor. In the middle of the tray lay limp sticks of simubread. The idea was to scoop the mush with the bread.

Barney let the silence build while he fell to eating, wondering how all this had come to pass. In Hinterland the old men must read the Crestmore bible once again, fingers on that passage about the "bastions of the whore." Like a malignant virus, the Activists had lain dormant until now, when they had the argument that no one could refute: "We have it in our power to topple the structures. The Abomination shall be humbled. We shall break the back of the Technology Beast. No more threats, people of Hinterland. Their missiles shall never strike again. In the heart of every town we shall build a generator, and their bombs will fall like rocks but won't explode." The members of the tribal council must have heard Tack's eloquence and voted to send Franklin, Denton, Ruff, and the others back to their wells and their ranches, dispossessed— the noble cause of Accommodation dead, displaced by the pointy-eyed wrath of the Crestmore zealots. His assessment made sense. It must have been thus.

Chewing, Barney looked up. He took a sip of wine, swallowed. "The strategy stinks. And it's juvenile. Union will smell a rat. Has Tack lost his marbles? All you Activists are crazy. Here's what'll happen, Franco. Proctor will run to Harvanth of Defense, and the two of them together will see the Unifier. Unsler will have to pay attention this time. He'll give Proctor permission to attack—selectively, of course. They won't stop until our production capacity is totally destroyed—all but the essential refineries, of course. Though they won't touch the helium. The irony of it . . . Union will destroy *our* technology. This is the Helium War of 1011 all over again. How many of these components does Tack want, by the way?"

Dart wiggled uneasily. "I can't tell you that."

Barney laughed. "Franco, don't be silly. You must. You've already blabbered too much. We're conspirators, you and I. You must confide in me."

Dart protested. "I didn't tell you anything of importance."

Barney cocked his head and smiled. "Of course you did. You told me about the hostage demand—another really jejune notion. I suppose Tack thinks that Union will give up the parts if we relent on the hostage question. Where have you people been these last few decades. This is no way to negotiate! You should have asked for microwelders, not for the components. Insane! Well, how many?"

Dart stared glumly.

"Franco, out with it. If you play games with me, I swear I'll cable Tack and expose your blabbermouth."

"Fifty thousand."

"So many? Why, that's almost one for each tribal settlement. Why the sudden concern for other tribes?"

Dart stared ahead unhappily. He didn't touch his food.

"Explain it to me, Franco."

"There's an alliance."

"What?!"

"Jonny has formed a tribal alliance. It's called the Counter-Union."

"Sooooo! Well, that explains a few things too. Far too many ambassadorial changes lately. *Hmmm.*

Jonny has ambitions, then. He wants to bring all of Hinterland under his protective umbrella . . . But eat, Franco, try this peppery stuff here. Not bad."

"I'm not hungry," Dart said. Then, after a moment: "What'll you do, Andros."

"I'm more discreet than you, Franco. I'm not going to tell you. But, as the saying goes, a hint is permitted. I expect to look out for the Accommodationist cause."

The Harvey Hare

In the alternating cycles between dumb pain and almost disembodied vision, Bono had lost track of the passage of time.

Somewhere in that murky period, a physician had installed a needle into his arm. Sugar flowed into his body through the hose that linked the needle to a bottle hung above him. He wore a strange pair of rubber shorts from which his wastes were pumped out. In lucid moments he could hear the pump cut in and out at intervals. The rest of him, up to the neck, was submerged in jelly that trembled with his every breath and exhalation.

Some chemical in the sugar or the gel interfered with his brain chemistry. Time and time again he dozed off to relive with minute variations a single experience: his last day on his father's ranch on the Plain of Baez, a vast expanse of mutagrass steppe closed off in the distance by the jagged blue line of the Sierra Blanca.

There he had hunted the giant Harvey hare, one of many curiosities created by radiation's disorderly invasion of the chromosomal world. He was again a half-naked fifteen-year-old armed with a crossbow, stealthily stalking through shoulder-high mutagrass toward the grazing beast. The Harvey raised its head from time to time, ears erect, listening. Then the head went down again and the hare fed invisibly on young mutagrass sprouts that issued green in spring and autumn. When the Harvey ate, Mycal crept forward, the wind in his face. When Harvey listened, he crouched. Cricks chirped harshly on all sides, and a flock of carries, sensing a feast, glided in a faraway circle against the sky.

Kilometers away, a large transport copter landed near the ranch house, and a group of boys clambered out. They stood about in a half-circle and threw rocks at a scarecrow while the pilot went inside. The copter belonged to the Academy of Action at Wellhead, and it had come to fetch Mycal for his first term. This meant the end of his carefree days.

Men on horseback soon rode off to find the youngster.

Oblivious to all this, Mycal crept forward. Fifty meters from the beast he picked up the musk scent of a female. He paused and checked his dark, oily bow, the cranked-back wire, the blunt bolt. Then, in the high tones of a boy whose voice had not yet changed, he called: "Har-vey! *Har-vey!*"

The she-hare rose, a large white apparition. She sailed from Mycal. He anticipated her direction. So when the hare zizzagged, they were both heading for the same spot like lines of a triangle on a collision course.

The hare was faster than the boy and reached the magic spot where obscure instinct made all Harveys stop for the cloying counterattack. The animal turned and stopped. Her red eyes were inexplicably sad. Her ears hung down, accentuating that pitiful look. Her paws were bent in the manner of a begging dog.

Then the telepathic pulse hit Mycal with full force.

He had only a second to react.

He felt a sensation of pity, love, and concern for the hare. The beast appeared to him not as it was— a white giant, a half-ton of muscle and sinew wrapped in a fluffy pelt that brought three hundred suds in Merillo. It now appeared to be a tiny, sweet, and utterly helpless baby rabbit, a lost little thing. Mycal's eyes watered with affection.

Tribesmen believed that the Harvey Hunt strengthened character. Mycal had already killed seven hares in the course of growing up. He knew how to choke down the pity. When the beast moved again, he let the bolt fly. She gave an agonized shriek and fell out of sight into the grass.

Her shrieks continued as he went after her, hard and pitiless inside. She lay on her back and spasmed, pink nostrils gushing blood, red eyes terrified. He felt the terror as if it were his own. Nevertheless, he knelt beside the beast and slit her throat with a wide-bladed knife.

She was his eighth hare.

Bono relived the experience time and time again. The dream changed shape. Sometimes he called and there was no Harvey. Sometimes he shot her and she fell dead at his feet. Sometimes he missed. Yet again he joined in her pity and embraced the hare with a rush of emotion, as the two of them cried in each other's arms like people.

Awakening with a shudder, he would feel the onrush of discomfort as pressure again descended on him. His breath grew heavy and he began to gasp for air. He could swear that a chemical interfered with his memory.

Bono had devised a method to escape the trauma. He concentrated on his heartbeat, on his breathing. He took one breath at a time: In . . . out . . . in . . . out . . . in . . . out . . .

Silvery, swaying, there was the Plain of Baez. In the distance stood the Sierra Blanca. Mycal stalked through the shoulder-high grass. The Harvey looked up, ears tall and trembling.

Careless in the Pit

French met Barney for dinner in The Mutant, a fashionable but discrete up-level eating place in West Tower. French chose roast veal with autumn potatoes; Barney ordered crick legs in wine sauce. Not every-

one in Union's structures ate flavored tankmush; the
very rich and very poor had access to real food, as
well. French picked up the ninety-sud tab; it was a
bargain considering the information he had gained.

They parted in the tubepark adjoining the restaurant. French found his official BTA tube, a red-and-
white-striped affair. He headed out to find Proctor. A
Flame had left the restaurant some time before and,
spotting French's tube in the lot, hid in the shadows.
Now he followed French at a distance. In his excitement, French did not notice the surreptitious pursuit.

The time was ten forty-five, or fifteen minutes after the scheduled start of the late-night jumpball game.
Tonight Proctor would be in the Leader Box, so
French made for Central's colosseum to catch him with
the news.

When French arrived he noticed at once that
Proctor had not made his appearance yet. The people
roared with unhappiness and stamped on the thin
plastosteel floor so that the colosseum trembled. A
band played on the field below, but crowd noises almost completely obliterated the sound.

The Leader Box was on the upper level, accessible
by the wide corridor that went up around the place in
a spiral. French stopped along the way and chose one
of a bank of empty telbooths. He closed the door to
dampen the noise, dialed Fred Clemmens at his cubohome. Clemmens was director of the technical di-
vision, one of three operations under French in the
Office of Intelligence.

The man appeared in the tiny screen, old and balding. A towel hung around his neck.

"Fred, what do you know about silcoplast?" French
asked.

Clemmens raised his eyebrows.

French went on, a little amused. "Ever hear of a
silcoplast wave modulator used in a telcom net?"

"Riv, what is this? Some kind of practical joke?"

"I am serious, my friend. Ecofreak will ask us for
fifty thousand silcoplast devices or components or
switches or whatnot; they claim they need them for a

communications system. I searched my brain, Fred, but somehow the demand didn't make sense."

Clemmens shook his head slowly. "It doesn't; not on the face of it. Are you worried?"

"Aren't you?"

Clemmens made a face. "Frankly, Riv, you've made me interrupt my vibromassage, so—"

"Do you have contacts in the SP industry?"

"Some, yes."

"Well, Fred, I want you to get on the tel and have the best sil chemists in here by tomorrow morning."

"You *are* worried. You sure? The SP centers are mostly in Husten, Norlens, and Laystruc. Should I—"

"Yes. Fly them in overnight. I think this might be a big one."

French signed off and went on his way.

Through vaulted doors spaced at regular intervals, he could oversee the colorful crowd and the green field below. The crowd was in an angry, ugly mood. Hate vibrations filled the air. Roused structure crowds were dangerous, especially sporting crowds. The leader had made them wait for more than half an hour. Clearly the people didn't know that they were waiting for Proctor.

French was walking between two openings—bare, scuffed wall on either side—when the noise suddenly intensified, then died down. He hurried forward. Even before he reached the next door, he heard the announcer's magnified voice.

"Here he is, jumpball fans. The games are on! Reston Proctor, the Chief Negotiator."

At the mention of the name, the crowd fell silent. It held its breath. Then a wild cheering started and grew in intensity.

French had reached the door and stopped to watch.

Light from the floods glared off the bulletproof, chemproof glass of the Leader Box. Proctor was not visible inside, and the crowd wanted to see him. It took up a chant: *"Proc-tor, Proc-tor, Proc-tor . . ."*

French saw movement in the box—a blue robe flashed. Cheering and whistling much more intense than before displaced the chanting. It lasted a long time; then, finally, slowly, it died out.

French walked on, thinking about Proctor's popularity. Media had issued two books in as many years glorifying Proctor: *Boss* and *BTA in Action*. For three years now a visishow ran on Saturday nights called "The Hunt," which depicted an organization much like the BTA, an "old man" who resembled Proctor, and a security chief—black like Darby Dickens. Proctor's engineered popularity was all part of the Secret Agenda. Hondo Weinberger, one of the Media Bigs, often lunched with Proctor in BTA's executive dining room. He was not the only one.

It was a measure of Unsler's decrepitude that he tolerated the obvious self-promotion of one of his agency heads—and a measure of Sidney's stupidity that he appeared not to notice. Or perhaps Sidney *had* noticed; hence the recent harassment.

Outside the Leader Box stood one of Dickens' men.

"Mr. French, I'll have to search you."

"Me, Harlow? For God's sake, surely you know *me!*"

"Sorry, sir. New orders from Dickens. Everybody must be searched. No exceptions. It's the Flames, sir."

"More trouble?"

"Not so far this week, Mr. French, but we're on a general security alert."

French handed over a pistol he had checked out of the security shop some days ago. He'd considered the gun precaution enough against the Flames. He said: "Here. Now you can be sure I won't shoot the Negotiator."

"Yes, sir. Go right on in."

French frowned as he walked down the aisle of the Leader Box, his eyes on the players. Some floated in the air, maneuvering with boot and elbow jets. Others stood on the ground in patterns of defense and attack. French scorned the game. He belonged to the diehard set that resented the game's debauchery by the addition of Fulbright's gravitron webbing. The classic collision of forces had become an awkward aerial ballet.

Proctor sat up front alone, absorbed in documents pulled from his briefcase. French lifted up his robe, sat down, and gave his report. Barney did not think the Activists would last long. He had hinted pointedly that Ricardo should look out for some electronic components ostensibly meant for a telcom system across four radiation belts—Barney hadn't said anything specifically, but that had come across clear as a bell. Sil components welded to copper. Those parts would play a key role in the negotiations, French said. Then he reported on the predicted plastosteel levy and the hostage demand.

Down below, three men in red crashed against the triple-decker flywall, zoomed down. Ground guards felled them with loud snaps of equipment.

Proctor stared at the crowd.

"Sidney Unsler . . ." he rumbled. "That's interesting."

"It doesn't make sense," French threw in. "Either they are incredibly naïve negotiators—or else I'm missing something. I think it's a diversion, Res, an attempt to make us focus on the hostage question. They'd rather we don't think about the things they really want. Technology. The sil components. Barney almost said as much. You just don't ask for the Underunifier as hostage—not in this day and age."

"Very interesting," Proctor mused.

French asked, "What do you make of it?"

Proctor glanced at French, a little wary. "You know how I feel about those intelligence estimates."

"They're the best we have."

"Sure, sure. Still . . . Rivera, I sense trouble. I suspect these Activists of yours, and the demand for Sidney makes me nervous. Suppose they insist on their demands, insist hard enough so that I'm forced to take it up with Unsler."

"So?"

"So I take it up with Unsler—and suppose Unsler says yes?"

French was genuinely puzzled. "Why would he do that?"

"Because he wants Accommodation. I can see it now. Sidney in Hinterland. Sidney hobnobbing with tribal leaders. Sidney forming close friendships."

"With Activists?"

"*If* they're Activists."

French didn't hide his irritation. "Res, they *are* Activists. I have no doubts about it. I've been out there." He gestured with an arm. "I've seen the sour breed."

"You're too brash, Rivera, too damned cocksure."

For a moment both men were silent. Down below, whistles shrilled and flags dropped from the rafters. French broke the silence.

"The key is in those silco parts. Barney's hint was —hell, it was a slap in the face. *Hint* isn't the right word."

Proctor shrugged. "Maybe. Maybe not. Maybe they *want* us to worry about the technology. Besides, technology is one of those things with Ecofreak. They always want some damned oddity. The last time it was laser drills—but nothing happened."

French wasn't satisfied. "I'm suspicious."

"You're always suspicious," Proctor countered. "You've got a fetish about technology. You were suspicious in '51, but nothing happened, like I said. Those people are like monkeys. They like to play with gadgetry. It's like sex with them. Because the Crestmore forbids it, *therefore* it has appeal." Silence. "Sidney Unsler. That may be a brilliant ploy." He thought about it for another second. "At any rate, we must wait for more details. How is the helium situation?"

"Flow is back by thirty percent—the usual thing. All the structures are holding. Four or five days' inventory, roughly."

"Air liquefaction?"

"The stand-by units are all operating and they compensate for the shortfall. But it's the usual problem. We're having one hell of an energy drain. Just not enough fusion capacity for everything—gravitron, services, *and* air liquefaction."

Proctor nodded. "High time we start the talks. The

44

ball's tomorrow, and the first session the day after that. By the way, I did wangle an invitation for Miri. It was like pulling teeth, but she's invited."

French smiled. "Thanks," he said. "Miri has been after me for months. Though search me why anybody would want to go to a Top Level dance."

"Women!" Proctor said in the tone of a confirmed bachelor who has long ago stopped trying to understand the mystery.

They talked for a while longer about concurrent talks with Maoling and toxic metals in a shipment of lettuce delivered recently. French noted some assignments, then left, retrieving his pistol on the way out.

He headed south by the intertower beltway. South Tower was a pattern of random lights ahead. He lived with Miri on Level 118. He wondered if she still waited up for him; he longed for her company.

What makes me disconsolate?

Laser drills, his mind answered instantly. Yes, laser drills. They symbolized, for French, Proctor's contempt for all technical matters, his preoccupation with politics and personalities at the expense of gut issues.

During the last helium round Ecofreak had demanded and gotten five hundred laser drills despite the tribe's weak rationale. They claimed to need them for dental work, which was patently ridiculous. French had protested at the time, but had been overruled. Later he had personally gone deep into Hinterland to find out how Ecofreak really used the drills. The track led him to a research center under maximum security outside Kaysee in Mokan Territory. French returned more suspicious than ever; but Proctor simply shrugged off the report. The pieces of the puzzle locked nicely. The Tacks came from the Kaysee region. Could those lasers have had something to do with Jonny's rise to power? Could the sil parts be another link in a technological chain?

He entered South Shaft and, bottom jets blazing, began the steep ascent. Podlike elevators clung to the walls. Hundreds of slide bars glistened darkly between the elevator grooves. The chasm was empty, the hour late.

Near Level 80 a group of white-clad men in tubes shot out of a feeder, almost colliding with French. The timing of their entry convinced him it was no accident. Among the men, he recognized several prominent Flames, including Clafto Meyer, the dark, swarthy plastosteel heir Sidney favored as his first deputy.

"Watch where you're going, pig!"

"Fratres, that's no ordinary pig. That's a BTA pig, a superpig!"

"We don't like BTA pigs, do we? Let's teach this guy how to drive a tube."

French assessed the situation coolly. His standard issue vehicle could not outrun the expensive jobs these boys had. He had retrieved his pistol from Harlow, but the goons must also be armed. Stare them down? Talk them out of it? French had cold memories of many bloody Branco confrontations, many close calls in Hinterland. Old instincts stirred. His fatigue fled under a rush of adrenaline.

The Flames had begun to maneuver, forming a circle about him, even as they all rose in the shaft at maximum speed.

French guessed their intention. They would try to upend his tube, to make it tumble around and around until the centriforces grew so great that he would be flung free.

One of the men lunged, sidejets ablaze. French saw the mindless grin of a youngster. The feint didn't deceive him. He turned quickly and saw two others almost upon him; he chopped out with the edge of his hand. A man reeled back, coughing. He punched the other and shoved his tube aside. From the corner of his eyes, French saw two others dart forward.

He couldn't win: this was their game. He did the only thing he could.

With a flick of his thumbs, he cut out jets and gravitron and overrode safety with his knees. His tube dropped from the circle of his pursuers like a rock.

French had practiced this maneuver years ago in training. The Death Drop. But this time there was no flexonet to catch him if he failed. An endless chasm yawned below. His fall accelerated, and his tube began to tumble slowly as it fell. French held on with all his might. He stared rigidly ahead. His innards liquefied. Physical terror clutched him. Forces tugged and wrenched. His knuckles grew white as he gripped the rail; his knees went numb against the tube.

The shaft turned, helter-skelter—now up, now down, a wheeling broken telescope of light. On one of the turns he saw the Flames in hot pursuit. But they came slowly, with jet power.

His mind wheeled. His brain lagged behind events. His thoughts flashed. *Flames. BTA. Proctor. Miri. Helium.* He had no time to reflect, but his body and mind were active. His eyes measured the height and counted levels. Around Level 20 he cut in the gravitron. Immediately his body grew heavy, his own weight nearly crushing him. The tumbling stopped slowly, but the inertial forces of his fall overcame the gravitron and he went on falling at a sideways tilt.

At Level 1, he cut in sidejets. When the tube had righted, he let the bottom jets blaze. Despite those actions, his tube crashed on the concrete of the Pit and burst apart in a shower of sparks. French fell free and rolled some distance from the impact point before the tube exploded. A long flame shot toward him and licked his face.

He rolled from the fire and lay where he came to rest. He felt a pain in head and shoulder. Scrambling up, he nearly stumbled over his own robe. Black clouds of smoke rose from the furiously burning tube.

Above him, the Flames approached. He stared up into the chasm for a second, an endless tubularity. From this perspective it seemed to curve, to lean over him. He couldn't see all the way up. The shaft walls closed in and came together in a point.

French ran toward a corridor.

Roused from the dull routine of duties in a lighted booth, a Pit guard waved his arms. BTA forces secured the Pit, but the guard did not recognize French. He ran past the man and into a darkness faintly lit by red lights. The guard yelled behind him. French ripped the purple robe from his body as he ran; it impeded his movements. He wore a simple gray jump suit underneath.

French understood helium like few other men. He knew precisely where Ecofreak pipelines fed each and every Union structure, how the gas was liquefied and where, how the cold stuff flowed to the drums. He knew the layout of the Pit in every detail. But his memories went even further back. As a boy he had explored the deep, dark catacombs below the Pit, the tunnels and bunkers of ancient Eastcoast on whose site Ricardo had been built. He knew where he was. He had several avenues of escape: sideways, up, or down. He stopped to orient himself.

That luminous exit sign up ahead would lead into one of the drum rooms and from there he could make his way into the interior of the structure.

He ran toward the exit, freeing his pistol as he ran. He heard voices and the sound of boots on concrete.

Ducking into the opening, he fired at movement behind him. He meant to do no harm, merely to show that he was armed and dangerous. In the narrow confines of the corridor, the sound of the blast was deafening and made his ears ring.

He ran through an instrument room, his face lit up for a second by green, red, and yellow lights from a panel. From there, through a door, beneath low-slung piping, he entered a gigantic hall so filled with the hum of vibrations that he couldn't hear his own feet hit the ground hard when he cleared some low steps.

Pain stabbed up his leg. He hobbled forward and ducked behind a huge, gray, loaf-shaped machine to catch his breath and massage the foot.

Hall A: six giant generators stood in a line. Beneath the painted, yellow, concrete floor on which he cowered lay tanks of liquid helium. Drums turned, half submerged in the liquid. From the generator casings gargantuan strands of cable, each fiber as thick as a man, carried the pulse into a vaulted ceiling and, through the ceiling, to the plastosteel framework of the tower.

He shook his head to clear the pain, blinked, then peeked past the gray-painted metal of a drum toward the door through which he had come, toward the stairs he'd descended.

His foot still hurt. He did not dare attempt the run until he had assured himself that his pursuers had given up the chase. Just in case, he aimed the pistol at the door. His hand shook so that he had to steady it with his left. The door opened a crack, then all the way. When he saw a white-robed figure slipping through, he pulled the trigger without thinking. The shape fell forward and rolled down the stairs.

French blasted away until the door closed.

In the fantastic hum of the hall, he hadn't heard the sound of his own shots.

He waited a moment longer. The man he had shot lay sideways on the stairs. Blood spread a large circle of red on his chest.

French stared at the dead Flame. *Now I've done it. Now they have a casualty!*

He was angry with himself, angry that he hadn't had sense enough to think before he shot. He could have eluded these goons. The consequences of his action came to him now: the death of a Flame meant big trouble for BTA. A bloodbath could follow . . . *Goddamn!*

He gathered himself from the floor and limped past other grav-drums to enter another hall where expanders liquefied helium, and stopped to decide on his course. The dead man would serve as a warning. No need to find one of the hidden passages to the catacombs. He would make his way to a small service elevator not far from here. His BTA master key would operate it.

He reached the lift without mishap. The elevator came, summoned with a button. He walked into the narrow box, punched 118.

When the register showed Level 60, French finally relaxed. He had been leaning against the wall. Now he let himself slide down to the floor. The pistol still hung from his fingers. Flames from the exploding tube had blackened his hand. Singed hairs curled at the ends. For a long moment French stared at the hairs as if they were a matter of the greatest interest. Then he broke his gaze.

He realized that he was very shaken. Energy had drained from his legs, arms, hands.

It took him a long time to put the pistol into its case.

He looked at his watch. The exquisite device, a gift of Miri's, had been shattered. The fine pieces of the micromosaic had been dislodged. The digits had stopped at 11:59.

Miri

Miri French spent her evening at a meeting of her coven on Level 120. Most of the session was devoted to a test of mantuition, the art of reading character from the aural energies that leave the human body by the extremities.

All ad-adepts had gathered in a small room. Two women and two men hired to help in the procedure waited behind curtains in a dark room. Groping in the darkness that prevented the acquisition of visual cues, Miri followed others to shake hands with the strangers. Then she retired to a cubicle next door to write down what she had learned from those brief touches.

Afterward, the coven elder had sought her out over tea. "Miri, your analysis was almost perfect. You're growing stronger in the arts. Soon you'll advance the final step. Frankly, that pleases me very much—because you're marked."

Miri reached up involuntarily and touched a birthmark on her cheek. From time to time the elders mentioned that peculiarity of hers. Each time Miri felt a vague uneasiness combined with an inner pulsation, as if a suppressed memory were trying to surface. But the memory bounced up against a barrier of some sort. To her, the birthmark was simply a blemish. To the elders it meant something else. For months at a time they allowed her to forget she wore the Madonna's Mark. But then, out of the blue, came another cool reminder —and Miri found this maddening. The mark meant, according to lore, that she had a role in history. Beyond that, no one would tell her anything.

Miri looked up at the coven elder, a fortyish woman whose face was smooth as marble from the spiritual abrasions of meditation. "Mother, I may be marked, but I'm still childless. In my group I'm the only one who hasn't passed through that experience. I can't become a full adept until I have conceived. Do you think Frenchy is sterile?"

Miri kept her voice under control. Even her eyes were steady. But the question stirred anxieties that ad-adepts were supposed to have put behind them. She hoped, with unseemly eagerness, that the Lady wouldn't test her to the utmost, that her Frenchy would be spared the grav-sterility that afflicted so many. Could she, a member of Madonna's cosmic body, be mated to a crippled male?

The elder smiled faintly. She reached over and patted Miri's arm. "You'll conceive, Miri. The mark assures it. Just don't forget to practice vision. Form a strong vision of maternity—but what am I telling you. You know all that. Tell me, are you bothered by something?"

"No, Mother . . . Yes, Mother, I sense—I have an odd intuition. Something is wrong. I think it has to do with Frenchy."

"Let me feel your hand."

Miri laid her hand into the elder's who, in turn, eyes slightly narrowed, sampled Miri's mood. "A party, a dance. Some sort of great event. You're worried about some future event."

Miri laughed. "You're right. I'm anxious about an invitation to a Top Level ball. The ball's tomorrow, but I still don't know whether I'm going, even though I want to very much."

"Anxiety is unnecessary. Now that you're an ad-adept, you could consult the Sybilline books. Then you'll *know* whether you're going or not."

Miri looked down at her cup. "It's a trifle, really. And we're not supposed to trifle with the oracle."

The elder rose. "Of course not, child, but we can

make an occasional exception. Have you consulted the oracle about conception?"

Miri shook her head.

"There, there. Now, that's not a trifling matter. You should trust yourself—and the Lady. Above all, Miri, avoid anxiety, practice vision. Practice, practice, practice. Until next week, then."

Saying this, the elder nodded and went her way.

Miri's tea had been laced with Millusion, and soon the effect of the drug manifested itself in a bell-like ringing in the head. She moved toward the assembly hall whispering with others. They settled on cushions on the floor. The lights dimmed and visions appeared on the large curving screen.

Miri caught her breath as Earth appeared, a green-white magnificence, turning slowly against a velvet darkness. She heard music. The picture faded and others followed in succession: brilliant visions of the world as it had been in ancient times, a riot of color and a shimmer of light, an exotic profusion of biological life, of jungles, prairies, animal herds, bird flocks, fish schools, and things that creeped and crawled. The proud, beaked head of an eagle, the moist nostrils of a hippo, the shadowy whisk of a deer tail, the rush of wind in tree tops, the radiance of a screen of fish in coral, the glistening sweat on the bodies of men rowing a log canoe, the lumbering of a polar bear, a drop of water on a leaf. . . .

The beauty of it brought tears to her eyes. Millusion enhanced her senses, enabled her to become the marvelously varied life shown on these secret, ancient tapes. She'd seen it all before a hundred times, but ever and again the vision was fresh. She sobbed as she watched, knowing it wouldn't last.

Soon the visions faded, growing lighter and lighter.

Now a throbbing, hissing, pounding, and drumming overlaid the music. The Male had entered the world and transformed it before her eyes. These too were ancient films—of tractors gouging the earth, of sky-lines forming and disappearing, of machines beating rythmically, of smoke, devastations, penned beasts, polar bears bleeding, whales quartered and melted, parched land, poison fumes, sludge lakes, landscape carved into geometrical formations by thousands of identical dwellings.

Miri held her breath and screwed up her eyes anticipating the blinding light and the explosions. They came. In their wake came pictures of today—of gaping craters, the uniform silver of mutagrass broken here and there by trees, the lope of Harvey hare, the flight of carries. She saw furtive mutant colonies hugging the edge of rad-belts, hiding in caves, burrows, huts, hovels. They hopped one-legged, roll-walked three-legged, crawled legless on rump-stumps. Beemen whistled bonily, tailed crick-eaters purred. She saw six children suck milk from a woman's six udders. Tribesmen on horses came to raid, poking spears into hovels, looking for reasonably humanoid shapes. Smoke rose from burning huts when the men rode away.

Last came a vision of the structures, one after the other, surrounded by Desolations. They flashed by faster and faster as the music rose higher and higher —and suddenly there was a single flower, sharply in focus, against a blurred green and a deep-blue sky.

The picture hovered before her eyes for a long time while the music hummed in harmony.

Then it was over, and Miri went home.

Frenchy was still out. Miri debated with herself, sensing her anxiety. Then, to keep her hands busy, she resumed work on a micromosaic, eyes framed by the rubber of her microscope, hands busy with wires thinner than hair. She worked for a while, absorbed by the task. Nevertheless, her feelings of unease grew. At last she rose and stepped into her meditation nook, eager to rid herself of the odd depression.

Against the wall hung Madonna's shrine. It featured the Gosmic Lady on an oval micromosaic of the finest quality. The rays of the sun formed her hair. The planets were her jewelry. She stood wrapped in spar-spangled night. Next to her, on either side, hung other, small pictures—trees, shrubs, animals. Suspended from the ceiling on fine wire and turning slowly with the movement of air in the room were tiny yellow birds, their wings extended.

Miri pushed a switch on the floor next to the prayer rug.

A low multitonal hum began to fill the room. It was electronic music, a slowly shifting harmonium piece whose sound resembled the sonorous chant of men.

She meditated on maternity. Suppose she were pregnant and carrying child. She imagined the ceremonies in the coven when she announced her pregnancy.

Miri opened her eyes. Suddenly she was frightened. Something had interfered with her meditation—a worry or an intuition. Frenchy was in trouble and she *knew* it.

She uncoiled from her cross-legged position, rose, and walked out of the room leaving the deep hum behind her.

She passed through her workroom, where the implements of her art were laid out on tables, and through there to a small but comfortable living room drenched in the orange blaze of artisun. She left through the front door of the cubohome, took the elevator down, nodded to the dozing guard, then crossed the lobby and walked out through a revolving door into the brightly lit street.

Frenchy's work demanded odd, long hours. As a rule she didn't worry about him. What was different about tonight? Why did she feel that something was wrong?

She made for Central Shaft, eyeing the airspace above the belt; she sought signs of Frenchy's red-and-white tube.

No one about. Past midnight. A strong current of air blew over Outer Ring. The air was renewed at night and it smelled fresh and salty. Ocean spray entered the ventilation intakes down below. The colorful banners of competing apartments waved and beckoned in the air: Union Manor, Galsworthy Square, Denver

Acres. Through glass portals she could see ornate lob-
bies and sleepy staffs lounging in chairs.

Going out to meet him like this made no sense at
all, but Miri had to do something. She could not stay
in the cubohome any longer.

She searched the empty airspace below the brilliant
overhead lights arranged in random, artistic patterns.

She was so intent on the heights that she missed
him. His call made her look down. Then she saw him.
He seemed to limp slightly as he approached on the
movebelt. His robe was gone, his face blackened by
soot, his long hair in disarray. She broke into a run
to meet him.

"Oh, Frenchy," she cried, when they collided.
"What happened?"

He said: "Nothing. Nothing, girl. But you—what're
you doing on the belts? Don't you know how dangerous it is?"

3

The Opening Ball

The ballroom slowly filled with people. They
stood on the dance floor talking and drinking. They sat
on a kind of peripheral balcony supported by pink
marble columns. Young men and women moved about
in separate groups to see and be seen.

The grandiose sweep of the place, the flash of lights
from chandeliers and jewelry, the shimmer of robes
and gowns, shadowy movements in endless mirrors
against the wall below the balcony, the bubbles in the
wine he drank—all this made Bono's head spin.

Something in his stomach laughed.

Fourteen harmonious tones rose side by side from
an electronic organ on a platform to Bono's left.

Crystalline water spurts from a fountain to his right pulsed in rhythm with the music.

He put his glass on a passing tray, snatched a full one, and turned to Dart.

"Wild, isn't it?" he said with an arching eye.

He ogled a group of passing girls. The curvature of rumps and breasts shone pink beneath oddly textured gowns that seemed to let the eye penetrate and then again not. Dark almond eyes glanced with provocation at the group in whose midst Bono stood—tribesmen in simple leather clothing that looked drab amidst the fire of diamonds and the sheen of silk.

He took a large swallow from the glass. Droplets of wine clung to his mustaches.

He throbbed with happiness. The pressure had fled. Morning had finally brought relief. Amid the foul stink of the gel, in the reddish darkness of the bathroom, Bono had awakened to his old self; he had scraped the stuff from trunk and limb, shaken it from his hand. Already, now, a giddy joy possessed him. No, it wasn't just the bubbly wine or the shine of glass, silk, silver, and waxed wood. Life beat again inside his skin. He was back among the living again, out of the realm of painful dreams.

He slapped Dart on the back with a hand a little out of control, hard enough to make the wrinkled oldster spill a drop of the wine he hadn't touched. "Come on, Franco! Cheer up, old man. Why that dark look on your puss? Tonight we see how structure Bigs live."

Dart said nothing. He meant to tell Mycal to curb his guzzling. His foolish, grinning face drew the snickering attention of the Bigs. His bucolic manner clashed with the sophisticated setting. Crestmore urged moderation—and modest shame in the presence of lascivious display.

Dart said none of this, gloomily aware that he himself had already made a hash of things. He followed Barney with his eyes. The Ambassador mingled with Bigs. Dart hoped Barney would stay away from Bono. What if those two had a heart-to-heart talk?

Maybe I should confess all, he thought; but then he

shrank back from the notion, repelled by the reckless madness in Bono's eyes. Quite clearly the chief was out of control on this first day of his Adjustment. He was a five-percenter, and God only knew what such a man would do.

Across the room Proctor, who had been searching for French, found him on the edge of the ballroom with Miri. The two were watching the crowd.

"There you are, Rivera," Proctor rumbled. "Hello, Miri." He took her hand. "It's been some time since I've seen you."

He eyed her opaque, long-sleeved gown, the fringed white stole across her shoulders, and noted that she did not display herself. Despite the chaste costume she was seductively full, but her femininity did little to reassure Proctor. He always experienced a kind of discomfort in her presence. She resembled a proud, black bird with that dark hair, beaked nose, and flashing eyes. The single golden ring suspended from her left earlobe reminded him that she was a witch of some sort, a member of some obscure cult.

He released her firm, warm hand, still vaguely troubled.

"You don't mind if I steal your husband for a second, do you? We have a small crisis on our hands." He smiled momentarily.

"Not at all, Reston. And thank you for getting me the invitation."

She analyzed the feelings conveyed by Proctor's hand. He gave her a sense of concentration, ambition, vulgarity, and repressed resentment. She had a vision of a small, fat boy, the butt of cruel jokes. It seemed incongruous in a man who lived in a world of abstractions, his vital energies chained to the power lust. At the moment Proctor was fearful of something—yet he seethed with suppressed anger. At Frenchy? At something else?

She looked after the Chief Negotiator as he led her husband a few steps away. How little of his power the man revealed in his externals, she reflected. Despite the blue robe and the ceremonial white sash that ran from his shoulder to his waist, Proctor looked common—a small bureaucrat.

Proctor stopped with his hand on French's sleeve. His mind lingered on Miri, who was one of the Schulheitzins, he now recalled—very high, Very Big, a family prominent in the arts but inconsequential in politics. Miri had made an odd match, marrying a slum kid—probably the expression of artistic eccentricity. She was a practicing micromosaiker.

Proctor released French's robe and brought his mind back to the unpleasant business at hand. "I've had a call from Blottingham."

French affected surprise. "Blottingham on Unsler's staff?" he asked, thinking: *As if the world were simply filled with Blottinghams! There's only one that matters.*

"Yes," Proctor said. "But he said he was calling in his private capacity."

"Meaning?"

"Meaning he was speaking for Sidney."

French raised his eyebrows. He hoped that the blood pounding in his neck was not visible.

"It seems someone from BTA killed one of Sidney's Flames last night," Proctor said, eyes sharp. "In a gunfight. Have you picked up something on that?"

"No," French said tonelessly. "What else did he say?"

"He gave me a few not-so-veiled threats. Fact is, Blottingham was furious; and if he weren't a bit afraid of me . . . Anyway, they want the man handed over, no questions asked."

"What did *you* say?" French asked.

Proctor snorted. "The obvious. I told them I'd find the man and hand him over."

French was taken aback. "You mean it?"

"Don't be absurd," Proctor said with deep scorn in his voice. "I protect my own. But we've got to gain time. Whoever did it should not have left witnesses. We can't afford open war with Sidney now." His eyes spoke about the Secret Agenda.

French nodded. *There's no help for it,* he thought. His eyes rested on the clump of tribesmen and he noted casually that Bono seemed quite another man from the reserved and hostile Activist French had received a week ago. Bono was bent double with laughter. *There's no help for it. I have to tell him.*

He took a deep breath and braced for the explosion. "Res, the BTA man who did the killing was—me."

Miri grew restless as the conversation between Frenchy and Proctor went on and on. The nobility had begun to clear the dance floor. People took up positions along the edges of the shiny, waxed surface. Eyes looked expectantly toward a double portal.

Miri watched Frenchy's red face and hangdog expression while Proctor spoke angrily with vehement, chopping gestures of his fat hands.

A group of men passed behind Miri. They stopped and drew her attention by a murmured conversation, their heads bunched in a knot. From time to time they glanced toward Proctor and Frenchy. Then one of them drew away from the group and came toward her, a young man with an olive complexion, glistening hair.

"Excuse me, miss," he said. His half-smile was unpleasant somehow. "Would you happen to know who that man is?" He inclined his head toward Proctor.

It surprised her that anyone might have to ask. "Of course. That's Reston Proctor, the Chief Negotiator."

The man shook his head. "No, no," he said. "The *other* one, the blond one. I think I recognize him from a recent encounter." At the words his lips curled oddly.

"Why, that's my husband, Rivera French."

His eyes bored into her, noticing her for the first time. He nodded. "Thank you," he said, nodding again. Then he rejoined his group and, arms extended, he pushed his companions on their way. None looked back at Frenchy.

Miri could not escape a faint shudder, but she couldn't attribute the feeling to anything in particular and assumed that she had experienced the man's aura mingling with her own. Whoever the man was, inside he was a bundle of contradictions.

Miri shrugged off the feeling and turned her attention to the double portal, sensing a sudden hush. In a second the electronic organ opened with a jangled version of the Grand Harmony, music calculated to grip the emotions as it rose, fell, rose, and built up to the grand finale. It brought tears to the eyes, but Miri resisted the emotion. She had learned to scorn this crude, visceral adoration of Unsler's power.

When the portals finally opened, she saw the Unifier in his golden robe, a thick black belt around his middle. Behind him stood members of the family.

She noticed that Proctor had been caught by surprise. He disengaged himself from Frenchy and, as the Unifier slowly walked toward the Ecofreak delegation, weaved his way rapidly in the same direction beneath the balcony. He had a part in the ceremonies.

Frenchy came back to her side with *that* look on his face.

"It's all right," she whispered.

She sought his hand and squeezed encouragement. Then she turned her head back to the ballroom.

Behind the Unifier marched Regina; and behind her, three abreast, and in several ranks, was the rest of the family.

Like her father, Regina moved slowly, one hesitating step after another hesitating step, in rhythm with the slow processional. She looked straight ahead with only brief glances to the side, spotting people she knew, nodding to them faintly.

She noted with pleasure that all eyes were on her.

Her red hair was piled high on her head, revealing the swanlike sweep of a delicate neck. The hairdo was called Medusa—hundreds of ringlets seemingly random but actually arranged with computerized precision. Emerald teardrops swung from her ears. Her sheer-robe with the coiling snakes, all oriented suggestively toward her middle, glistened in the light of chandeliers. Tiny bells tinkled on her neck. Volcano burned in her blood and surrounded her with a nimbus of seductive scent.

She glanced to the side again, where her eyes encountered Clafto. He stood a little back, half in shadow, surrounded by several of his sparks. She saw anger in his eyes and felt a pulse of fear. So far she had kept Clafto at bay, but obviously Clafto still hoped.

She broke her gaze and looked ahead again with a defiant lift of her chin. Clafto would have to resign himself to his fate—yes, even if Sidney pressed and pressed and pressed. She would not be his tool, not anymore.

She dismissed both of them from mind.

She could not see the tribesman. Her father's golden form blocked her view. If Sidney weren't nursing a broken leg, he would be beside her now, and then she could look past her father. She imagined the curtsey she would give Mycal, the look she'd have on her face: a trace of a smile, a tinge of a pout in the lips, a boldness in the eyes followed by a drop of lashes. She had practiced the look in the mirror.

The plan swam before her mental consideration. It pleased her that Serenita had blessed it—although it was just a wee bit devious. But Regina didn't care. Her energies flowed and raced, stimulated by a little drug mixed just for her ladyship by her physician.

This time I shall achieve it, she thought with determination.

French watched her from the sideline with a brooding look. Proctor's last words still rang in his ears: "Never, *never* disobey me again!" *I should have done as he'd ordered,* French thought. Part of his mind noted that Regina looked fit to kill—a veritable, if slightly vulgar, goddess. She was ravishing and knew it. *If I'd had some staff with me,* another part of him brooded, *all this would never have happened.*

I should have stayed behind that drum and killed them all.

Half measures, he thought. *Half measures. Now we're in the soup.*

He felt Miri's eyes on him and turned. She smiled.

French felt a sudden rush of affection, put an arm around her waist, and pulled her close. So long as he had Miri . . . Her body heat penetrated through the silk. She was soft to the touch and yet he could feel her strength. Nothing daunted Miri. She could have been a Branco chick—a fierce, passionate smuggler's fem. He tweaked her hip, eyes on the scene.

The Unifier had stopped before the delegation.

An attendant noble disengaged himself from the entourage and carried the ornate key to Ricardo forward. He knelt down and held the pillow high so that the Unifier could take the key. Then Bono stepped forward. The two men shook hands and the key was presented.

Ceremony, French thought. *Ornate gestures of goodwill. Meanwhile we're just waiting to knife one another.*

His mind went back to the long, arid session with the sil chemists that morning. They had explored every conceivable possibility, but ultimately they had not been able to resolve the central question: Why would anyone want to *weld* silcoplast to *anything?* It could be done with copper, aluminum, and plastosteel. Simple: all you needed was a clean room, a molecular welder, and tightly controlled conditions—dust and random electrostatic fields had to be absent. Virtually every structure had the necessary facilities. But why do it? Such combinations had no possible use in any kind of communications system.

At the center of action, Barney and Proctor had now joined the group and toasted each other with glasses from a tray held by a brightly clad servant. Behind the group Regina and the family waited patiently.

The Unsler clan always amazed French by its size —all those brothers, uncles, aunt, cousins, nephews. They all had a kind of dull sameness, the same long face, pouched eyes, drooping nose. Only two people stood out. One was Regina—a beauty. The other was Harvanth, a fat, ruddy man. He had married one of the Unifier's four sisters and had brought into the

Unsler clan a blustering kind of energy. They had put him in charge of Defense, an unimportant job that even a stupid man could do.

The toast over, Unsler turned to introduce his family, and Regina advanced toward Bono. French watched with interest, wondering how the strict constructionist would react to the girl.

Bono blushed when she came forward, her hands lightly grasping her long gown. She bent down before him in a curtsey so low he glimpsed the movement of unsupported breasts. His blush grew darker. Blue eyes locked into his. Then her lashes dropped and she withdrew. Bono felt an involuntary twinge in his bowels and caught himself staring at her center with stupefied intensity. Someone else had come forward and pronounced a name, but Bono barely heard it.

He'd—he'd *never* seen anything quite so . . . It was really obscene, but she had definitely hypnotized him! He had to resist looking at her again, at all those undulating snakes. They pointed to a spot in her body that now shimmered darker, and now not.

Faces and names flashed by him. He shook hands and bowed absently, while his mind touched furtive memories of short, guilt-laden sexual encounters. He knew very little about women, really, it came to him now. Strict-constructionist training discouraged experimentation. Chastity was the word—at least until you formed a harem. Bono had trespassed on that command, of course. Drunk on fiery Wellhead whiskey, he had stumbled into the dark shacks on the other side of the refinery, where the mutants lived. But those experiences had never been altogether pleasant in retrospect. You couldn't call him an innocent, not really, still . . . Bono had never seen such display before. She was a princess, after all, he noted with inward shock. The Unifier's only daughter . . .

The last of the family came and withdrew.

Bono looked about at the vast glimmer and shine. Wellhead was very far away. The ballroom lay in a hush. No one moved; people stood on the edge of the empty dance floor. Unsler's family had arranged itself on both sides of a throne. Only Regina stood a little apart, alone. Her lashes were down.

Dart whispered fiercely from behind: "Dance. You're supposed to ask her to dance."

Now he remembered. Dart had described the whole procedure in the afternoon. The dance.

He walked toward her, rigidly averting his eyes from the snakes. He looked at her neck instead, at a narrow red band around her neck, at little silver bells. He bowed. Again she curtsied, in response, and her nipples flashed.

Then he held her and they swung out on the floor.

The Birth of Hairy-Scary

For some time, Proctor had conferred quietly with members of the Group. He had just spoken with Justin Todd, an old friend in the Ministry of Engineering, on whom he would rely to help hide the Interdiction. Todd's people, jointly with Proctor's, supervised helium delivery. And then Hondo Weinberger had also been by, his hair gray and unruly. Hondo was the architect of the surreptitious Media campaign.

Proctor obtained perverse pleasure from meeting the Group here, in Top Level, but enough was enough.

Roger Belmonte strode toward him, the black commander of Ricardo's police and garrison. With a slight shake of his head, Proctor told the soldier from a distance that a meeting was inappropriate. Belmonte changed course. The red-and-gold jacket suspended from a button on his shoulder swung at the turn. Soon only the feather on the man's triangular hat showed above the crowd.

Proctor looked around for French, eager to chew on someone. The evening had been a sinister replay of 1051, when Tack had chased the same seductive bitch with such disturbing consequences. *Can all the intelligence forecasts be wrong?* Proctor wondered.

For a single, frightening moment Proctor imagined a scheme whereby Ecofreak arranged a charade to let BTA's intelligence forces think that Activists had won.

Once that notion was firmly set, they would swoop in for the kill, bypassing BTA in a bold bid for Regina, intermarriage, the whole lot. The thought made Proctor tremble. Under those conditions, there would be no Interdiction, no Secret Agenda.

French! Goddamn, where was that man? He had blundered last night, gunning down a man. Had he also blundered in his estimates?

Proctor searched the crowd.

Then at last he saw them. White-robed men had blocked his view, but he picked out French and Miri just as they joined the dance. They turned around and around. Miri's fringed stole flew through the air and light glanced off her single golden earring. Proctor watched French lead his wife across the ballroom, corner to corner. He lost the couple for a second; then he picked them up again, somewhat closer this time.

A strained expression on French's face caused Proctor to glance back toward the spot where French and Miri had started. That group who had blocked his view—had they been Flames?

His searching look fell on Clafto Meyer flanked by three husky young men. They wove their way through dancers on the floor clearly in pursuit of French but at a sedate, leisurely pace. Proctor comprehended the situation in a flash and experienced concern for his Deputy Assistant. BTA had no power in Top Level, while Sidney's Flames came and went here every day. On second thought, French was no fool—a hardy man, a veteran of Hinterland. He had brains, good instincts . . .

Proctor glanced back to his left and saw the couple again just as French broke off the dance and, pulling Miri under the balcony, raced for an exit. He nearly collided with a tray-bearing servant.

From the other direction, Clafto and his followers followed in hot pursuit, now running. They pushed rudely through the dancers, heading toward the exit.

Suddenly Proctor exploded in anger. It boiled up in him, hot and steaming. He had felt the fury ever since Blottingham's telcall, ever since that pear-shaped wonder had threatened him. Damnation! He had watched the bloody arrogance of this noble brotherhood too goddamned long, thank you! They could ravage the helpless masses of Ricardo all they liked, but BTA was a far cry from helpless. BTA was Proctor.

Deep down, Proctor sensed a memory, but its content was out of focus.

A counterthrust, he thought, casting caution to the wind. *Goddamn, I'll mount a counterthrust.*

Turning cool, icy as rapidly as he had flared, he thought about the matter with shrewd calculation. Sidney's Flames all came from Very Big families. BTA could not kill such men without severe danger of retaliation. But if the counterthrust was to have its desired effect, it had to be something . . . shocking, jolting, memorable.

Proctor turned this and that around in his mind. Then he had an idea and began to elaborate on it. As he did so a smile faintly lit his features. The idea was neither very practical nor very rational, but he found it irresistible for that very reason. Nobody would believe the Flames, and therefore it might just work.

He gave his plan a name: Operation Hairy-Scary!

Proctor snapped his concentration and began to look about. He would have to have a talk with Belmonte after all. Tomorrow night, when BTA swarmed over the Acropolis to pick up Flames, the police had to be conveniently blind.

Invitation

As they had danced through the hours, Bono had fallen ever more deeply into a trance in which nothing seemed to matter but her scent, her feel, her warmth. He moved with the tide, aware that he was drunk with stimulation and false hopes. *The girl's crazy about you,* he thought. *There is no other explanation. She has refused all others, and her eyes shine with a kind of admiration.* Seconds later he took it all back. *She isn't really in love with you. It's just this damn Adjustment thing. You're making it all up.*

Shame possessed him, and he blushed recalling the

stupid conversations between dances. They had nothing in common. "You are a rancher, Mr. Bono?" "Yes, ma'am." "Where is your land?" "In the Merillo district, on the Plain of Baez." "You dance divinely, Mr. Bono." "Ma'am, I . . ." He had stood beside her like a tongue-tied clod. Choked up, plain and simple. A chasm yawned between them. Yet . . . yet she clung to him for dear life. He could not be imagining it all. Her eyes sparkled in such an odd way . . .

They danced near one of the exits from the ballroom. She had more or less guided him toward it, and now she stopped.

"Come," she said, and she pulled him through.

The heavy door closed, shutting off the noise of people, the jangle of music. In the odd silence, in a hall lined on both sides by mirrors and lit by lamps fashioned in the shape of candles, her eyes gazed into his, and then he found her in his arms.

Her lips sought his in a hungry, almost angry kiss. After a moment she disengaged her mouth with a wrenching sigh, as if it caused her pain to do so. His legs trembled with weakness. Bright, languid, yet teasing eyes looked into his. He bent to kiss her again, but she turned her head aside and shook it slightly.

"When?" he asked in a voice harsh with emotion.

"Tonight?" She raised an eyebrow.

"Where?"

She reached up and pulled his head down so that her lips could whisper in his ear. "In my domain, you silly. Where else? Top Level West. The tower nearest to Hinterland." She even managed to give that word a romantic sound. Her breath tickled and heated his ear.

"But how?" He need not have whispered. They were alone, observed only by mirrors on either side. "I don't know how to get about. I've been inside the embassy all week."

Once more she pulled his head down. Her teeth gingerly bit the lobe of his ear, causing him to tremble all over.

"Outside the main lobby—where you came in? Turn

left and walk to the garage that faces Outer Ring. One of my people will bring you to me."

She let go of him and drew back.

He took a step toward her, but she shook her head again.

"Later," she whispered. She puckered up her lips in the semblance of a kiss. Then she walked away from him, hand extended, reflected in mirrors.

When she had disappeared, Bono turned and walked back into the ballroom. For the first time in hours he became aware of his surroundings and noticed that the crowd had thinned. He picked a path along the edge of the dancers, walking next to columns, unaware of the knowing looks that followed him. He mused in a kind of strung-out way, thinking that it was true after all: she *did* love him, by God! That meant that he would soon be violating a sacred law of the Crestmore doctrine, but the thought left him indifferent. He knew the verse—who didn't! "Thy seed shall not mingle with that of the whore." So it was written. But he could hardly wait to pollute the pure tribal blood, he thought with an inward chuckle, didn't give a damn, was delighted to do it, in fact. He picked up the pace, making for the lobby.

Suddenly, small, wrinkled Dart stepped out from behind a column and blocked his path.

Bono frowned.

"There you are, Mycal," Dart said, eyes searching and disapproving all at once. He sidestepped and continued beside Bono. "Ready to go home, call it a night?"

"I have other business," Bono answered curtly. "You go on alone."

"Mycal!" Dart grabbed him by his sleeve and stopped his eager forward rush, raising within Bono a sudden fury.

"What *is* it!" Bono grunted.

"If there is one thing I have," Dart said dramatically, "it's the courage to oppose. I oppose your whoring after structure flesh!"

"Hold your tongue!" Bono growled, glancing about

furtively. His face had gone red, more from anger than embarrassment. "I have business. I am *not* whoring after anything." He tried to pull free, but the wrinkled claw held on to his sleeve tenaciously.

"The talks start at nine tomorrow," Dart said. "It's nearly one in the morning. You must be rested and sharp. You can't risk the future of the tribe."

"Let *me* worry about that," Bono spat back under his breath. He jerked his arm loose. "What I do is none of your business, Dart. Remember that!"

He gave Dart an angry stare, turned, and walked away.

Pursued

French pushed through a swinging door and pulled Miri behind him. Cooks in white tunics looked up in surprise. French swept the gleaming kitchen with a glance. His eyes came to rest on a heavyset butcher. In front of him, stuck point down in a wooden block, he saw a big, sharp knife.

He glanced at Miri and noted that her uncomprehending surprise of a moment ago had yielded to cool awareness. He let go of her hand.

"Keep with me, no matter what," he whispered.

She nodded as he moved forward.

French stopped before the butcher, eyes on the knife for a second. "Which way out?" he asked, looking up.

The butcher stared back with an open mouth, clearly a stupid man.

"The *back* way!" French added, feeling strong tension.

Precious seconds fled. Then he saw the exit, half obscured by large pots hung on the wall. French grabbed the knife as he passed the butcher. It would replace the pistol he had left at home—one did not go to Top Level social events armed.

Past pots and pans he ran out, Miri breathing hard behind him.

The stunned butcher yelled: "Hey! *He-ey, you!*" The door cut off his voice.

Senses sharpened by danger, French looked about with a flashing eye. They were in a narrow room. To the right, a row of women stacked plates into a battery of dishwashers. Ultrasonic cavitators hummed. The women did not notice them. He ran forward, pressed into motion by the certainty of pursuit.

Near the opposing door stood a wheeled cart loaded with stacks of dirty porcelain—precious, skin-thin stuff from Narodnik. He drew up short before the cart and gave it a shove. It sailed down the way they'd come, its tiny swiveled wheels wobbling. The butcher opened the door just in time to collide with it. French heard the crash of breaking, skidding china as he pushed Miri ahead and out.

They ran through a maze of corridors, seeking the exit toward the garage, but found only toilets, broom closets, pantries. French felt fatalistic about this crazy chase. Clafto's face back in the ballroom, when, for a second, he had confronted French, had been too damned cocksure. French was certain that Flames would be blocking all the exits.

He kicked himself for his carelessness and softness. He should not have allowed Miri to come, should have anticipated this, shouldn't have let her talk him into it. Would he ever learn to say no to Miri?

He raced ahead. Miri's silk swished behind him. Now was the time for some of her magic, he thought wrily. They needed a spell that would transport them to their cubohome. *Never mind,* he thought, *I'll bet Clafto has the place staked out.*

On one of the turns they suddenly saw Flames coming toward them and turned in the other direction, running for a door up ahead. They ran to the door, went through. On the other side French found and activated a lock. *Thank God for little favors!* They had a second or two for deliberation.

The room was dark. It took him a moment to see what it was.

An empty dormitory! Beds were stacked five high

to the ceiling, but clearly the place wasn't used at present; the mattresses, seen in the dim red light above the door, were bare. An idea came to him and he decided to take a chance.

He pulled Miri between a set of bunks. "Quickly. Get down," he ordered. "Crawl under the bed." She complied, and he lay down beside her. "Don't move. Don't even breathe."

She settled down. For a second her gown rustled. Then all was still.

In a flash Flames bounced against the door, tore at its handle, kicked the metal. This was followed by the silence of their consultations on the other side, and then by the dull reports against the metal of a heavy shoulder backed by body weight.

The lock snapped at last and a big man tumbled in, bringing a flood of light and, immediately behind him, a group of Flames. Clafto yelled: *"Up ahead, through there!"*

Boots ran along the aisle of the empty dormitory. A door slammed. It was still. The gamble had paid off.

"Come," French whispered.

He ran to the door through which Clafto's herd had just departed, locked it. Then he led the way back. On the opposite end of the long corridor he saw another door just like the one Clafto's men had broken down. Another dormitory? One for women, one for men? Another lock?

His guess turned out to be right. They plunged into darkness. Once more he saw a red light at the end of a bunk-lined aisle. He locked the door and moved forward.

Stopping below the night light at the other end, he glanced at Miri, saw tension in her face.

"Are you all right?" he whispered.

Miri nodded. She was tense but confident. She had never seen this side of Frenchy before—his concentrated instinct and power. The knife in his hand glowed red in the light above the exit. Tiny bits of meat and fat caught in the serrations of the blade brought to mind that Top Level ate imported food, not hydroponic substitutes.

French turned to the door, grasped the handle firmly, and slowly opened it. Light drew a narrow line down his face. He saw a wall. He opened the door wider.

A guard!

A heavyset young Flame leaned against the wall out there, a pistol suspended from his slack hand. He was evidently bored by his guard duty. French saw him yawn, saw him scratch his head.

Very, very slowly, French closed the door.

"Wait here," he whispered to Miri.

He gripped the knife, the doorknob. Five steps should get him to the Flame and surprise would work for him. His throat was tight with excitement.

One last glance at Miri's face, then he leaped out of the darkness into the light.

His sudden, flashing attack totally overwhelmed the Flame. The man didn't even have time to raise his weapon. His big, florid face turned slowly. Large, watery eyes stared. Then French drove the knife into the man, stabbing up through guts toward the lungs. Moist eyes, wide open in innocent surprise, slid past French as the figure sank slowly to the floor. Blood appeared at the man's mouth, nose.

French grabbed the pistol. Three quick steps carried him back to the dormitory door. He reached in for Miri and pulled her out.

She stopped and stared at the dead man. His eyes were still open, still innocent but glazing. A wound in his center had begun to ooze.

She took it all in with cool objectivity. Recycled. Back to the womb of the Cosmic Lady, she thought, and she reflected that he would be reborn again and would start his interrupted journey over as a baby.

"Come on," French said, his voice edgy. He had glimpsed a door down the hall with the word GARAGE painted in black letters on its gray surface.

In the garage itself, dark at the point where they entered, but light up ahead where through arches

French could see the upper portions of Outer Ring, he led the way toward a clump of jumptubes parked closely together.

"Get in one of these," he told her. "Quickly. Get down so you can't be seen. I'll look around."

He waited until she had disappeared in what turned out to be one of the tubes of the tribal delegation. All the tubes in this cluster bore the circular Ecology symbol on the door, and French was reminded that the ancient greek letter, *theta*, symbolized death. He hoped it wasn't an omen.

They were on the third or fourth floor of the parking lot, a simple arrangement with open sides. Thick, rectangular columns supported the roof.

French ran to the spot in the shadow of the columns from which he could oversee the downshaft. He recoiled when he saw motion. Peering out more slowly, he recognized Bono and another man descending in jumptubes marked by the Unsler flower.

Sooooo! French thought. *Will my troubles never end? My noble strict constructionist already pants after the only fem he should avoid like the plague. Proctor will—Proctor will have a heart attack!*

He headed toward the street side and saw what he had hoped he wouldn't see: Flames spaced at regular intervals on the sidewalk below. That way was blocked too. Now what?

Armor

Regina ran out of the shower, still drying herself, to see if Selma had laid out the costume. She wanted to be ready and in position by the time Bono arrived.

Yes, the girl had done her work.

The ruffled blouse and leather shorts with suspenders lay on the end of the large, canopied bed under the supervision of four large teddy bears lounging against the pillows. White knee socks with tiny red pom-poms on top—also ready. On the floor waited red leather shoes with thick, high heels.

Regina smiled, pleased with the display. Shorts, suspenders, especially the crossbar on the suspenders made of carved bone—all this would combine into a signal. A tribal touch, but not excessively tribal. The leather conveyed a hint of armor, of inaccessibility. Yet the shorts were *very* short and would give full play to her thighs—a touch of the necessary enticement.

As if the poor boy needed any more enticement!

She slipped into panties and pulled them over her flat belly, across the shadow of her navel.

Should she wear a bra? Decidedly. Absolutely. She squeezed several in a row, standing before a cabinet with its drawer open, and picked the stiffest and most opaque one she could find.

More armor.

In a way she felt sorry for him. He was a very nice boy. She had found him clumsy and innocent. As for dancing, he hadn't the faintest. Most clubfooted, clumsy. Not like her Jonny at all. She could *like* him, she decided. She might even learn to love him, although now it was all pretense.

Her arms behind her back, she pressed the fabric together and the fibers locked.

She put on and buttoned her ruffled blouse and slipped into the leather shorts. The horn buttons of the suspenders gave her a bit of trouble. They refused to fit into the button holes.

Serenita had approved the plan and had called her a clever girl. The nun had come in the afternoon for consultation. For once she had not worn her usual nunnish costume but a long, blue robe and a simple cloth around her head; she was a very tall woman and surprisingly erect for someone her age. In her left ear had been a golden ring, and that ring now puzzled Regina. She had seen the identical ring on a woman at the ball . . . Or had she? Oh, never mind.

"He will understand when it's all over," Serenita had said, seated primly on the edge of a backless, hassocklike seat in the conversation pit. Her understanding had surprised Regina, for the proposal was a bit unethical. She meant to use Mycal, to make him into a tool of her own designs; and Serenita should have disapproved of that as contrary to the teaching of charity. But the nun had nodded. "Now you must do anything you can to escape that worthless brother of yours." How true. How true. "Afterward, when it's all over, you can explain everything to him. He will understand and forgive you—I'm sure of it."

Yes, Regina mused, *he's a sweet boy.*

She pulled on her socks and slipped into the shoes. Fully dressed now, she walked to the tall mirror by the shower door to look at herself and found the image pleasing.

The hairdo, of course, would have to go.

Five minutes in that marvelous, computerized machine her hairdresser had devised—he said it was the only one in all of Union, designed exclusively for Her Ladyship—and she would have two girlish braids on either side with a red ribbon in each, in place of this randomly curled Medusa pile on her head.

Then she would go up into the garden and wait for him under the stars.

Agony in the Garden

All around Top Level's lobby, Bono had seen pictures of Union's thirty-nine structures. Some were shown at night in a blaze of light, some in daytime against clear skies, yet others half shrouded in clouds. The sight of so many structures had filled him with awe. The reality of Union's some odd million people had impressed itself on his awareness.

That was one perspective on the subject.

Another was the inside view, what he had observed in the last fifteen minutes or so: the Acropolis at night —or in the daytime, for that matter. In structures there was no difference between the two.

Ricardo—a bright shining of glossy surfaces, deeply

shadowed recesses. Everywhere light had bounced off bluish drilla-glass panes, large and small, convex and concave—like the eyes of an insect magnified a thousandfold. Ramps, railing, flights of stairs cascading down or towering up. Squares, alcoves, fountains, mechanical birds chirping in artificial trees. Gigantic micromosaics blinking from tiny particles as he passed. The slithering, reddish, scaled surface of movebelts. Colorful clusters of flashing signs in empty shopping arcades. The breathtaking drop down Central's shaft, passing level after level in a succession of bright–dark–bright all the way down to the mixing bowl. And now this sweeping vista that stretched before him—West Tower's broken lights seen through the translucent roof of the hoselike intertower beltway.

She lived up there.

She lived up there. She lived in this city. Yet another perspective on the subject.

Ricardo, fruit of a tree. Regina, sweet meat of the fruit.

Bono explored the image. A map of the helium pipeline in that Top Level lobby had suggested it. The pipeline resembled a gigantic red tree overlaid against the American subcontinent. Its trunk ran south and north. Its branches reached from coast to coast. At the end of each branch hung a structure. The roots of the tree reached deep within Texahoma and sucked helium from five red pools, all of them near Wellhead, where the gasfields had been discovered three hundred years ago—a new formation since the wars, perhaps caused by the wars, gasfields whose methane was rich with helium.

The gas came from the ground and went through refineries. Cryo-expanders stripped off the methane, leaving pure helium, which traveled through slender pipes up the trunk of the tree. Once he had put his hand around it. His fingers had almost touched his thumb. And yet that small artery sufficed to raise these magnificent constructions.

His admiration for the structures was excessive, of

course. Regina colored his thoughts. Wherever she was, there was magnificence.

The poisonous fruit of the helium tree held a sweet kernel that he would taste. How could he reject the structures?

He wanted to *get* there. "Show me how to drive one of those things," he said to the servant who traveled beside him. Bono pointed at his own jumptube, which the man operated by remote control.

Later he sat in a dark lobby of "Her Ladyship's domain," as the servant called it. He paced up and down, nervous like a caged beast. At last a thinnish young woman with large eyes appeared at the door. She had a face perpetually in an expression of astonishment.

"The mistress is waiting for you in the garden. Please follow me."

She led him through halls and rooms, a veritable warren of rooms, some small and cozy, some large and expansive, but all of them incredibly wealthy and beautiful—with mirrors, tiny fountains, glass tables, cabinets, soft crumpled couches, statuettes, glistening mobiles, tables and chairs, exquisite micromosaics. The lights were dim and he sensed in the shadows more rooms, more nooks, more mysteries. He heard a faint whisper of music.

He had a vague thought of paradise and underneath that a tremor of anxiety.

I'm not worthy . . .

He couldn't believe any of this. The experience had a dreamlike, unreal quality. He followed this girl through a . . . museum of wonders. He smelled perfume. Somewhere she waited—for *him!* It boggled his mind.

A devilish part of his brain reminded him that he had come to Ricardo to destroy it.

Madness, foolishness!

He meant the Crestmore doctrine. Right now he could not understand what the fuss was all about. Perhaps Myron Crestmore had had a point at one time. But now the mad antagonism between Structure and Hinterland made no sense at all. The two had lived side by side for centuries.

Heretical thoughts, chided his devilish self. *My, my, Mycal! How you can twist and turn the facts when you want to . . . when you want* HER!

Bono shook his head in protest as he followed the girl over carpets of iridescent sheen, delicate tiles, polished parquet.

Nothing new, this doubting. He recalled his adolescence, when he had stared at refineries, compressor stations, copters, laboratories, rockets, cannon, temp-control devices . . . He had thought then that all these things were also Technology. He had smiled inwardly when he'd been told that tribesmen only used Technology to defeat Technology. He had always wondered. Now, after all these years, the doubts had simply come to the fore again in the presence of structure life—which didn't seem so terrible after all.

I really had no concrete idea, he assured himself. *No idea at all what it was like.* It was enchanting— the whisper of music, the strands of faint scent floating in the air, the warble of water somewhere, the girl hiding somewhere here—

Well, yes, dammit, the girl! They don't know anything back home, he thought with sudden irritation.

The servant had stopped before a glass door. Through it Bono saw a stairway curving out of sight. His own image—boots, beaded leather clothing, dark-bearded face—was mirrored faintly in the glass.

"The mistress waits up there. Go on up."

He pushed the door open and felt an inrush of humidity, smelled a garden.

Nodding to the servant, completely intent now on what lay ahead, he went through and climbed the stairs.

Halfway up he noticed open sky above, glimpsed through a curving dome of glass faintly reflecting light, a deep blackness richly sprinkled with a wash of stars. He had not seen the sky in days. The Milky Way clouded across his vision overlaid by closer, brighter luminosities.

He went on around a spiral.

Bono stopped at the head of the stairs and saw a garden under a roof formed by numerous small domes. Telescopes stood in a row on his left. Lamps on two sides behind a profusion of plants bathed the roof in a faint light. A graveled path stretched ahead. Olive trees, palms, tropical bushes, flowers in a riot of color filled the place, closely packed and lush, exuding a rich organic smell.

The garden must have cost a fortune to install, must cost a fortune to maintain. The whole place had to be completely shielded from gravitron—like mush-tanks.

He sought her with his eyes and saw her at last half hiding in a small, moon-shaped clearing off the path, smiling from the depth of a large piece of canvas upheld by four steel stems that fanned out of a thick stone base. She had crossed her legs and her chin rested on two upheld fists.

She took his breath away. She had transformed herself from a sultry goddess into a sweet, lascivious child—braided hair, white ruffled blouse, and tiny shorts that gave full play to a pair of thighs the color of milk above the tan.

She smiled at him for a long, breathless moment. Then, with the grace of a kitten, she jumped up and ran toward him. She nearly leaped into his arms.

He kissed her with mad abandon.

He kissed her, hugged her, and held her close because he didn't know how to go on. In those dark and filthy shacks in Wellhead, bored naked woman had waited while he had dropped his pants. This situation called for a ceremony of disrobing. But where to begin? She did not help him. He had to make the first move.

Regina, for her part, began to weaken rapidly. He was so deliciously inept. She fought the urge to yield, to help him. *She* was aroused! *She*—who had been subject to the most sophisticated methods of seduction used by men who fancied they knew a bit about the art of love. *That* she could handle. *This* was something much more dangerous for all its innocence.

When Bono began clumsily to grope around her back for an opening—she felt the roughness of his hands as they encountered the rigid strappings of her suspenders—she nearly panicked into submission. But she pulled herself together. She *had* to follow her plan, no matter how inconvenient. When he intensified his search with something approaching frenzy, she suddenly slipped out of his grasp and stepped back.

Her face was blank with desire. She shook her head. Her eyes brimmed with affection.

"We mustn't," she said. "Not *that*."

"What do you mean," he rasped, completely out of breath, chilled with irritation.

"I can't strive with you, little darling. Not yet."

"Why not?" he barked, his eyes in a terror. "Why? Why not?"

Bono had a terrible premonition that she would elude him. He felt a dark confusion. Everything about her told him she desired as much as he. The sensation of her own lust merely amplified his own.

"Don't be so furious," she whispered. "I love you, truly! But I've been disappointed before."

At that moment, strangely, she *did* love him—or maybe it was just her hormones?

"I love you," he breathed, and he took her in his arms again, possessively, fiercely. But she blocked him from her softness and resisted his artless tugging.

Did he truly love her? she wondered. Or was he, like she, under the venal spell?

"I know," she whispered. Whatever they now felt was real enough in its way to be a substitute for love. "I know, Mycal. But I won't be hurt again. I need your true commitment."

"You have it," he said hastily. "Truly. I love you." Once more he began to seek an opening on her back.

He still hasn't grasped that it can't be tonight, that I must have more . . . She wished it didn't have to be so; she wanted to conceive, so much, so much. *Con-*

ceive? That was a stray thought, and she put it aside. What she wanted, obviously, was to yield. But this time she was determined to win. Like crazy, menacing laughter, another world was there, in a corner of her mind—a future much like the past, a future which might become worse after Daddy died and Sidney became ruler of all.

My plan, she thought. *My plan.*

Slowly but firmly she pushed him back.

Bono saw her shake her head. "I must have more . . ." she said.

"Name it," he cried. "I promise you! You'll have it." He was all fervor and conviction. He would give her the Milky Way itself, rolled up in a canvas bag.

She looked at him with an expression so sweet, so filled with longing, he forgot the lust he felt, that subliminal rage that was ready to burst forth, that strange vacillation between hope and despair.

Her look was questioning, timid. "Do you *really* love me?"

"Truly, I do!" He made a step toward her, but she retreated.

"Then take me with you to Hinterland."

Bono felt a surge of joy. Was that all? Was that all her little heart desired? Nothing he longed to do more, nothing easier. He relaxed again. He would possess her yet. He could meet her price—and more. To have her by his side was his own most fervent longing.

"Yes," he effused. "I'll take you."

Once more he made an advance, thinking that now the bargaining was over. But then he saw with a wary eye that those words were not enough. She retreated farther, all the way to the moon-shaped clearing off the path. She walked behind the lawn chair, put it between them.

"Darling," she said, "please don't be angry. I shouldn't have asked you to come. But I *so* wanted to see you again. We won't strive tonight. Please don't expect that. I won't do that until you've made your commitment."

Bono was devastated.

"But how?" he asked. His voice had the sound of suppressed tears, a choking. "What do you want me to do?"

She looked at him; she hesitated. Now she would learn the extent of his commitment. In this moment, she cared as much for his commitment as she did for what it would bring her—escape.

She took a deep breath.

"This round," she said, "*I* must be the helium hostage. Only then will Daddy let me go. Ask for me, darling. And when I see it reported on the Media, I'll be yours."

4

Meditation

French lay on the bed in his underwear, one leg propped up. His eyes rested on Miri's dark silhouette. She stood by the foot of the bed and undressed before him in the half-light from the bath. The chaste gown fell to her waist.

"I must meditate," she said, as she turned.

French smiled and nodded, admiring her cool. They had just escaped death and had been shown into this dingy cubicle empty of furniture but filled with an unusually strong gravitron hum. A cold and musty room. A late hour. Unusual circumstances. Nevertheless, Miri remembered her spiritual chores.

She sank down to the floor. Over the bed's edge French saw her shoulders, neck and face. Her eyes were closed. She sat with her legs crossed and her hands on her knees. In the mood of relaxation he now felt, with the anxieties of the past hour still there like a residue at the bottom of his perceptions, her very posture aroused him. The physical alignment of her body signaled two kinds of receptivity: spiritual and sexual. His face softened, and he watched her profile through eyes clouded with a kind of tenderness. He often watched her like this, thinking the same thought.

He waited a long time. Miri tripped out in a trance, her spirit in other dimensions. She sought the limpid light of truth, a state of quiescent calm. Such states came very rarely, she said. Instead she usually had visions—silly, prophetic, disturbing.

As he watched her, he saw again a faint light around her head—or thought he saw it. French was never certain whether or not Miri really radiated a kind of strange energy or whether he merely imagined it. To watch her meditate was itself a kind of meditation. It engendered images.

Devotee of the Cosmic Lady . . .

French knew next to nothing about the Cult. They taught magical practices—like this technique which draped Miri's head and shoulders in a nimbus of light. He swore he saw a light, although its subtle radiance faded when his concentration slipped. Secretive, the sisters of the Cult. They claimed and had very real powers. They claimed to see the future in visions or in books or oracles—but darkly, darkly. Not with the precision French needed for his work. Prophecy had its limits. They had a doctrine that thoughts took on reality if held with strong emotion. Ritual lustrations and such things. Miri left, Saturday evenings, to partake of the mysteries. When she returned she was always receptive—oh, she was receptive!

French approved of the Cult, not so much because he approved of the occult or the transcendental but because he disapproved of nothing Miri loved. He was not religious himself. He saw the world in its irreducible particularities, not in collective symbols. If he longed to worship, he could always reach out.

You are my Cosmic Lady, he thought. *When I embrace you, I embrace the world. When you smile, it's sunny. When you frown, it's clouds . . .*

He watched her and waited.

Deep in meditation, Miri felt Frenchy's enveloping presence. His mood penetrated her sensitized psyche —and yet she had induced it or amplified it by her visions. His adoration sparkled with erotic tension. He would soon grow restless, she knew. She smiled inwardly and let the visions of maternity slowly fade away until nothing was before her eyes but the darkness behind her lids.

French decided he had waited long enough. He leaped from the bed and tiptoed up behind her. Kneeling down, he began to massage her skin gently. She radiated heat. The Cult also taught them how to control the body temperature. His hands pressed passionate.

He rubbed and massaged and moved closer and closer until he pressed up against her.

Miri pretended not to feel him. She detached herself from her body and perched her soul in a corner of the room like a yellow bird. From there she watched him and watched herself as if she were looking at an ancient etching illustrating some book in love yoga. But then came a point when the urgency of nerves summoned the bird back from its perch. She became one with her body, and with a low moan she twisted out of the lotus posture and drew him into her arms.

They rose after a moment and jumped on the bed, giggling.

The rush of breathing subsided at last. They rolled to the side, touching in silence. Gravitron vibrations pulsed in the air. French placed tiny kisses on her forehead. Her breathing grew shallow. She fell asleep.

He wormed his left arm out from beneath her and set his watch for six o'clock. He wouldn't get much sleep, but every little bit would help. The light was still on in the bathroom. Should he disentangle himself and put it out? No. He closed his eyes and immediately saw shadowy dream images. In contemplating them he passed over to the other side.

French started. Six o'clock? Yes. He felt a searing

pain against his wrist. He fumbled and turned off
the heat-alarm. Miri's legs still held his body in a
scissor grip. They lay much as they had fallen asleep.

He had to get up, but his body resisted. It seemed
as if he hadn't slept at all. Miri was warm. Perfume
lay on her skin like a wraith over waters. Her
breath moved against his naked arm.

He hovered between sleep and waking thinking in
rhythm with her breath. Miri-mine, Miri-mine . . .
Sleep reached for his awareness again, but he shook
it off. He had to get up, had to. His lips sought
Miri's birthmark. Then he gingerly lifted her leg,
rolled out of her earthy grip, and walked barefoot
and naked to the showers.

All shivering business now, he made a plan.

He was in the Ecofreak embassy and he somehow
had to get out undetected by Flames. Barney had
saved their life the night before. They had left Top
Level surrounded by tribesmen. The Flames hadn't
dared to cause an incident, not with men who controlled helium. But they had followed the group all
the way to the doors of the embassy. Despite strong
protests from Franco Dart, Barney had taken them
in; but in deference to the Activist, Barney had
put them up in an unused wing. Therefore the strong
gravitron vibrations. Someone had failed to do the
necessary maintenance around here.

French took a shower pondering his situation.

He expected that the Flames were still out there,
waiting. If he wanted to arrive at the first negotiating
session on time—without the humiliation of doing so
under Ecofreak protection—he had to get away now
undetected. That meant a disguise of some sort.
And it would be best to leave Miri here, where she
was safe, until he could fetch her with a group of
men.

He shaved with a dirty old razor someone had
left behind. Then he rummaged about in the cubicle's built-in closest trying on odd pieces of tribal
clothing that visitors had abandoned here. Judging

by the pattern of beads, this cubohome hadn't been used in years.

In the midst of these activities, French discovered a section of wall patched over with a plate of plastosteel screwed into place. He realized at once that the cubicle abutted a service chasm. His troubles were over. He could get out with no trouble at all.

Soon he was at work with a stiff saniblade from the shaver. The plate came off easily. Behind it gaped a ragged hole in the eroded wall, and gravitron sparks flew about. The suction pulled him but he resisted. Only his blond locks moved toward the opening.

French wrote a note for Miri. Then he put on the tribal tunic—a little too small—and a tribal hat—a little too big. He crawled out into the humming darkness, reached inside and lifted the plate. Chasm vacuum sucked the metal back into place. He was on his way.

The Hostage Demand

According to tradition, the first session of the helium round was scheduled to begin at eight in the morning. Based on the same tradition, no one expected the Ecofreaks until a quarter to nine at the earliest. Ritualized discourtesy belonged to the negotiations as much as did the toast upon arrival and the Top Level ball.

Promptly at eight forty, French slapped his knees and rose from his chair in Proctor's office. He waited until the speaker had finished. Then, with a glance at the senior members of the negotiating team who had assembled for a last-minute session, he said: "I'd better go and do my chores."

Proctor nodded, and French left.

By hallway, elevator, and another hallway, French reached BTA's lobby. He nodded to the guards on his left and took up a stand before the door. Arms folded across his chest, he stared through glass at shallow stairs that fanned out and down to the sidewalk and the slow edge-lanes of the movebelt. Morning crowds filled the belt. French lifted his eyes to the airspace above and surveyed the jumptube traffic coming and going. From time to time utility jumpers and levi-limos passed in the middle, spurting blue flames from tailjets.

French preferred idle waiting to the gloom of the meeting he had just escaped—where the Office of Intelligence in general and French in particular had been under sniveling attack.

Everyone in the meeting, and above all Proctor —who had set the tone and whom everyone had avidly aped—made much of Bono's behavior the night before. French's characterization of the man as a strict constructionist had been ridiculed and questioned. How could BTA enter the negotiations with such poor intelligence estimates? The performance of the Office of Intelligence had been most lackadaisical on this issue. And other such bosh!

They called themselves negotiators, French thought with scorn. At cocktail parties they told tall tales of fancy dancing and eyeball-to-eyeball confrontations in practice they demanded hard guarantees, well in advance, that everything would go smoothly and that no one would get the slightest bit of heat.

French could understand Proctor's anxieties to some extent. Proctor worried about the Secret Agenda. He feared that Ecofreak had made an end run. The big corporate interests and Bernard Unsler both wanted Accommodation. The corporations sought unimpeded trade with Hinterland without the paternal interventions of BTA. Unsler followed his oldest ambitions: to rule the entire American subcontinent, as his predecessors had done. These two interests conspired with Ecofreak to bring about Accommodation at last, lulling BTA by a show of Activism. At least, that was Proctor's thesis.

It was nonsense, of course. Nevertheless, all the

men had sagely nodded. Then they had begun to blabber something about Regina Unsler. French had quietly suggested that five-percenters often suffered from behavioral aberrations. A chorus had shouted him down, hands waving in deprecation.

A most inauspicious beginning, French thought.

Yes, inauspicious.

When he had arrived early that morning, still in his ill-fitting tribal clothes, he had gone to report to Proctor and had found Dickens in Proctor's office spread out on chairs and couches with his security chiefs. They were planning Operation Hairy-Scary. The mere fact that they were in Proctor's office rather than in one of the conference rooms of the Office of Security had alerted French. The name of the operation had also given him pause.

Hairy-Scary: a strangely juvenile code name for what seemed very serious business.

Dickens and his people were busy with several simulators and with intricate three-dimension maps of Ricardo's towers. Spots on the maps had been marked *points of attack*. In the brief time French spent in the office, he learned the name of the operation and gathered that Sidney's Flames would be the target. Trays of stale refreshments and mounds of narrow printout scripto pointed to an all-night session.

His misgivings grew when he saw Proctor in the midst of it all. Proctor's eyes were red from lack of sleep, and yet they gleamed with boyish excitement —disturbing in a man of Proctor's usually stony reserve. French was reminded of the fact that he knew almost nothing about Proctor's background; nobody did. He came out of the past, ready-made. French soon gathered that Proctor didn't want him there. The Negotiator scowled at French's tribal costume and sent him off to gather the negotiating team for a meeting at a later time. He waved a hand. "Get into some decent clothing." Then he turned back eagerly to Operation Hair-Scary.

Playing little games . . .

French rocked back and forth on his heels. He liked neither the exuberance surrounding Hairy-Scary—ostensibly an action triggered by Clafto Meyer's murderous pursuit last night—nor the pessimistic approach to the negotiations.

Men should sleep at night, he told himself. *When they stay up all night, they lose perspective.*

A glance at his watch told him it was a quarter to the hour. The delegation should be here by now. He pulled down on the stiff new robe he had bought from the commissary in the BTA complex. Tillinghast, the manager, had been obliged to come in early to sell French a robe. He hadn't dared go home for proper clothes, and neither could he receive the delegation in a mockery of their own dress.

Punctual to the minute, Ecofreak arrived. Their jumptubes fell down from the traffic and settled on the sidewalk. Little doors opened. The tribesmen gathered into a clump and then, in unison, they came up the stairs toward the glass door. French put on a smile while his eyes searched the ascending delegates.

Bono was not among them. Dart walked at the head of the group.

French experienced a twinge of anxiety. His mind flashed a hazy memory of jumptubes in a shadowy garage, the Unsler flower . . . He pushed the glass door open, face still frozen in a smile.

After a series of perfunctory handshakes, French led the delegation toward the negotiating hall—a cavernous expanse built in the burgher style of another age and somewhat overwhelming. It was a vast glitter, sparkle, and shine from chandeliers and huge mosaics made of precious stones. In the center a large oval table rested on sinuous legs. Chairs carved from egg-shaped pieces of obduplast stood around the table. Smiling uncertainly, the BTA complement, minus Proctor, already waited.

Gnarled hand on his robe sleeve, Dart pulled French aside. His eyes looked at the Deputy Assistant and evaded him at the same time.

"The chief of mission has been detained," Dart said stiffly. "He is receiving additional instructions from home. I wonder if we could delay the start of the meeting briefly?"

"Of course," French said. He pointed to his right, where coffee, whiskey, and tiny pastries shaped like human thumbs were laid out over immaculately white cloths on tables. Servants stood waiting. "We can refresh ourselves while we wait. The Chief Negotiator has also been detained."

French moved toward the coffee, eyes on Dart.

"I understand that you have had extensive experience in structures," French said. He bent down and worked the silver handle of the coffee urn. Coffee steamed darkly into his cup. "You were First Secretary here, I understand."

"Yes," Dart answered absently. He peered toward the entrance over his shoulder. At that moment Bono appeared at the door, blinking in the brilliance of the room.

"Excuse me," Dart said. "I see that he has just caught up with us."

French nodded. He took a sip of coffee, followed Dart with his eyes.

A small figure before the taller tribesman, whose forked beard and hollow eyes gave a forbidding image at the moment, Dart stopped in front of Bono. Even from a distance, French saw that Bono had not slept much, if at all. But his features showed strain. He didn't have the languid air of a man who had spent his night striving.

Dart's hands gestured fiercely as he spoke. Bono looked past the older man with an indifferent expression in his eyes, observing the tribesmen, who placed ornately worked leather folders before each seat on the Ecofreak side of the table, premarked with name plates. Then Bono glanced at Dart and said a single word. A harsh gesture of dismissal followed. Bono stepped past Dart and walked toward the table.

French caught the eye of a Union negotiator, held

an index finger into the air, and nodded. The man stepped to a telset and punched numbers. The call would summon Proctor.

Following Bono's lead, the tribesmen settled around the table. Ecofreak would obviously shun the preliminary talk and drinking that, based on experience with this tribe, was an almost necessary preparation for sensible negotiations. But if the tribesmen wouldn't come to the refreshments, the refreshments had to go to the tribesmen.

French beckoned to a servant. "Please serve these things at the table," he said. Then he went to his own place, next to Proctor's in the center, opposite Franco Dart.

Bono reached for the carafe of whiskey and poured himself a glass full. The liquor tasted sharp, warm. Bono hoped that his weird excitement did not show in his externals. He experienced a kind of breathless intoxication, a kind of careless abandon a man felt only in the hunt, leaping, say, from boulder to boulder in the mountains after a wounded goat, without time for reflection, at the mercy of reflex.

He poured himself another glass and sensed Dart's disapproving stir.

Down the hatch! *God—some breakfast.*

I'm free, I'm loose, Bono thought. He kept his face rigid and his lips in a kind of pout, but he was amused, he wanted to laugh.

I'm awake, he told himself.

Tack was far away, plotting some kind of nonsensical war, like a child with lead soldiers, yes. Bono had once bought all that talk of war; but now he had awakened, finally. Here he was, on the scene, plotting love. Amazing how one could just chuck all those years of habit and go right against the grain of the past!

Men rose around him. He looked up and saw that Proctor had entered. Bono rose also, keeping himself in control despite internal bubblings.

Proctor approached the table, blue robes swishing. He carried folders under his arms. His chin was out.

He took up a position across from Bono, bowed. Bono returned the bow. Proctor waited until the assembly had settled down. Then he opened a folder and began to read the welcoming remarks in a hurried monotone.

Bono sat entranced by an internal vision of Jonny Tack. The vision amused him in a perverse sort of way. He saw Tack kicking furniture, saw him hit out with a balled fist. "Perfidy," he would bellow. "Treason!" *And what if Union yields the parts anyway? Wouldn't that be doubly amusing?*

To act, to leap out over a chasm certain that angels stood beneath to catch you on their wings—it had a mind-blowing exhilaration.

Bono followed the vision. If Union failed to yield up the parts, he would be a fugitive hunted by Tack's agents all over Hinterland. He wouldn't be safe anywhere except in the radiation belts or high up in the icy wastes of Canada. No matter. He would wander forever . . . perhaps with her. One act of defiance after all these years would be worth it all.

Proctor's voice rose slightly, revealing that he neared the end. Bono began to pay attention.

". . . And so, gentlemen," Proctor wound up, "as we again look forward to another five years of constructive cooperation with the great and noble tribe of Ecofreak—whose purposes, ideals, and aspirations all of us in Union deeply share—I welcome you around this table where, though disagreements might surface and conflicts may erupt, we have always, in the end, signed an accord of mutual benefit."

Hands clapped politely.

Bono rose, a little giddy.

"Gentlemen of Union, Chief Negotiator, men of Ecofreak . . ."

To his left, Dart gestured with some vehemence. Bono looked down and saw a folder in Dart's hands extended toward him. It was the official opening statement. Its every word had been carefully weighed; every intonation and nuance had been honed in daylong conferences. Bono waved the folder away.

"I'm a simple man," he began, really believing that

at the moment. He moved his eyes, looking at Proctor, French, then sweeping the line of yellow-robed BTA officials, all of whom, having seen him gesture the folder away, now stared at him with new interest.

"I'm a simple man from the steppes of Texahoma. I've never been inside a structure before. I was prepared, like all of my countrymen, to bring to you suspicion and traditional hatred. And is it any wonder? We are worlds apart. You live on the coasts in these gigantic machines under the drumbeat of gravitron, while we farm the land and herd our cattle through endless oceans of rolling mutagrass . . ."

A strong emotion helped him speak. Words rolled off his tongue unasked. He saw without reflection an exchange of glances between French and Proctor. He heard a sound from his left where Dart seemed to be gagging on something.

"For too long a time, too many years, your missiles have threatened our settlements. But we've held your life in our hands. Ever since the Helium War of 1011, when we forced your corporations to give up control by guerrilla warfare, we've had our hand on the helium valve. And so we stare at each other across the Desolation that circles you and keeps us apart."

The tribesmen to either side stirred in discomfort.

"There is much beauty here," Bono continued with a sweep of his hand, indicating the blaze of lights in the room. But he saw in his mind's eye the beauty that was Regina, her face inclined over his face as they had talked on a low divan all through the night. "There is beauty here and art, great skill," he continued. "Structure-man has made the High Culture, and may it live forever. May we—our scientists and yours—all together seek an alternative. to gravitron, an alternative that doesn't kill as it lifts."

Dart coughed. The old man seemed to be dying of coughing—a harsh, distracting sound.

Bono went on. The words came of their own accord. He was high with fatigue. He realized vaguely that he was speaking to Regina, to himself, not to this assembly.

"But Hinterland mustn't be despised. We have our life as you have yours. The land belongs to us. Our eyes look out over the steppes. We walk the high sierras, we sail the lakes and rivers. We give you what you need to live and in exchange you give us the products we don't want to make for ourselves. Ours is a life of mutual dependence. Why then do we threaten each other? We have helium and you have the Technology we need—to communicate, to increase our comforts. Is there sense in constant tension?"

He looked around at the assembly, lifting his eyes from the empty whiskey glass to which he had been addressing himself.

"There is not," he affirmed. "We have everything to gain, nothing to lose from maximum cooperation. Let us strive together"—the word made him halt for a split second—"for the best possible deal we can find, in a spirit of love and mutual respect."

He sat down amid uncertain applause.

Dart's face was immediately at his ear. The sour old-man's breath hissed.

"Have you gone mad? Why didn't you use the prepared text?"

A BTA man rose, cleared his throat, and began to read the 1051 Helium Contract.

Bono turned to Dart. "I didn't say anything that wasn't in the text, more or less. Just different words. My own." He saw that Dart was frightened.

"Mycal, there's a world of difference. For God's sake, don't go on like this! You're endangering our lives. Yours and mine. Jonny will be furious."

Bono shrugged. "He doesn't need to know. If we get him the silco-parts, he'll be delighted. He doesn't have to know how we conducted the negotiations."

Dart was breathless. It seemed to him that Bono's eyes still held a glimmer of madness, a residue of the night before. He reached for the prepared text bound in a folder, opened it, and flipped to the last page. He pointed to Jonny's initials in the approval box in the corner.

"He approved it," Dart whispered. Although Dart's

voice was low, Bono could sense the heavy charge of emotion in the words. "He put his initials on this. That's tantamount to an order." Dart hit the expensive fiber paper with a wrinkled knuckle.

"We need flexibility to negotiate," Bono returned curtly. "I'm no tape recorder, parroting his words."

The BTA official droned on, reading the contract.

"The cable," Dart insisted in a whisper, meaning the random-coding radio communications system that linked the embassy with the Texahoma camp but which, as a result of tradition, still went by the term *cable*. "If you want a change in direction, you can cable home. But without his approval, you can't deviate from your instructions. Jonny will string us up. I can't let you do it, Mycal. Withdraw your statement now and read this."

Bono fixed Dart with a stare. "You're merely an advisor. You can't tell me how to negotiate."

Dart remembered that he had the courage to oppose. "Do you know why I'm on this delegation?" he asked in an angry whisper, recalling Jonny's words again. ("Go with him, keep your eyes on him.") "I'm here," he went on, "because I opposed your nomination. And Jonny sent me along to keep an eye on you. And it's a good thing he did. You gave them an altogether false impression with your off-the-cuff ramblings."

Dart felt redeemed by Bono's blunder. *I might have blabbed a little to Barney,* he thought, *but I didn't disobey any direct orders from Jonny Tack.* He wondered where Bono had spent his night and suspected that he knew only too well. Of such liaisons came bad policy. Bono's incoherent babble, the mad look in his eyes, his rumpled clothes convinced Dart that more trouble lay ahead. Union bureaucrats had a phrase that described what he now felt about the chief of mission: Bono had "blood on him." Any moment now the hounds could close in. Dart had known it, had known it from the start, had told Tack as much in no uncertain terms. Dart didn't mince words when he opposed. And if the hounds already bayed in the distance, Dart wished to be far away when they arrived.

"You've heard the old accord, Chief Bono," Proctor said. "What is your initial position for the next round?"

French eyed Bono with interest. The tribesman's opening remarks, clearly invented on the spot, had had a very different sound than Bono's initial observations in the hall of reception. Now the Ecofreak chief, who had lowered his eyes toward a leather folder, looked up at Proctor. His face revealed nothing.

"Ecofreak has no *initial* position," Bono stressed. "Ecofreak has *one* position. We intend to abide by it. I believe it's fair and reasonable and will benefit both sides. With your permission, I'll read it."

Proctor nodded.

They would have certainty, at last, French thought. If they had been deceived in their estimates, now they'd know the truth—or at least as much of the truth as Bono would reveal in his opening sally. French found it significant that Barney had been excluded from the delegation. He hoped with all his heart that Bono's statement had been mere talk, rhetoric, not the exposition of an Accommodationist view.

Men opened folders. French looked down at his own sheet. He held a stylus at the ready.

Bono began to read, very slowly.

French made a checkmark next to item one. The plastosteel demand, as Barney had told him—and as French had noted that night on the fiber napkin with the imprint of The Mutant in the corner—was eight hundred thousand tons. No surprise there. Bono read sixteen conditions that dealt with delivery. BTA men recorded the points. So did six cameras through holes in the ceiling.

Next came a list of products. French grew more alert. The item slipped by almost without notice. Five thousand clock movements, three helicopters, *fifty thousand switches,* eight hundred visisets, ninety thousand lectroshavers of brand "Brasomat," five hundred thousand sensitized sheets of scriptoplast . . .

The list went on and on.

The last item on the BTA prediction was the hostage demand. It said: "Hostage: Sidney Unsler, Underunifier (expected to yield on this point if 33 percent of plastosteel demand is met)."

French felt his muscles tense as Bono's voice rose. The chief was almost finished. French glanced at Proctor, but the man's face was impassive, the thick neck solid; the huge chin stuck out as if daring the world to hit it.

"And finally," he heard Bono say, "the hostage demand."

In that moment of intense waiting, French recalled wryly the origin of hostage demands. They went back to ancient days, the troubled era of the LNW's, when the taking of hostages for political purposes had been a random and unpredictable phenomenon until, in this era, it had become institutionalized. It was symbolic, nothing more. Yet now, how much emotion stirred in French as he waited!

Bono had laid aside his folder. His eyes were straight on Proctor.

"This round we shall require only a single hostage," Bono said. "However, by reason of the unremitting threat that Union missiles represent, we shall demand unusual proof of your good intentions."

Bono paused. He reached for the carafe of whiskey and poured himself a tiny glass of the clear liquid. French watched him tilt it back. Dart appeared upset by this small interruption in the proceedings. His deep-set eyes stared at Bono with an expression of tight-lipped disapproval.

Bono held the glass in his hand. "This round," he said, and French detected a slight trembling in the voice, "we demand that you make available as hostage Regina Unsler, the Unifier's daughter."

Silence.

Bono lifted his little glass, tilted it back. He shook it, as if to extract a tiny drop of whisky at the bottom.

"And furthermore," a stunned French heard him say, "it is our demand that you make this known to the public of Union immediately by a special visicast."

Silence.

French had predicted most of the negotiating points —save one. That one deviation spoiled it all. He remembered an image he particularly liked: Each helium round was a knife fight in the dark on wet and muddy ground. At the moment, in a kind of slow motion, Union's feet were slipping on the mud. Slowly they came off the ground. Slowly Union fell toward the ground while the opponent, equally slowly, came in with a flash of light caught in the metal of the blade.

French controlled his astonishment and looked about.

Bono filled his glass with whiskey. Two tribesmen at the far end of the table whispered, heads close. Most of the rest stared gloomily at folders and hands.

Then Dart suddenly rose from his chair. The short, wrinkled man turned from the table and on wobbly, curved legs he hurried toward the door.

Proctor appeared to be frozen. French glanced at him anxiously. The chief negotiator stared at the list before him, chin down, as if it had been hit with a sledgehammer.

"Your demands, Chief Bono," Proctor said, looking up at last, "are unprecedented, to say the least. I propose that we reconvene here tomorrow morning, at which time we shall give you our initial reaction."

With that Proctor moved back his chair.

French leaned over, whispered, "The specs. We've got to have a look at the drawings. Ask for documentation, Res."

Proctor shrugged. With a sinking heart, French saw the man's intense disappointment, although Proctor hid it well.

"Details," Proctor whispered tiredly. "Details. We've been stabbed in the back."

"Please," French pleaded. "We *must* have the drawings."

From across the table, they both heard Bono speak.

"Mr. Proctor, I can agree to your proposal that we adjourn. On one condition. The hostage demand must appear on Media today."

Proctor had himself under excellent control. French knew how Proctor must feel. Everything about the session had Accommodation writ large about it—front, back, sides, top, and bottom. French skirted a suicidal thought: His estimates *could* have been wrong. But now, it merely *seemed* so. Seemed but weren't! He simply couldn't imagine that he and his staff should have blundered so badly. The evidence before French now must have another explanation.

Proctor spoke. "Your demand is most unreasonable. At this point, traditionally, we analyze your demands. For that we need both time and complete documentation. We have no problems, in principle, with your hostage demand. But we expect to negotiate a package in secrecy before we go to Media."

Across the table, Bono tried to control the shaking of his hands. His hands were sweaty. They left moist marks on the folder before him. Until now, he had always dismissed Dart as merely tiresome, but suddenly the little rat had shown unusual initiative—walking out of the negotiations! What had possessed him? Bono had a vision of Dart dictating a communiqué for transmission to Tack. But that was unthinkable. Dart was a coward at heart. Even so, Bono had to get them to announce the hostage demand. At once. He had no time to lose. She would see him tonight. She'd see him the moment Media made its report.

"We have the documentary package for you," Bono said. He gestured to Sonder. The burly tribesman passed a large roll of drawings and a thick book of specs across the table to his technical counterpart from BTA, Clemmens, a balding, older man. "As for the announcement, it is the minimum requirement for another meeting."

Bono rose from his chair and gestured to the tribal delegation. All rose and bowed.

Ultimatum

Regina came up out of groggy sleep, angry, resist-ing. Something pulled incessantly on her arm.

Her dream had been a mass of confusion, anxiety, and fear. She had tumbled in the air through clouds. Sideny had chased her in a tube, his finger pointing. Someone had buried her beneath a mountain. No, it had been a grave. Dead? Dying? And Mycal had glowered above her with a spade in his hand. Earth had tumbled on her—or had it been grass?

She tried to turn away from the insistent, nagging pull. But the pulling persisted. She heard Selma's voice. "Miss Ginny. Mistress."

Regina opened her eyes and saw the maid's face. Beyond the girl was the intricate pink-silk construc-tion of the bed's roof and sides.

"What is it? What time is it?" Regina mumbled.

She felt as if she had not slept at all. It seemed only moments ago that she had lifted Mycal's head gently from her lap. She had been bone weary. She had left him asleep on the divan where they had talked end-lessly through the night. She had left him and gone to curl up on her own bed. And now this person . . .

"He wants to speak to you on the tel," this person said with a hunted, harried look in the eyes. "He in-sists that I wake you up. He's been calling for an hour, every five minutes."

Regina shook her head and blinked. There was a pain behind her temples.

"Who?" she asked. "Who insists?"

"It's *him*," Selma said. Her facial expression and in-tonation said the rest.

"Tell him to drop dead," Regina said and turned her head back into the pillows.

Once more she felt a tug on her arm. Selma's voice had an edge of panic.

"Miss Ginny, please, he threatens—"

Regina sat up. Eyes flashing, she cried: "All right, all right. I'll talk to him."

She leaped out of the bed and strode off into the sitting room outside her sleeping chamber. Fury boiled in her. She threw herself into a chair and activated the small-screened tel.

"What do you want," she said, staring at the screen.

The image of her brother did not appear. All too often he turned down the visio. He liked to come into her room as a disembodied voice. She reached forward and turned down the visio on her side too, just as his voice came over the box.

"How was it?"

"How was what?"

"Striving with that bumpkin."

"You're disgusting," she said; her voice conveyed revulsion. She wanted to cut him off, to take the tel and fling it against the wall. But she didn't dare.

"Ho, ho, ho! Look who's calling who names. I was told all about you, femmy. As for disgusting . . . you *threw* yourself at him. Well, let me tell you something, Ginny. I won't have it, understand?"

She heard the sharpness of his voice and could well imagine—without any help from the screen—the tight, angry look on his long face, the cruel turn of his lips. She should have known that her activities at the ball would be reported to Sidney. She had put him—and Clafto—out of her mind. But Clafto had tried to dance with her several times, and she had refused him each and every time. At the end he had glowered with dark fury. Now she reaped the consequences.

She didn't answer. She wondered what he might say next. She was afraid, but for once she felt defiant as well. By tonight Media would broadcast the news. Her father would hear of that and know that Accommodation was possible again, that Ecofreak sought her. They would call her into his presence. She would be safe again and forevermore, safely tucked away in Hinterland. But for the moment she was fearful and wary. She did not dare give Sidney any hints.

"Well?" he said. "You heard me."

"I heard you."

"And . . . ?"

"And what?"

"And what're you going to do?"

"What do you want me to do?"

"You know what it is. I don't have to tell you."

She knew. He considered her a plaything for his favorites. Clafto was Sidney's latest favorite. He stood next in line as Underunifier should Daddy suddenly die. Until Sidney changed his mind, of course. Then it would be someone else; and after that it would be someone else again. And in Sidney's mind, whoever it was must be her lover, her husband if Daddy ever died. She imagined the future as a succession of husbands, one after the other. Each one would be executed when he fell from favor. Today Sidney couldn't kill them. But in the future he would. For a moment she felt desperate. Then she remembered: This time she would escape. Serenita had known it, and somewhere deeply she also knew, despite that horrid dream which even now lay beneath her consciousness like some pressure.

"I'm still thinking about it."

"Damn you, bitch," he growled over the tel. "Weeks ago—*weeks* ago I told you to take Clafto! Thought it had happened. Now this morning he tells me how it really is. You deceived me, Ginny. You shouldn't do that, you know. And last night you made a whore of yourself—with a tribesman! *Again!*"

"I did no such thing," she answered quietly. She wished she *had*.

"He spent the night."

"We talked."

"I bet," he cried with a little laugh. "I bet you did! Well, my sweet, there's an end to that, as of now. Clafto will come to you tonight, and you'd better receive him. If you don't, I'll personally open the doors for him. *And* for his friends. Tell that to your staff, chippie."

Regina shivered. She wouldn't be here. She would go and hide somewhere. He wouldn't *dare!*

"I'll go to Daddy," she cried. "I can't stand it anymore!"

"Ohhh? You will, will you? Good luck, fem-stuff, good luck to you. And if you get through to him, tell him that, that . . ."

He can't think of a threat terrible enough, she mused.

"Let me tell you this, Ginny. You go to our father, and I'll make sure that you regret it to the end of your days."

Sister Serenita, she thought. *I'll go to St. Theresa of Carmen.*

"And don't think you can escape me, Ginny. My men are stationed at all your doors. You can't get away. Don't try."

Hysteria put clammy claws around her throat. Regina buried her face in her hands. Her mind raced, seeking alternative routes of escape. She couldn't find any. *Maybe I'll have to yield to Clafto. Sidney will have his way with me one final time. Then I'll get away forever.*

It wasn't the physical thing she hated; that she rather liked. It was the humiliation of it all. Another man's will imposed on her. And now, with that strangely sweet experience behind her, her memories filled with the long talk she had had with the archangel, trying to assure him that she truly loved him—although she didn't, and this morning she knew that—it seemed to her terrible and repulsive to yield to Clafto merely because her brother commanded it. Mycal had given her a feeling of what it might be like again . . . true love. She could yield to *him,* although she did not love him and meant to use him crassly—as Sidney tried to use her.

But I'm in desperate straits, she thought. *He'll forgive me.*

"Well?" the voice over the tel probed. "What do you say?"

"Nothing," she answered. "I have nothing more to say to you, Sidney."

She reached forward and cut him off.

Immediately, she punched out the numbers of her father's office; she kept the visio off. In her fluffy nightgown, her hair in disarray, her face puffy from sleep and kisses, she didn't want to be seen.

"Top Level," the switchboard operator sang, and a woman's face appeared in the screen.

Regina identified herself and asked to be connected with her father.

"We'll switch you," the woman said. Her voice was cool. The screen went blank.

Regina waited. The seconds multiplied into a minute, then another. *Too late,* she thought. HE *must have gotten through before I did. His people are everywhere.* Her spirits sank. She saw in her mind the corridors, the large offices filled with her father's many aides. A wall about him. He was behind them, remote and inaccessible even to his own flesh and blood.

After another minute, a second face appeared. She recognized Blottingham, Daddy's chief of staff—and one of Sidney's friend as well.

"Miss Unsler? Am I speaking to Miss Unsler?" He ran a hand over the short hair on top of his head, cut into the shape of an egg. "Your visio is off."

"This is Regina."

"The Unifier will return your call as soon as he is out of conference." His tone was crisp but cool, and Regina knew that she had failed.

5

The Random Oscillation Effect

French stormed out of Proctor's office and rushed past an astonished Mrs. Sedlig toward the elevators. His energetic strides translated anger into kinetic energy.

Mrs. Sedlig peered after him, her head slightly bent,

over thick rimless lenses that she wore on her nose for reading.

She was a small, faded person, whose gray hair held in a bun at the back, red-rimmed, almost lashless eyes, fussy fingers nervously checking packages for signature were as much a part of BTA's atmosphere as Proctor himself. She had been his inseparable companion since the days of Defense; and though she didn't look it, she was a survivor type, having come through the clerical purges when secretary machines had invaded the bureaucracy and only a very few, the most loyal, the indispensables, had remained in such positions. Like Proctor she lived alone and had never married or entered a contract. She drew her total psychic sustenance from her work; and this room, with its scatter of comfortable couches and little coffee tables, the holograms of helium refineries on the wall, the tribal flags in stands, the huge potted artificial plants she tended as if they were real, was her real domain. From her teak desk next to Proctor's door she guarded his privacy, filtered the messages, and watched the rise and fall of issues and of men.

As she watched French disappear down the hall, striding angrily, his purple robe swinging, she had a clear intuition that Rivera French was on the way down. She inferred this from a number of little signals, not just from the shouting match in Proctor's office which she had overheard as a dampened sequence of sound through the wall. She gathered it also from the frequency with which Gregory Korn, the DA for Compliance, was called to Proctor's office—he being French's chief rival—and Proctor's own mutterings when she took him coffee or emptied his in-box. She stored the information away in her meticulously ordered memory, thinking that French was altogether a vulgar man, much too impulsive, his Branco heritage worn outside for all to see. Then she returned her attention to a thick decision package.

Down the hall French had stopped in front of the elevators and waited, fuming. His breath still steamed with hormones generated by the bitter exchange.

The postmortem of the negotiating session had left a foul taste in his mouth. Proctor had gathered his chief aides for an emergency meeting. His strategy had soon emerged: a replay of the laser issue of five years ago. Proctor had proposed that the silco-parts be offered to Ecofreak in exchange for a withdrawal of the hostage demand—and, of course, delivery of a Helium Interdiction. "We have nothing to lose by trying," he had said, "and, frankly, we have nothing left to try."

French punched the elevator button again with unnecessary force.

He had known it, had felt it in his guts, could have predicted this would happen.

In the office he had argued with something approaching fury that the Secret Agenda had to be achieved some other way. The sil components could not be delivered. A brief glimpse at the Ecofreak drawings before the meeting had convinced him that the parts had some sort of military significance. But Proctor had shrugged that off. He could be ruthlessly single-minded when it came to his own objectives. At last French had walked out in anger, leaving the field to more compliant Deputy Assistants. He, for one, wouldn't risk Union's millions—not even to remove the Unslers from rule.

But you shouldn't have said it, he thought. *You should have kept your yap shut.*

Opposing the Chief Negotiator did nothing for a man's career—least of all if Proctor turned out to be right in the end and became Unifier. But there was a point where ambition had to be subordinated to responsibility.

The elevator doors slid aside. French was about to enter when he saw Darby Dickens come out. He stopped the DA for Security.

"Darby," he said, "in all this turmoil I haven't had a chance to talk to you. Did Franklin tell you about my situation?"

Dickens nodded gravely. He was a tall, black Structure Panther whose exemplary neatness never failed to surprise French. After a night's work, his jump suit was completely free of wrinkles. His sleeves were carefully rolled back to his elbows. His olive arms were thick and solid. A golden watch gleamed on his wrist.

"We'll rescue Miri, never fear," Dickens assured him. "That'll be the first sweep tonight. But it'll be late. We must wait until the crowds thin out."

"I want to go along," French said.

Dickens nodded. "Have my boys issue you a chemgun and mask and meet us in the stadium at half past ten or so. Gomer will be in charge of that sector. Look him up."

"Thanks," French said. "By the way, Darby, what is all this about, Operation Hairy-Scary?"

A grin lit up Dickens' face. "You don't know?"

French shook his head. I haven't had a chance to ask Proctor."

"Well, let it be a surprise, then. I'm sorry, Riv, I don't have time to explain. I'm on my way to Res now. Hairy-Scary is turning out to be one of his pets—if you know what I mean."

"Darby—"

"Later," Dickens said, moving off and waving.

French punched the elevator button again. Darby enjoyed all this. Nothing like an operation to break the routine of guarding doors and grav-drums. But if Proctor planned something foolish, would Dickens restrain him?

It came out of the man rarely enough, thank God, French reflected, thinking about Proctor's penchant for practical jokes. But when it came out, it was usually something approaching the sordid. It seemed as if practical joking and perpetual bachelorhood went hand in hand. French recalled "Operation Sulphy Ovum," when a hundred crates of rotten eggs had been delivered to Top Level three years ago. Proctor had been most indignant, had promised a full investigation when Blottingham came calling in the wake of the stink. Yet everyone suspected that Proctor himself had planned each detail of that operation.

The elevator came, and French got in. For a second he considered the many hours between now and half past ten. Miri would be in that small room, waiting. A powerful pulse of longing caught him, and he realized he didn't give a damn about silco-parts, Ecofreak, Proctor, or anything else—not until Miri was safe.

As he strode off toward his office two doors down, he made a mental note to call Dachshund Jones, Number One in the Kayring Gang. He would hand Miri over to the gang for safekeeping. Nothing less would give him rest.

People had filled his office. The lights had been turned off. Schematics were projected against a wall. A computer console stood on the right. A three-dimensional articulation of the component turned slowly in the upper half of the screen while an odd, random, zigzag curve flashed like lightning on the bottom.

Clemmens had assembled the technical staff for an examination of the sil components. Two sil chemists from Norlens had stayed to help. But why in this office? Then French realized the reason why. Operation Hairy-Scary, whatever the hell that was, had preempted all the conference rooms.

French stepped in, wondering if Professor Fulbright of the Central Technical Institute had arrived. "How are we coming? Anything new?"

Dark, shadowed faces turned toward him. Clemmens stood next to the computer screen with a pointer in his hand. He turned to French.

"We've stumbled onto something new, Riv. Should've thought of it long ago . . . but we're industrial technologists. This is a rather advanced research notion. Lindy here suggested that Ecofreak might be using the ROE. That's a long shot, of course, but we haven't got anything to lose. We're boxed in . . . Professor Fulbright is here."

French took the cue. He searched the blue-white

faces until his eyes found a small man with angry eyes and a sparse goatee. He walked over to Fulbright and shook his hand.

"How do you do, Professor? Glad you could come."

He turned back to Clemmens at the screen.

The Random Oscillation Effect. Curious. Over the years French had read articles about the ROE in the scientific press. Great promise, little performance.

"Well, Clemens, what have you decided? What use could they make of the effect?"

Clemmens shrugged. Computer lights were reflected in his bald skull. "We haven't the faintest, Riv. It's a useless phenomenon—useless precisely because it's random. A laboratory curiosity. But suppose this little gadget *controls* the oscillations . . . ?"

Clemmens let that one sink in.

French thought for a second. "Atomics?" he said. *God,* he thought, *if it's really so, Proctor has to be stopped!*

Heads nodded around the table.

Clemmens said: "If this little switch can modulate the oscillations, Ecofreak could neutralize an atomic attack. But how?" Clemmens raised his hands. "We can't figure it out. This isn't the whole assembly—only the part they can't make themselves. And from this little bone"—Clemmens tapped the console screen with his pointer and tiny dots of white appeared on the blue surface where he tapped—"we can't reconstruct the whole beast. At least not in an afternoon."

French looked down at the professor.

"What's your assessment, Dr. Fulbright?"

The physicist snorted. He had a high, crackly voice. "It won't work," he pronounced. "I've told your staff as much, Mr. French, but they persist. I've spent thirty years of my life trying to control the ROE and haven't done it yet. I find it a little difficult to imagine that simple tribal engineers should have solved the puzzle."

The man's offended ego sent out angry vibrations. French didn't say what he had on his mind. Those simple tribal engineers had proven their mettle in field

109

after field. The Crestmore bible thundered against Technology, but Hinterland was filled with heretics, as it were. He recalled a fancy laboratory he had once nearly penetrated on the outskirts of Kaysee in Mokan Territory—clumps of buildings in a rolling valley beside the remnants of an ancient highway. French had seen white-clad technicians moving about like monastics beyond a fence. Roofs had bristled with antennae. He had found odd chemicals in the waste cans of that lab. That had been one of those missions to follow up on the laser demand, a job he hadn't left to subordinates.

Clemmens cleared his throat. French sensed a tension in the room.

"You will admit, won't you, Professor Fulbright, that you've never tried to weld copper and SP?" Clemmens asked.

"I'll admit no such thing!" Fulbright bristled. "I have avoided meaningless experiments, if that's what you mean. But my students and I have simulated *all* possible combinations of sil and common materials. The mathematical foundations have been laid. They yield no results."

French looked back at Clemmens.

"Suppose for a moment, Professor, that they use a new kind of mathematics."

Fulbright snorted. "Preposterous! What new mathematics? There is only one kind. Models of the Universe, Mr. Clemmens . . . perhaps, perhaps. But surely you don't mean a new math!"

Scientists were childish in proportion to their fame. French knew that Fulbright could be of help—but it would take time.

"I meant a model, professor. Perhaps a five-dimensional approach, that sort of thing. I'm an engineer myself and don't pretend . . ."

French wanted to leave. In that bitter meeting with Proctor, he had had an intuition. Recalling the negotiating session, it had seemed to him that Bono had acted against tribal instructions. Perhaps the man had fallen for the girl and meant to extract her by using the negotiations. Proctor rejected that thesis out of hand, saying it was incompatible with the parallel demand for Media announcement of the hostage request. Bono could have the girl for the asking. She was a notorious whore, warming the bed of just about anybody who wanted her badly enough. Nonsense, nonsense.

Nevertheless, French was sure. He wanted another look at the tapes of the ball and of the morning session.

He waited for Fulbright to finish while he eyed Clemmens. The two men clearly clashed. French decided he had done the right thing in calling in Fulbright. Answers would surely come from such collisions.

". . . I welcome your inspection of our models, Mr. Clemmens," Fulbright was saying. "We have a good set of models. Five-dimensional models, ten-dimensional models, Mr. Clemmens. Thirty years is a long time, you know, and I pride myself on a modest reputation in the field of vibration."

Personal gravitron—the Fulbright invention everyone knew about—had made the professor famous. He had discovered a method of sensitizing fibers in gravitron chambers so that they gave temporary lift to individuals. Police used it and so did sealing crews. It had made jumpball possible—alas.

French rose to leave. "I'll be back shortly, gentlemen; in the meantime, please continue. Professor, thanks for your help. We must break this mystery somehow and do it quickly."

He turned and went off toward the Psychometry Department of the Office of Research.

The Courage to Oppose

Dart scurried down the narrow stairs with occasional, furtive glances over his shoulder. He appeared unaware of the slightly comical, almost theatrical image he projected as he tiptoed down the carpeted steps, the very picture of guilty stealth. He tried to make himself small and inconspicuous, although there was no one about.

A nervous litany ran in his head. *I hope, I hope, I hope,* he repeated.

Dart hoped that no one would interrupt his clandestine communications with Jonny Tack. He hoped that the technician on duty in the comroom would not raise any annoying little questions about Dart's authority. He hoped, above all, that Tack would receive the message well. In a situation of this kind, where a man had to walk a tightrope between two chasms, one couldn't be sure of the outcome. It took a man of courage to do what he was about to do—no, more than that, a man of subtlety.

He held several sheets of scriptoplast in his hand. He had labored long and hard on the precise wording of the message. Time and again he had pushed sheets through the renewal slot above the desk in his room to erase unsuitable variations. Now he had a version he could live with.

He hoped that his words would convey the picture just . . . so. Not too hard on Bono—just in case. Not too tolerant either—in the event . . .

At the bottom of the stairs Dart stopped to orient himself. He had been down here many times in the old days, but things had changed. The comroom should be to the left. Yes, there it was. He saw the sign painted on a glass door and moved forward.

I talked to him, he reassured himself. *I asked him outright. This shouldn't come as a surprise to him. I said to him:* "Mycal," *I said,* "are you acting on your own authority on this? Do you have a secret

*mandate from Jonny Tack?" I was very direct with
the man. I came to the point. I didn't mince words.*

Bono's eyes had shied under Dart's penetrating
gaze. The chief had scratched his ear, had glowered.
"My arrangements with Jonny are none of your concern, Franco," he'd said. "When I want your advice,
I'll ask for it."

The memory made Dart feel the fury he had felt
then.

Further discussion had followed along those lines.
Bono had not been direct. He hadn't denied, hadn't affirmed.

*Well, my boy, you can't blame me for drawing my
own conclusions. I hope they're right. I hope, I hope.*

Dart's entrance into the comroom startled a lone
technician. The youngster lounged in front of a large
console with many buttons and a keyboard. He
shoved a book into a drawer.

"You're certainly busy," Dart snapped, taking advantage of the situation. "What's this you're reading?
Let me see it?"

"Yes, sir," the young man said, swallowing. He
opened the drawer and held out the book: *BTA in
Action*. It had Proctor on the cover.

"Uh-hum," Dart said, eyebrows raised. "Propa-
ganda. And theirs at that. Don't believe a word of
it. You men certainly live a cushy life around here,
don't you?" He gestured at numerous pinups on the
wall. "When I was First Secretary around here, we
ran a tighter ship."

The youngster gulped. "Yes, sir."

"Got an emergency," Dart said. "Get cracking on
this message to Tack. Priority. Security Code One."

Dart held out the sheets, and the technician went
to work. He pulled out a book and looked something
up. From a cabinet with little metal drawers opposite
the console he selected a plastic card, inserted it
into a slot on the console. Then he sat down before
the keyboard.

Dart relaxed. He felt in control.

"Does this door lock?" He gestured toward the

frosted glass. "I don't want to be interrupted. This is a Priority One." He wanted to drive that point home.

"Yes, sir," the technician said. "At bottom, there, under the handle."

A small button activated the electronic lock. The bolt slid home with a buzz.

Over the technician's shoulder, Dart inspected the words as they appeared on the scriptoplast fed into the machine from a roll. The youngster sweated. Priority One was not an everyday occurrence.

QUERY GROUNDBASE READY TO RECEIVE PR s1, Dart saw on the sheet.

They keys were still. Nevertheless, the machine clacked rhythmically in readiness.

That single line would cause quite a stir back home. Dart imagined men around the console, one man breaking away to fetch a supervisor.

The clacking intensified. It seemed as if the machine were gathering strength. Then the keys began to move with great rapidity. A message appeared.

QUERY RICARDO REPEAT/CONFIRM PR s1 SHOW ID CODE

The technician looked up at Dart with a question in his eyes.

"Confirm," Dart said. *They don't want to believe it,* he thought.

1Ø834 PR s1 CONFIRM STOP STANDING BY FOR GOAHEAD, the youngster typed.

The answer came immediately. QUERY RICARDO IS PRESENCE OF JT DESIRABLE/NECESSARY

Is presence of JT desirable/necessary . . . The words caused a rush of delight mingled with anxiety. Jonny must be available for communications, else base camp wouldn't have put that question to them. A dialogue with Jonny would be most desirable. Above all, Dart had dreaded a long wait for a response from Tack, unsure how the man had received the message.

"Desirable," he said to the waiting technician, who now typed the word.

SEND MESSAGE RICARDO STOP WILL SEND FOR JT

The technician spread out and smoothed Dart's sheets of scriptoplast and began to type slowly. He had difficulty deciphering Dart's small and crabbed hand.

Dart watched through deep-set eyes, anxious that every word should make it across the vast distance to Texahoma. He felt the excitement rise, mixed with a good deal of fear now . . . now that he had made a commitment to act.

He wondered what it was like in base camp. Did the sun shine? Did rain beat a drum on the canvas of the tents? Did the steppe wind blow, ironing the mutagrass? *So much depends on the weather*, he thought anxiously. *What if it rains and Tack's in one of his ugly moods?*

The Tacks of Kaysee had a mean streak. Genius had its price. The Tacks paid it in the coin of occasional madness. Old Tack had had his share of that blood, and Jonny had inherited both: his father's gifts and curses.

At last the message had gone through. The technician's hands rested on the keyboard.

MESSAGE RECEIVED RICARDO STOP STAND BY STOP JT MAY WANT TO DISCUSS

Dart tried to guess Tack's reaction to the message. Would he frown? Would his eyes be puzzled? Would the muscles of his neck tighten in anger?

Dart's heart beat hard behind his wrinkled throat. He nearly shivered with tension. The machine clacked evenly. Its internal hammers drummed a tattoo against the retaining bar, eager to tap out another message. Then the machine's noise intensified and the words came.

FRANCO OLD BUDDY IS THAT YOU QUERY

It's all right, Dart exulted, staring at the words.

He noticed the half-anxious, half-admiring look on the young man's face. Few they were, few indeed, the men Tack addressed as "old buddy."

"Tell him, 'Yes, sir,' " Dart said.

The technician typed.

The machine responded immediately. Dart imagined Tack next to the machine, his hand on his hip as he dictated.

HOW DO I KNOW IT IS YOU OLD SCOUNDREL QUERY SEND YOUR PERSONAL ID CODE AND WAKE UP HEAR

Dart smiled. It would be all right. He recognized the tone. Jonny was in one of his funning moods.

"Four nine two," he said. "Five eight seven. Nine nine one."

The youngster typed.

Jonny Tack

Tack stood next to a console, his legs wide apart. One of his hands rested on his hip. His head was shaved with the exception of a thick sheaf of hair at the crown which, in the shape of a bushy horse-tail, hung down blond and shiny over his back. A pinched and angry expression sat on his face.

He waved his arms and yelled: "Somebody fetch me a chair."

Men stirred into action. Seconds later a wood-and-canvas seat appeared behind him. He fell into it.

"Is is Dart?" he asked.

The man at the console looked up from a list and nodded.

Tack stared up at the sagging canvas roof, at the wires that ran along a wrinkle toward the pole-supported tent tip.

"Write," he said to the operator. "Franco, you old skunk, I read your little message, but it's sneaky as hell. What're you trying to tell me?"

Tack glanced about. A ring of men had formed a a distance. "Clear the hell out," he yelled. "Out, goddammit!"

Tack glanced about. A ring of men had formed at the heels of his boots sunk into the canvas flooring. His horsetail fell over the bright-green back of the chair.

He wondered how long it would take to get the story out of Dart. The old man always hedged his bets. Nearly in his grave, the old coot, but ambitious as hell. Sometimes that could be useful in a man, especially a suspicious little ferret like Dart.

Tack weighed all the factors while the machine clacked, grew agitated, and the keys began to flash.

Dart hated Bono. But Dart was a gutless little rat. He wouldn't dare accuse Mycal of anything unless it had substance. Come to think of it, Tack was not sure Dart had made an accusation. The message had been vague, full of odd hints. An irregularity in the hostage demand . . . ? What in the hell was that supposed to mean?

"What's he saying?" Tack asked.

The operator pulled up on the yellow cable paper to read the message.

" 'My message, I believe, is clear and concise as to facts,' " the operator read. " 'In essence I am asking for confirmation of the fact that the hostage demand can deviate from your signed and approved instructions.' "

"Double-talk. Garbage," Tack shouted. "No, don't type that."

He stared up at the canvas ceiling again while the operator waited.

Something had been done up north. Had Bono changed the hostage demand? Dart would never come right out and say it, if left a chance.

"Write: 'Did Bono present the Ecofreak demand to BTA? Yes or no?' "

Keys clattered.

"Yes," the operator said after a moment.

" 'What was the hostage demand? Give the name, only the name.' "

Sidney Unsler. It had better be that. A bold, clean jab right at Union's solar plexus. The Number Two man in Union. That should extract the sil components in a hurry. Tack remembered the loud, whining arguments about the negotiating strategy. All kinds of devious schemes had been proposed. Tack had

117

listened to all the garbage. Then one night he had smashed his fist on the table and had told the talkers what he wanted. A simple, head-on strategy. No monkey business.

He glanced at the operator. "Well?"

The man shrugged. "They haven't answered yet."

"Goddamn," Tack yelled. "Can't they spell?"

Just then the machine clattered briefly.

The operator rolled up the paper and leaned into the machine. When his head came back up, Tack saw agitation in the face, a kind of cringing.

"Well?" he called sharply.

"Sir," the man said, in a whisper, "Regina Unsler."

Tack leaped to his feet. His face turned purple. Veins bulged on his forehead. He was a very tall man; his head almost touched the inclined roof of the small tent. Two great strides brought him to the console. He tore at the yellow cable paper. It came away from the machine with a sideways rip.

He stared at the blank letters. They spelled REGINA UNSLER.

"Confirm," he croaked to the operator, choked with emotion.

He had nearly forgotten the little bitch. She recalled a troubled time: those sweaty nights, his father's thundering anger, the humiliation of six months' penance in the steppe with the herds. All that rolled around in him now like a down-dipping tornado.

Above all he remembered with a shudder the meeting with his father in the old man's Wellhead home. "Stand there, by the door," the old man had ordered. And while Jonny stood there feeling small and intimidated, his father cleared a large space in the middle of the gloomy room ringed by pictures of the ancestors going back nearly to LNW XIII. His father pushed the table against the wall as he moved furniture. That done, the old man turned with a flash in those eyes beneath the bushy gray brows.

"I'll teach you to sully Tack blood," the old man thundered, a fist in the air. "Defend yourself like a tribesman." Then his father beat him to a pulp.

The old man had been strong like an ox to his dying day. Tack remembered spitting blood on the carpet on hands and knees when it was over. Then he'd been sick. The old man forced him to clean up the vomit with a bucket and cloth like a mutant slave.

"They confirm," the operator said.

"Write," Tack said. " 'Dart, I want to hear it all. Every bit of it. From the start. I don't want any double-talk or I'll have you skinned, hear? Straight, Dart. Straight.' "

As he waited, Tack tried to give Bono the benefit of the doubt. Bono might have found some information unknown to Ecofreak before. Regina might be better insurance that the components would be delivered. But as Dart's message began to clatter over the machine, it rapidly disabused him of such notions.

He found it easy to construct a picture from the words: "five-percenter" . . . "tub" . . . "ball" . . . "dancing all night" . . . "refused to go home" . . . "disappeared from the" . . . "no sign at breakfast" . . . "late arriving at" . . .

The machine finally stopped. Tack stared at the yellow paper. He said: "Tell him to stand by."

Around the low walls of the tent many consoles formed an electronic wall. In the middle a thick central pole supported the roof. Tack began to walk around the tent. He folded his arms behind his back, unaware that it was a mannerism he copied from his father. His head was tilted forward. His eyes stared at the slightly cuffed tips of his boots.

He let it all sink in without resistance. He was surprised by his own reaction, so bland, so mild. So he had been betrayed. It was so simple that he almost laughed. The Brotherhood of Action had nursed a snake. The poisonous viper had turned and struck.

Very well, very well.

He walked in a circle. On his boot tip a rock had torn the shiny skin, revealing the white leather flesh beneath . . .

The Bono clan had its roots deep in Texahoma, but the family extended far across Hinterland. Tack recalled Bonos as far north as Chica. Bono fem-folk, in addition, linked the clan to many shades of political conviction. The poison must have crept into the inner circle through one of those capillaries. Tack conjured up an image of Gordon Bono, Mycal's father, and recalled that Gordon had never been an enthusiastic Activist. He'd had an independent streak —ever off to tend his property. Yes, Tack thought, the Old Man had said as much once. A loner, Gordon Bono.

And so's his son! he thought with sudden fury. *So's his goddamned son!*

Not a mainstream Activist. A little distant, a little aloof. Smart, smooth in a way. Tack had picked him for his quiet, brainy manner. The kind of man who would get along with Union folk, but bright enough to read them. And Tack had thought him strong— not a talker, not running at the mouth all the time.

But he had been wrong. The man was weak. *I sent Union a five-percenter, a shaky-waky, a jelly-ass. "Oh, please Mustah Union, suh, make this pressure to stop." Not a man who would bite his tongue and tough it out. A wobble-knee.*

Then a complex emotion of rage, jealousy, envy, and longing possessed him.

He saw Bono ride Regina's wicked, foamy saddle through the night. He saw them strive. He felt a pain and, mixed with it, he felt a treacherous twinge of ex-citement in the loins. It recalled the Pact of Chastity.

Mycal Bono! he thought with bitterness. He who had refused, with a handful of others, to join the cru-sade Tack had proposed to the Inner Circle. Most had sworn a solemn oath to shun fem-folk until the struc-tures fell. Bono had not said a word, hadn't explained himself. But when the others stepped forward, Bono stood his ground with a few. He was a bachelor and had no reason to refuse. It seemed to Tack doubly contemptible that Bono, the five-percenter, the one man in twenty who couldn't take gravitron, would tiptoe after structure ass the day he hit Ricardo. And he had known where to go! Tack's face darkened.

The House of the Lord must be swept clean. He would trace down the linkages that led through Bono blood to the treacherous Accommodationists. He had been too soft on them. He had let them scatter to their wells, herds, farms. The Lord's brush would sweep through the heap of Accommodationist garbage. He would order an action as soon as the structures were down. Until then he needed all the support he could get to hold the fragile Counter-Union together.

The thought of the structures brought him out of murky reverie into the cold, bright present.

What if he didn't get the silco-parts? What then? His base of power would begin to crack. The tribes would drift apart again. His father's dream would crumble; the structures would still stand.

No, he thought with vehemence. *Never!*

He broke his stride and crossed the tent to the manned console.

Dart's Triumph

Bono lay on the bed of his locked bedroom and spoke on the tel with Regina. He was puzzled, worried, yet delighted all at once. Despite tear stains, Regina's face was beautiful. Her tone had a kind of desperate edge. Bono had tried to discover what bothered the girl, but she'd avoided his questions. Instead she had pursued a single objective: to get him to come to her domain.

"Will you come?" she asked again.

Bono drew closer to the tel. He lay on his stomach and cradled the small device in his hands. The bedroom was large and comfortable. Thick white hare rugs lay on the floor. Photos of Hinterland scenes hung on the wall. An orange lumiglobe burned on the night table to his right.

"Of course I'll come," he said. "You know I'll come. But I thought that you were adamant. No message on the Media—no togetherness."

"Did you ask for me?" Her voice was anxious.

Her manner disturbed him. She revealed a state of unnatural excitement. Her head flicked to the side with short glances as if she expected an interruption. Could she be afraid of something?

"I asked for you," he said. "They have the demand. I told them to announce it on the Media. But it wasn't on the news."

"I know," she said indifferently. "I watched. Can you leave now?"

"Of course," he answered. "But . . ." He hesitated. He longed to be with her, but he could not go through another night of unsatisfied desire. "Do you really *want* me? I didn't satisfy your condition."

She shook her head furiously from side to side. "That doesn't matter anymore. I shouldn't have been so cruel—not for my sake, not for yours. Hurry, and be careful, very careful."

She's afraid, she's anxious. Something is wrong.

"I waited and waited for you to call," she continued in a burst of words. "I called and called the embassy, but you couldn't be reached."

Regina sounded like a woman in love, and Bono felt buoyed up by her longing, which he shared.

"Now you have reached me," he said, thinking back over an afternoon filled with angry altercations between himself and the delegates. They had sought him out singly and in groups to demand explanations. He refused to discuss the matter, but in the process also discovered how totally indifferent he felt about the helium round. Only she mattered.

"Tell me," he said. "You mentioned that I should be careful. Why? Is something wrong?"

"Nothing," she answered, but Bono saw a furtive motion in her eyes. She appeared to change her mind. "There—there are some strange men outside. I— I don't know what they might want . . ."

"I'll be right over," he said, alarmed more by her manner than her words. "Right away."

He undressed and took a quick shower. The rush of water enlivened him, and his sense of dull fatigue gave way to exhilaration. He dried himself before the mirror, pleased by his lithe, hairy, healthy body. For a second he felt again what he had felt the night before: an irrepressible good humor.

"Hey, man," he said aloud to his mirror image. "Hey, you know something? I don't give a shit about the Crestmore prophecies."

He grinned at himself.

The grin reminded him of another Bono—his younger self. A flash of insight sobered his face. Then he broke into a grin again. It had occurred to him that all those years at the Academy of Action had been a sham.

He combed his hair and beard. He gave a twirl to his mustaches. He thought: *I really don't believe in that religion stuff. Hell, I don't want to change the world. Jutting nonsense.* At the moment the world seemed marvelously beautiful. There she was, almost within reach. He frowned for a second, thinking of her strange mood. Well, he would console her.

He left the shower and quickly dressed, whistling a tune. The words went: *"I am a kid from Texaho, the prairie she be my hooome . . ."*

Across the room hung a photograph of the many-peaked Sierra Petra. He stared at it while his right foot wiggled and worried into his boot. Then he heard the drumbeat of feet outside. He looked at the door. Someone called his name.

"Bono! Are you in there? Open up!"

He recognized Dart's voice and heard its harsh, commanding tone.

Bono instantly grasped the situation. Damn! He

shouldn't have showered. No matter. In all leisure, he pushed his foot into the boot. Resistance would be useless. He would think about Regina when all this was over.

Outside Dart hammered on the door and repeated his call.

Bono opened the door at last, and the little man nearly fell in. One of his fists was raised. In the other he held strips of blue scriptoplast. Several of the delegates stood grimly behind him, hands on the handles of ceremonial daggers. They appeared to be under the command of beefy Dulsol, the chief of embassy maintenance, who held a pistol.

Dart lowered his arm, composed himself, and inspected Bono's face. The forked beard stood out aggressively, the mustache tips were turned up. Dart felt sorry for the young man. He had the face that should make structures crumble. But he lacked the special something . . . that vibrant quality of leadership.

In the center of the room Dart took up a dignified stance, one foot out in front of the other.

"Better sit down, Bono."

He eyed the ex-chief with displeasure now. Bono had a little grin on his face. That grin would fade away in a hurry. In no time at all Bono would be on ice.

Bono smiled, amused by the little man's obvious air of self-importance. He decided to humor the little rat. He walked to the bed, sat down on its edge, folded his arms across his chest.

"Let me read you something, Bono," Dart said.

He arranged scriptoplast sheets. "I have a cable from Jonny Tack," he announced. Bono saw sparks of triumph in the deep-set eyes. "Let me read you what the leader says."

Dart looked up at Bono and noted that the man still grinned.

" 'I, Jonny Tack, Leader of the Counter-Union, apprised of certain treasonable activities by my appointed chief of mission, hereby remove him from that post and order him delivered to me under armed guard. I appoint Franco Dart acting chief of mission until such time as a new chief can be appointed.' "

Dart lowered the scriptoplast and looked at Bono. He said: "This much you have need to know. There is a good deal more, of course. It might interest you to know that I am also provisional ambassador."

Bono came to his feet and made for Dart. For a second Dart retreated, thinking this an attack. At the door Dulsol lurched forward with a grunt. But then Dart saw Bono's eagerly extended hand.

"My dear Franco," Bono cried, grinning, "let me be the first to congratulate you."

Dart withheld his hand for a moment and viewed Bono with dark suspicion. But the man's eyes seemed sincerely pleased even if that grin was insolent; and congratulations *were* in order. Dart took Bono's extended hand, shook it, dropped it, and withdrew a pace or two with a sideways glance at the waiting delegates.

"You have a big job ahead of you, Franco," Bono pursued. "Good luck to you. Now, I suppose, you'll put me under arrest? Or do I start for home tonight?"

"Take him away, men," Dart said, almost in a whisper, and Dulsol's huge hand soon grabbed Bono's elbow, jerked.

Bono walked down the hall thinking about Tack, thinking that this move was typical of that ox. He had not checked with Bono, hadn't called for his side of the story. Tack had acted from emotion—as always.

The guards led him through the ornate parts of the embassy and from there into a neglected, empty wing. Two men walked in front, two behind. As the group turned a corner, Bono saw coming toward them another and similar complement: two guards, a young woman, two guards.

In the narrow, dilapidated corridor, the groups had to squeeze past one another. For an instant Bono looked at the girl and she at him. Her situation seemed like his own. Her eyes flashed a knowing look, but he had never seen her before. She wore a long, blue gown and had a white stole over her shoulders—rather formally dressed for a prisoner.

In a moment she was past and he continued on toward whatever prison Dart had decreed.

The Little Speech

Eight Flames of the inner circle supped around a low rectangular table, seated on legless, cushioned chairs. The lights were dim, music subdued. Pink-robed servants chosen for their small size and delicate features hovered around the guests or moved about in the obsequious small-step. They served Peacefreak duck in dark wooden bowls and hot Maoling wine in shallow, pearl-white porcelain cups.

"This casual—dare I say haphazard?—meeting pleases me the more in that no *conquest* past or prospective will be feasted, and we are joined merely as close friends."

Through the faintly blue curtain of incense smoke that rose to the ceiling from a slit in the table, Clafto Meyer listened with a smile as Luke Payne began his little speech in fautless Latin.

The dinner had been called on short notice as a kind of secret celebration. No one *quite* said out loud why they were gathered here, the men closest to the Fire, but each one knew the reason, and each knew that the others knew; and so what Payne said had a special significance. It was titillating precisely because he did not say it all.

Payne lifted his shallow cup, held it in both hands; he spoke with his face inclined over the wine. He was the fifth man to try a little speech, but Clafto was sure that Luke would outdo the rest.

"As I taste the fire of this wine and savor the fey aroma of the steppes, I disagree with Jackson, Clafto. The question is before us: What is the peak of all delights? To Jackson it's a blooming rose whose soft red petals gently cup a dew-bedecked, delicate, pink interior. And he would be a hairy bumblebee with leave to plunge into that rose to bathe in the dew and suck the nectar. And if the petals should close at night, he'd gladly gambol in that soft prison until dawn."

To the sound of appreciative chuckles, Luke Payne looked up.

He is delightful, Clafto thought. *He has improved on Jackson's little speech and hasn't had his own say yet. It'll be bawdy, so much is certain.*

Clafto was glad that he had dropped the hint this morning after his talk with the Fire. It pleased him that the senior Flames had organized this feast. Sidney's second in command deserved such small, such thoughtful attentions. Clafto found it especially appropriate that he should be held in such esteem. Unlike the others, he wouldn't be replaced. None of Sidney's earlier favorites had complemented the Fire's personality to such an admirable extent. Sidney had said as much this morning.

He looked about at the Flames and thought: *They vie for my favor. Next to Sidney I'm the most important man in Union.*

"The peak of all delights?" Payne asked rhetorically. He had a scar from ear to chin on his left side, a special mark of initiation acquired in Sidney's gymnasium. In a face somewhat flushed with wine, the scar was white. "To me delight is in the doing. I like to make things. I like to cook, to bake. I love the smell in the kitchen, the heat of the stove. My favorite activity is to bake a little cake, a tidy little loaf, you understand, with a neat little crack in the middle, nicely rounded and browned. A puckered little crack, my brothers, and hot inside."

Through an arched opening opposite Clafto's seat at the head of the table, he saw a servant appear over the shiny marble floor of the outer hall. The servant came toward them in a hurry.

". . . To make my favorite cake, I first take two eggs and I put them on the table. Two eggs," he said, stressing the point, "if you see what I mean. Then I pick myself a little pot. Not too large, not too small;

a round little pot, white and red with a bit of black in the right places. I put the pot next to the eggs. Then I take a little lard, smooth, silky lard, gentlemen, just enough to cover a finger, and with it I smear the inside of the pot, not too fast and not too slow, but all around the lip and then deeper and deeper. I *probe* the pot, I *plumb* its depth with that lardy finger, slowly as if I were caressing something . . ."

The servant stopped next to Clafto, bent down, whispered.

Clafto rose. "You must excuse me, friends," he said. "Something has happened."

He followed the servant out of the room, through the arched doorway, across the marble. The blue light of an active tel shone from an alcove. He sat down before it and looked at one of the sparks of his group —Silvester.

"Well, Sil? What's up?"

"We've got her," Sil said. He seemed out of breath. "Eerie fem, cold as ice."

Clafto raised his eyebrows. "Show me," he said.

The image in his screen began to move as Silvester lifted the tel on the other end and pointed it toward the center of a murky room. Clafto saw the wife of French seated demurely on a chair. He could not see her features clearly, but he recognized the blue gown and white stole.

The tel returned to its original angle and Silvester's face reappeared.

"How did you manage that?"

Silvester shrugged. "The embassy door opened, and there she was. It looked like she had been pushed or shoved out. She certainly didn't leave of her own accord. We let her walk down the street a bit, then we picked her up."

Clafto frowned. Although he couldn't decipher precisely what BTA might have in mind, he feared a trap of some kind.

"Where are you now?"

"Upstairs in the Cosmos Club. In the private rooms."

"Good. Stay there . . ." He thought for a second.

Silvester had three others with him. The group was too small if BTA had ideas of a rescue. Word had come from Blottingham in mid-afternoon that unusual things were going on in BTA.

"I'm having dinner with some men of the circle," Clafto said. "After we're done, I'll come to get her—with a larger party. Just in case BTA is setting us a trap. It might be late, but we'll be there. Meanwhile, don't let her get away." Silvester nodded. "Cheers, Sil. And good work."

Clafto switched off.

Sidney would be delighted. The wife of French was better than nothing—precious bait. She would lure the man. But it bothered Clafto that she had been so easy to capture. Why had she been expelled from the embassy? Where was her husband? The situation demanded extreme care.

He returned to the dining Flames.

He stood for a second before sinking into his cushioned seat.

"Fortune smiles," he said. "We've caught the female. Silvester has her upstairs in the Cosmos Club. I propose a little venture, brothers. Let's dine in leisure. Then you might accompany me to the Cosmos with some of your sparks. From there you might escort me to West Tower Top, where I have a little chore or two before me . . ." He smiled. Faces smirked back. "Then you might deliver our prize to the Fire. He told me this morning that he has a personal interest in this little matter."

In the Stadium

Half past ten.

French walked downstairs and stopped in one of the entrances of the hexagonal BTA stadium. The place echoed with voices. People moved about. Someone experimented with the lights, dimming them on and off, switching entire sections. Once this room had been the

Hall of Burgesses. Now it was a gymnasium, ball-room, assembly hall. Basketball goals hung from the ceiling. The floor gleamed with painted lines for all manner of games. Bleachers pressed up against ancient marble.

BTA staff milled about on the floor. Some wore jump suits and toted chemguns. Some wore robes and had obviously come to watch the evening's entertainment—whatever it would be. French had still to learn the details about Operation Hairy-Scary.

He didn't see Dickens, Gomer, or any of the other leaders.

French suppressed a pulse of irritation. He moved into the stadium, carrying his chemgun. Its barrel was telescoped down so that the device was barely more than a pistol with an over-large stock. He sat down on a bench to wait.

A deep breath and its slow exhalation failed to break his tension. Since that moment in the elevator when he'd looked forward to this hour, French had had a wretched time. His only consolation was that his preparations for Miri's security had gone well enough. He had called her in mid-afternoon. Reluctant tribes-men brought her to the tel, and French reassured himself that she was all right. He recalled now the warning she had given him. He had asked her how she was, and she said that *she* was all right. But she'd had a troublesome intuition, premonition, call it what you will. About him. She urged him to be careful. He couldn't get more out of her with tribesmen watching the conversation.

French wondered what she could have had in mind, then shrugged it off. He could take care of himself. Everything would go smoothly.

After several attempts, he had reached Dachsy Jones less than an hour ago. The leader of the Kayring Gang had wrinkled up in embarrassed pleasure at the sight of French—embarrassing French in turn. Years ago Dachsy had been Number Two and French a youthful runner in his service. But now their roles seemed reversed, at least so far as Dachsy was concerned. Dachsy had scratched his short-cropped head, shy like a youngster. He insisted on calling French "sir." When French explained the situation, Dachsy offered to rescue Miri himself with men from the gang, all eagerness to help. But French shook his head. All he wanted was a safe place for Miri. They made an appointment for eleven, eleven-thirty, at The Scuttlebutt, a coffeehouse controlled by the gang.

French stared out over the stadium floor. People moved about aimlessly, restlessly. If Dickens didn't show up soon, French would be late for that appointment.

Miri's safety mesmerized him—had distracted him all day long. French had never before experienced the tension between personal and collective concerns as deeply. The sooner she was safe, the sooner he could devote himself to the job at hand.

Proctor's single-minded madness had intensified rather than diminished during the day. The man had convinced himself that Ecofreak would deal with him if he held out the silco-parts. Which was true enough. French had the same conviction. But it was wrong— dangerously wrong.

Proctor's eyes had narrowed sharply during their last meeting together. French saw himself reporting wearily, exhausted by the all-day session with Clemmens, Fulbright, and the staff. That session had deteriorated into a brawl of words at the end. Clemmens and the staff withdrew to one pole, Fulbright to the other. French tried to mediate between the two, but the combatants were beyond reason. At last Fulbright stuffed his briefcase angrily and left in a huff. French had to tell Proctor that no consensus had been reached. The silco-parts *might* be oscillation control devices, as Clemmens had insisted they were; or they could be "components for some magical prayer machine," as Fulbright, in a moment of white fury, had shouted in a shrill voice.

Proctor said: "Let's hope they are oscillation what-you-ma-call-it. I don't think Ecofreak will risk much over prayer wheels."

We are losing our minds, French thought in the stadium, rubbing his eyes.

Right now, with Miri in the Ecofreak embassy and Flames all over the place looking for him, French saw the Secret Agenda in a very different light. Politics did not seem important. Even the plan itself appeared to him a fabric of madness.

Preposterous notion, French thought. An old incident served as model for the plan. Eight years ago three gravitron drums had failed suddenly in South Tower one summer night. For reasons that were still under investigation, the backup units failed to come on line and structure collapse began in South with a series of horrible thundercracks. The ensuing panic shook Ricardo to its foundations.

But there was a big difference between that event and what Proctor planned, French reflected. Eight years ago the trouble had been quickly fixed. No revolutionary group had waited in the wings, ready to exploit the panic. This time the trouble would last as long as Proctor wished. And the Group would be poised for a coup.

French yawned and stretched his arms toward the ceiling.

Could Proctor hide an Interdiction for five days? he wondered, slumping again. Even with the full cooperation of the Ministry of Engineering? In five days, reserve supplies of the gas would be exhausted. At that point the grav-drums would begin to heat up. Automatic temperature-control devices would begin to slow down their revolutions. The gravitron would thin out in the cables. Thundercracks would resound again. And there would be no helium in the pipeline, no way to fix the problem. Panic everywhere: panic in the towers, panic in Top Level, panic in the Ministry of Defense. But one voice would be calm in all that uproar—Proctor's voice over the Media and the public address system. "The Unslers have gambled with your safety, people of Ricardo. But I can restore the helium flow if you give me the power . . ."

Unreal, French thought. *Unreal.*

He shook himself and stood up. Exhaustion robbed him of objectivity. The plan wasn't all that bad. He had thought about it often in the past and it had seemed a reasonable, even a clever scheme. Nothing less than the threat of structure collapse could shake Unsler's grip over the instruments of power, could wake the people from their dreadful apathy. It all seemed crazy now, but French was tired and depressed.

Where in the hell was Dickens?

A catnap in the cubohome Dachsy would put at their disposal would refresh him enough so that he could come back and do battle again, French thought. Clemmens needed help. Before French had left Proctor, Proctor had ordered plans to be drawn up, schedules to be fixed. "Proceed as if we were going to deliver those parts," Proctor said. "I haven't made a final decision, but should I decide, I want everything ready to go on short notice. As soon as you have a delivery schedule, get back to me."

He has to be stopped, French thought. *I have to make him see reason.*

A change in the low buzz of voices around him brought French back to the present. His eyes sought the origin of the excitement. Two men rolled a wooden log into the stadium as one rolls a barrel, on its edge. A bald man naked to the waist came behind the log with an ax in his hand. *What in hell . . . ?* French watched the men set up the block in the middle of the stadium. The bald man approached it. He hefted the ax back and sank it into the wood with a dull report.

Then French saw Dickens emerge from a narrow door between two sets of bleachers. His assistants came behind him. French rose and made toward the group. He wanted to know what that block signified, half suspecting that Proctor had flipped.

6

Caged Birds

A group of Flames in shimmering white robes moved above the intertower beltway. Passengers down below glanced furtively at the westbound assembly, reserve in their faces. Prestigious family signs blazed in bright colors on the nobles' tubes—Sidney's companions. Best to be inconspicuous and to keep the eyes low.

Miri rode in the middle of the group surrounded by at least three circles of Flames—a blue stone in a silver setting.

Clafto led the group. He wore a red scarf around his neck. He had bathed and oiled his body for Regina after dinner. *A suitable love offering for the slender bitch,* he mused with an inward sneer, picturing her, relaxed at last. Leaving the Cosmos, he had been a little apprehensive. But they had dropped down East Shaft without mishap and had made it to the beltway undisturbed. They hadn't even seen a man from BTA. Blottingham's rumors were absurd. Clafto had suspected as much. Ridiculous notion. Proctor wouldn't dare challenge Sidney. Proctor *was* popular and this *was* a helium year, after all. Even so, the Chief Negotiator had to think about the future. Bernie would die sooner or later. Then Proctor would have a new boss.

Clafto's thoughts returned to Regina. He would jut her with a vengeance. To jut the little bitch would put the final touch on his new status in the Circle of Fire. Too bad Sidney had had to force her into compliance. But that would steal nothing from the pleasure of her lascivious *corpus*. Clafto imagined all the ways in which he'd force her to give him pleasure. He would exercise her until dawn.

Behind him, masked by other nobles, Miri rode, her face serene, eyes closed. Right now, right here, she would prove the Teaching, the subtle power of the Lady. Madonna sat at the Eternal Wheel and spun Time's gossamer thread. She wove it into the many-colored pattern of Fate. The Lady was transcending, omnipotent Mind. *Miri* was the Lady; she herself was part of that Substance. And if she could rise above the Bondage of Attachment, she too could weave a pattern with her mind. Any pattern she chose. The pattern of love; the pattern of death; yes, the pattern of escape. Miri had never tried to do this. It had not been necessary. But now the time had come for a test.

She imagined a bird in a cage. She made the vision sharp and clear behind closed eyes. A Flame operated her tube lest she escape as Frenchy had the other night, so she could devote herself entirely to her project: the yellow bird and a cage whose bars she imagined to be silvery white like the robes of her captors.

She set the image firmly in her mind, complete with all detail: the litter at the bottom of the cage, the tiny cup of water, the cage door and its latch, open windows across the room, a blue sky and a fluffy cloud beyond the windows. Next she imagined a hand reaching down. The hand unlocked her cage. In a flutter of wings she made a straight line for the window, and in seconds she soared high into the air.

Next Miri *felt* her freedom. She made herself feel it with as deep and real an emotion as she could muster. The Teachings said that strong emotion helped the process.

This done, Miri opened her eyes and took a deep breath—always a pleasure after intense concentration.

Meanwhile the group had entered West Tower's shaft, and the tubes were rising. She was as much a prisoner as ever, but now she was certain that she would be freed. She had formed a clear, sharp image of her desire; she had watched it serenely. "Detached Desire," the Cult called it. At the end she had blessed the results with a powerful but directed pulse of feeling . . .

Above her in the shaft, Clafto's mind ran at random over recollections and anticipations. At the moment, he thought about Luke's little speech and found it had been superb, despite the interruption. Worthy of *"magnificatio."* That ending, when he'd broken the eggs and hurled them into the sweetened crack of the hot little loaf . . . *dolce,* truly *dolce.* In the end he would drape Regina over the back of a stool, head down, fingers on to her toes. Then he'd crack his belt over *her* little loaf just to remind her of past rejections. From this his mind went on to imagine other things he might do to her in that bent-over position.

Under the sway of such rousing thoughts, he nearly missed the feeder street—a narrow "channel" (another clever theme for a little speech)—through which they would approach Regina's palace. He activated sidejets just in time, and his tube roared into the feeder. He checked his advance, glanced back. The group followed, and he went forward pleased by his send-off. The brightest Flames, the choicest of the choice. Once he had slipped into Regina's "burrow," the whole assembly would continue on—a triumphal parade. They would deliver French's wife to Sidney. No man who dared to touch a Flame could hope to escape the consequences.

He had nearly reached the end of the feeder when gray-clad men in large numbers appeared at the mouth of the channel. Some were in jumptubes at his level, some on foot on the ground—weird figures in gas masks. Chemguns pointed in his direction.

With an expression of painful surprise, Clafto turned and looked back at the group. Beyond them crouched more men. He thought of BTA just as the invisible gas reached him and he lost consciousness.

Selma burst into her mistress' favorite room. Through wide-open and somewhat bulging eyes she took in the scene at a glance.

The poor woman sat on the divan, a clump of misery. Her legs were up. She hugged them against her body. Her chin rested on her knees. Selma saw her rocking dumbly back and forth among pink pillows on the white divan.

"They're gone, mistress!" Selma cried. "They've left."

Slowly Regina looked up at her maid, a dull expression in her eyes. They mirrored hour-long agonies— a roller-coaster ride of wild, turbulent hope followed by the sickening drops into suicidal despair. She felt like the gut-strings of one of those guitars made by Bluegrass Territory that had lost its tension after much play.

"Who?" she asked in a hollow voice. "Who's gone?"

"The men, the Flames."

Regina dropped her head to her knees and stared down at her toes again. Ten little gnomes, side by side. *One little piggy went to market, one little piggy went . . .* The toenails glistened with iridescent sheen. The polish changed colors slowly with every shift in temperature, however small. Made especially for Her Ladyship. Her pedicurist had sworn it was the only formulation of its kind in Union.

Gone . . . left . . . ?

She didn't believe it. All her faith had drained away like liquid from a cracked gourd. Faithless humanity. Mycal, the traitor. It was well past eleven, and he hadn't come. His passion must have cooled in the sobriety of day. He had lied to her on the tel in the late afternoon. He would not help her escape, and she feared setting out alone. Regina, the traitor. Regina, who had betrayed herself, whose courage had fizzed like a punctured balloon. In the glass-domed garden upstairs stood jumptubes placed there on her orders. Two of them—one for him, one for her. When Mycal hadn't come, she had dressed to make her escape alone, through the roof. But she had shrunk from the venture and had slunk back defeated. She'd undressed, had made herself ready for the inevitable.

Selma watched her mistress rocking, reminded of a child.

"Mistress, aren't you glad?"

"Glad?"

"Yes, glad. The men are gone. Don't you want to get away? Don't you want to visit Sister Serenita?"

"They're not gone, Selma. I know it. It's just a ruse. Just something nasty that Sidney would do."

Selma had her mouth open, ready to answer, when they both heard the melodious chime from the front hall.

With a dull, resigned emotion, Regina understood why the Flames were gone. They were no longer needed. Clafto had arrived. She would be shamed after all. The days of hope were nothing but illusion. It would be like before. Four times now Sidney's chosen of the moment had stood before her portals waiting to be admitted.

I'll be like a rag. I'll submit like a thing, a soulless thing! And tomorrow ...

Something. She would do something tomorrow ...

"Let him in," she said to Selma as the chime sounded again, twice in a row, impatiently. "Let him in," she sighed.

An Empty Cage

French kept his finger on the button, and the pressure produced the first six notes of the Ecofreak tribal anthem.

The steel cable of his self-control threatened to snap. Tension and anxiety overrode the dull fatigue he felt. Conflicting needs tore at him and filled his mind with flashing pictures. Miri. Miri came first. In the press of troubles around him, he grasped for fundamentals. Self-preservation. The family, however tiny. But French also feared for the larger family— BTA. He would go to see Proctor the moment Miri was safe. Now he understood the chopping block. Proctor had to be stopped. His politician's flair for grand gestures would extract too high a price. *What's the matter with everything?* he thought. *Has the world gone off its rocker?*

French rang the bell again. Worry and fear gathered his throat into a lump. Why didn't Ecofreak open the goddamned door? He wanted Miri *now!* He wanted to have her safely hid away.

Behind him Gomer, his flat face empty of expression, watched at the head of a small group of men. Gomer was an elderly man with a somewhat shapeless figure that did not make a good appearance in the tight-fitting, zippered jump suit he and the others wore. Gomer watched French, disliking what he saw. The grim, desperate look, reflected in the glass and polished brass of the well-to-do housefronts, had come upon the young DA when they had swooped down on this spot, approaching from either end of Outer Ring in a hurry, and—hadn't found a single Flame!

Thoughts ran through Gomer's mind, thoughts about love and about slum kids who had risen too high. He for one didn't have the rank to traffic with the famous DA, Intelligence; but he knew what every man knew about the man—a real romantic, he was. No man would *marry* in this day and age unless he thought he genuinely loved. Love? Why, it was like astrology —not very reliable. But you couldn't convince some people of that.

Gomer hoped that the girl was inside, safe and sound. French had a reputation. People said he had a crazy streak, and it was not merely a fable. In his early days he'd volunteered—yes, volunteered!—for sixteen missions into Hinterland. If that wasn't evidence of madness . . .

Now he saw French release the bell. The blond DA stepped back and kicked at the portal once . . . twice . . . again. The thick bronze door, decorated with pastoral Hinterland scenes in relief, gave a dull gonglike sound.

Balled fists. Flashing eyes. French looked as if fire would spout from his nostrils. Gomer could not escape the thought: *A low-level man who has made good.* Something about French brought to Gomer's mind a sense of the elemental, the crude, the uncontrolled. He must have looked like this in the East Tower slums —a gangster from Branco, with no hint of the polish he had acquired in later years.

French felt the cable of his self-control snap. He kicked the door again, his blood in a boil. On the next kick a small, square window opened in the door. Black eyes, brows, the nose of a tribesman filled the aperture.

"I'm Rivera French. I've come to get my wife."

"She isn't here."

The statement came like a fist into his stomach. It took his breath away.

"What do you mean, she isn't here? Where is she?"

"I don't know."

French controlled the urge to leap at the tiny opening, to grab for the face.

"Open up," he husked. "Open up this instant. I want to see the Ambassador."

Gomer heard the deadly tone and winced, wondering if he should step in to restrain the man. But then he decided it wasn't his place.

"Ambassador Dart doesn't wish to receive you."

"Ambassador *Dart?* Where's Barney?"

Thoughts raced through French's mind. Dart had walked out of the negotiations. Last night he had opposed giving them sanctuary.

"Mr. Barney is no longer Ambassador," the man said.

"Why? What happened?"

"I'm not at liberty to say."

Silence. Gomer watched French thinking. The blue eyes stared at the door, fixed to a spot next to the square opening. The DA's face was flushed. Muscles worked in his cheeks.

"What did you do with her?"

"Mrs. French was asked to leave."

"When? How long ago?"

Gomer noted a change in the DA's tone. Now it was cool, icy, but somehow even more disturbing.

"Seven, seven thirty."

"Did you see Flames on the ring?"

"I saw nothing, mister. I wasn't here."

French abruptly turned from the door and made for his jumptube. Before Gomer could react, French jabbed the device alive with angry fingers. Instantly the tube rose up and curved away with a scream of jets.

"Mr. French—Mr. French—"

But the DA heard nothing. Within an eyewink he disappeared from Gomer's view around the bend of Outer Ring.

Escape

"Mistress, mistress, it's *him!*"

Regina felt confused. She would have been angry with Selma if she had had the energy to be angry. What did that silly female want?

"Of course it's him. I told you that before."

Selma shook her head with great exaggeration. Her bulging eyes were wide open with some kind of mindless astonishment. "Not *him,* Miss Ginny. The other one, the man from Hinterland."

Regina lifted her head sharply, uncoiled her legs, and jumped to her feet. Her fatigue fled. The vigor she felt surprised her in a subliminal way. She saw her own image in the gold-laced mirror opposite. But this was not the girl who had sat in a miserable clump. The breasts were out, the chin was high.

"You mean . . . ?" she whispered.

Selma's head went up and down with an exaggerated affirmation.

Regina felt blood throb in her throat. One of her hands fluttered up.

"Bring him in," she said, "but give me time to slip into this."

Earlier, in anticipation of escape, she had worn a zippered fortress of a jump suit. She slipped into it now. It fit her snugly. The smooth silk over thermal fluff slid along her skin. The outside was made of miraculous polyhide with molecules so tightly linked a knife could not have pierced it. Her seamstress had designed it especially for her. No other lady in Union . . .

She saw movement from the corner of her eyes—and he was there!

With a gladness that made her sob, she flew to him. Her tears moistened his face; she mumbled incoherently. Her lips sought his with a kind of hunger. Her hands caressed his face. Gradually she calmed down, withdrew a little, looked at him. Mycal's eyes echoed her own gladness, but his face was drawn and pale, his clothes dirty and rumpled. Soil clung to his hands, dried blood marked numerous cuts. She hadn't noticed.

Regina had a vision of Mycal fighting outside against Flames to be on her side. She asked him what had happened. Had he been accosted in the street?

Bono shook his head. "I'm in trouble, Regina."

Inwardly Bono didn't *feel* like a man in trouble. He had passed through a kind of eerie hell and stood in heaven now—supplicant before the Queen. Behind him lay the pulsing darkness of a labyrinth of service chasms. He had escaped through a hole in the closet of his prison which had been blocked by a loose plate. He had groped and stumbled in the depths while tiny sparks electrified the air and clung to his beard like microscopic fireflies. Great shudders of machinery coming alive and dying terrorized him. Large rats shadowed his progress. They ran along ledges he couldn't see; they crouched on cable strands and stared hungrily through luminous, greenish eyes—Norway rats, the only mammal besides man to adapt to gravitron. Once he almost fell to his death when a section of railing turned into flaky dust beneath his hand. Now he was here once again in the sparkling palace amid traces of exquisite perfume. A tiny music lilted on the air, almost below the level of hearing.

He saw confusion in her eyes. "I'm no longer chief of mission. They removed me and locked me up. I escaped to come here."

Regina understood him now, and her heart leaped with pleasure. Now nothing stood in the way of escape. If Mycal no longer had duties in Ricardo, nothing would keep him here.

"Why?" she asked. "What happened?"

He glanced aside to avoid her eyes. "You see, I . . . I exceeded my instructions. I asked for you as hostage."

"And you shouldn't have!"

"I shouldn't have."

"Oh, darling."

She hugged and kissed him again, dimly aware that she did more than merely that required to secure his cooperation.

"I'm in trouble too," she explained, breaking away. "I've been told to stay away from you by my brother, Sidney. I can't hide you and I can't stay here either. Will you escape with me? The two of us? Together?" Hope sparkled in her eyes.

"But how? *You?* Me? Alone?"

She nodded eagerly and took his hand.

Bono followed her in a kind of daze up the same stairs he had mounted the night before with such sure anticipation. Everything moved too fast for him, he couldn't keep track. He lagged behind himself, trying to catch up. His life had become a voyage on a mountain stream with sudden twists and turns and mind-boggling drops and flings. Water, rock, embankments. A boiling and tumbling all around him. Here he was, about to abduct Unsler's daughter at her instigation. To take her where?

She stopped upstairs and pointed with a beaming face at two jumptubes as if they were statues she had just unveiled. Next to each on the gravel path lay a thick, fur-lined parka. On each parka sat a yellow mask of some sort attached by coiling lines to tubular devices with straps. To wear on the back? Oxygen?

"There," she cried with a note of triumph. "See, I've already planned our escape."

The Block

At first she heard the dull murmur of voices. Then, overlaid against that background, she heard the echoing fall of footsteps, movement. She lay in some sort of large place on a kind of narrow cot covered by a rough blanket. The blanket had been tucked in around her, under her feet. Someone had removed her shoes. Her head buzzed and ached. Nausea troubled her stomach.

Miri opened her eyes and closed them again.

From a place high in the ceiling, bright floodlights blinded her.

She found the spot where memory had failed. She had been on a feeder street in West Tower's Top Level headed for Regina Unsler's palace. She recalled a swarming of gray-clad men, crouched with chemguns in their hands. Then had come a rush of darkness, a feeling as if her eyes were turning inside out. And then—*poof!*

Darby Dickens' energetic voice cut through the confused noise around her.

"Up, up, up, you birds," he cried. "Quickly now. You too. Get up! Don't pretend, my noble friend. We know when the effect wears off."

Miri smiled to herself with eyes closed. Darby's voice told her that she had been saved. A hand had reached down to free the yellow bird.

She wiggled an arm from the tightly wound blanket and, shading her eyes, sat up to look for Frenchy.

From her immediate right came a voice: "Ah, Mrs. French, you're up. Here, let me give you a hand. No pains, I hope. Your tube bounced about a bit after you lost consciousness, but we caught you before you had a chance to fall."

She didn't recognize the helpful young man. His hair was cut in bangs across his forehead. He wore a button on his jump-suit collar, and she recognized a management intern. He pulled her up from the cot and she stood for a second in her stockings, unsteadily, leaning on his arm, smiling her thanks. Then, eyes still shaded from the glare, she looked around for Frenchy.

The stadium. She had been here before for official dances. Then the ceiling had had a low-slung belly of festoons and a band had played on a stand. Proctor danced with Mrs. Sedlig in her memories—the pale secretary blushing crimson from the honor. Now she saw only BTA staffers packed on bleachers. A chopping block with an ax in its center dominated the middle of the room. *What is it for?* To her right Darby marched among supine nobles laid out in rows, nudging now this, now that Flame with the tip of a brightly polished boot. One by one the Flames came to their feet, groggy, confused.

She did not see Frenchy anywhere.

Several thoughts crossed her mind more or less at once. She wondered what this was all about—the crowd, the block, her captors on the floor. The crowd scene stirred her artistic interest. The room suggested drama—a scene for a mural, perhaps. At the same time she wondered where Frenchy was. *Why did they assign a trainee to wait on me?*

"Quick, now, gentlemen," Darby called. "We can't be napping all night. Let's move."

Miri said to the trainee: "Is my husband here?"

"No, ma'am."

"Where is he?"

"He went out with another party, Mrs. French. They haven't returned."

The intern avoided her eyes. Miri grew troubled. How many groups searched Ricardo to find her? Didn't they communicate?

"What party did he go with?" she asked.

"He went to the embassy to get you—but of course, you weren't there."

"And?"

He ducked her eyes, but she stared until he answered.

"Mr. French broke away from his party and went off alone."

Miri sucked in her breath. She had had that dark

145

premonition. He had not listened to her. He hadn't counted to ten, as she had asked him.

You are sound, secure, calm, and unafraid. She sent the telepathic message with the strongest pulse she could muster. She hoped that he would be calm enough to receive her message. *I am well and safe,* she signaled. *You are calm, reasonable, confident, courageous.*

"Mrs. French," the trainee said. He took her by an elbow. "Now that you're awake, may I take you to an apartment we've set aside? Mr. Proctor has instructed me to—"

"No," she broke in. "I'll wait here for my husband."

Yes, she would wait. She'd wait until French returned.

The intern still held her elbow. He tugged at it, clearly agitated and embarrassed. "Ma'am I—"

She turned her head and looked at him.

"I wouldn't advise that you watch this." He gestured vaguely.

She followed his gesture and saw the chopping block. "Why?"

"All right, Flames and Sparks," Dickens bawled to the nobles. She saw him march up and down in front of the figures in white; they all stood, finally. "Out of your robes, all of you. Undress. Quickly. Down to your Adam's costume. *Move!* We haven't got all night."

Undress? Strange . . .

"What'll happen?" Miri asked.

The youngster glanced away, embarrassed. "Ma'am . . . it'll be harmless, but it won't be pretty. I urge you—"

She shook her head. "I want to see."

She threw off a pulse of annoyance. Why couldn't women witness ugly scenes? At the same time, she felt a stir of suspicion. This was more than a rescue operation, and BTA didn't want her to watch. Well, she would!

"Hey, you. Get with it, man. I told you to strip."

Darby addressed a swarthy man Miri now knew as Clafto Meyer. She thought: *We're all connected.* She remembered a small commission from the Meyer family she had received some years ago, brought by a senior servant of that household. It had been for a series of inlays for wooden furniture. Since then she had graduated into portraits.

To her right Clafto experienced a rare emotion. He felt genuine, gut-wrenching terror. Like flashes of successive lightning in a dark and fearful landscape, his mind fed him information and insights: BTA had dared to touch him! Clafto Meyer, the plastosteel heir, the Flame nearest to the Fire! Even now some black man yelled at him in a tone . . . Clafto didn't understand the man. His ears buzzed. But he heard the arrogance.

"You!" the black yelled. A finger pointed. It came out of a dark fist at the end of a dark arm. Around the dark wrist glowed a golden watch. "Get out of that robe. I won't tell you again."

Clafto understood now and burst into protest. "What *is* this? Who're you to tell me to undress . . . ?"

He heard the death of his own protest. Around him Flames and Sparks were more compliant. Some already stood naked with hands up front to shield themselves from scrutiny.

"All right, men," the black man yelled. "Strip him."

Miri watched the ensuing, feeble struggle as BTA men overcame Clafto and stripped him bare. They left only socks and boots. The naked form . . . so noble in art. But here nudity was used as a weapon—to underline BTA's superiority.

She saw movement from the corner of her eye. A man—unusually tall, muscular, bald, and naked to the waist—approached the chopping block. She turned her full attention to him, plagued by an indecision in her mind: Was this an elaborate psychodrama staged for the benefit of the Flames? Or was there more to it?

Behind the bald, half-naked man rolled a camera on wheels. The camera circled the block until the technician operating it found his angle. Miri now became aware of other cameras spotted about the stadium and aimed at various spots.

The bald man worked the deep-sunk ax out of the wood, tested its weight in a hand, took a step back. He lifted the ax far back over his shoulder, and with a loud shout—"Haay!" he cried—he sank the blade into the block.

Miri glanced at Clafto to see his reaction. The handsome, hairy man was fearful. His eyes shifted incessantly. Three men held him, two on each side and one in the back. She found this excessive because Clafto didn't resist. Did they expect that he would . . . later?

This can't be real, Clafto told himself. *I don't believe this. Why the butcher block? What significance the ax-wielding gesture, the loud cry of the man?*

"Mrs. French, I really think you should leave now."

Miri shook her head. She was tense with expectation. She thought: *Surely they don't intend to harm these nobles!? Even Proctor wouldn't resort to low barbarism? Or would he? Could this be a practical joke? He is said to be quite a practical— No.* She doubted it. This—whatever this was—was more than just a joke.

"All right, men," she heard Darby call, "take him to the block. The rest of you, look lively! Don't let these birds panic."

Clafto's guards began to move him forcibly. She heard him cry: "Hey, what is this? Stop! You can't do this. I swear I'll—" His voice disappeared in grunting struggle.

Miri felt the man's hysteria. It spread like an acid stench on the air, choked the throat. Clafto would not walk and had to be carried. He struggled all the way to the block, where the ax-man hefted his weapon with a satisfied but eerie look on his face.

It's like a scene from a cheap visishow.

Meanwhile other BTA staffers had swarmed out to take up positions on either side of the naked formation. Miri watched in growing disgust. Clafto's guards, now joined by two others, forced the noble up against the block in such a way that his genitals lay on the rough surface of the wood. Four men held the madly struggling Flame. The fifth crossed opposite and rudely grabbed the man's parts. He stretched them out a little, away from the body.

Clafto's yell of pain shot through Miri as if it were her own. The chemblast nausea rose up in her again. *Degradation in the venerable stadium. Savage rite. Disease of the Cosmic Mind.*

"All right, you," Dickens called to the naked nobles. "Turn around. You won't have to see this. You'll feel it soon enough. Go on, turn."

The nobles turned. Miri saw her own disbelief mirrored in their faces. But why did Darby make them turn?

"Mrs. French, please—"

"Please, for God's sake, people, this is—this— Oh, God, let me go!"

Miri's eyes focused on Clafto's face. She dared not look down again at the man's stretched genitals. She'd had no idea that the organ could be pulled so far from the body. A great burst of sympathy for the man went out from her to him, so patently fragile and human now—he who had chased Frenchy and her yesterday. *Was it only yesterday?*

Darby turned and signaled to the bald man, who nodded. He lowered his ax blade over Clafto's genitals in the way of a man taking aim. Then he stepped back. Clafto made one last effort to get away, but the pain restrained him. The bald man swung his ax back over his shoulder.

Miri turned away. She couldn't watch this. The ax wielder's loud "Haay!", Clafto's piercing scream, and the dull report of blade on wood all came simultaneously.

Head still averted, Miri said to the pleasant intern: "Take me away, now."

"But, Mrs. French," he now protested, "you don't understand . . ."

"I understand," she said flatly. "Take me away."

Clafto's momentary swoon receded. He had almost lost consciousness under the brutal impact of emotion that had enveloped him. His eyes had gone black. Now he was back again and he felt release.

He felt . . . release?!

The pain in his genitals was gone, or less intense.

He opened his eyes, bent his head. He was still whole! The ax blade sat embedded in the wood of the block, but it was a long way from his exposure, on the other side of the sawed-off stump. Two men were hurriedly smearing a red liquid on the wood from little bucketlike containers.

His captors hustled him out of the room. He went willingly. He was halfway down some kind of hall when the next man's loud screams echoed through the corridor. His guards pushed him into a room. Behind a desk sat a man in a gray jump suit; the room was empty save for that desk and a chair.

"Here, put these on," the man said, pointing to a blue jump suit, crumpled underwear, and a white robe on the chair. Clafto recognized his own clothing. Gladly, hurriedly, he dressed.

"Now understand this," the man commanded. "BTA won't be harassed by Flames or Sparks or anyone. No more killings, no more attacks. Remember this well and pass it on. Next time the ax will be right on target. Take him away."

Men took him to his jumptube in a garage. They watched him until he had cleared a guard booth and had entered the movebelt.

Clafto spurted away at maximum speed, a hollow sensation in his stomach. Proctor had dared the ultimate humiliation. It could only mean that the rumors were true, that revolution was brewing. No, more than that. Revolution had succeeded, else how would Proctor dare . . .

Memories of Narses

Proctor sat behind his desk and watched the action in the stadium over the same visimonitor that had shown him Ecofreak's entrance into Ricardo a few days ago.

His face was pensive, with a touch of puzzlement. Below the hardened surface of his everyday consciousness, something stirred. He almost had it, but it kept eluding him. It was a memory that would explain, he knew, why Operation Hairy-Scary pleased him so—despite the risk, despite its terrible timing, its potentially high political costs. But the memory would not hatch.

A buzz on his communicator made him reach out. The voice of the night-duty secretary told him that Clemmens waited outside to give a report. He told the man to send Clemmens in. Simultaneously he turned down the audio on the visiset, and the loud screams faded away.

Clemmens came in and sat down with a sheaf of scriptoplast in his hand. Somehow his presence underlined with a vengeance French's absence.

"We still don't have word of your chief, do we?" Proctor asked.

"No, sir."

The men exchanged glances. The glances said: *We both know Rivera French, and both of us are worried.*

"Where do you think he is?"

"I'd hate to speculate," Clemmens answered.

"Go ahead. Go ahead and speculate."

"He's looking for her. That'd be my guess. And you know where he is likely to look."

"Sidney's domain."

"Yes, sir."

Proctor shook his head. It was more of an incantatory denial than a conviction. "Surely not. The man can't be such a fool. Madness. Sheer madness."

Clemmens made a wry face. His expression suggested that French was capable of madness.

Proctor deliberately dismissed the subject with a wave of his hand. *Unfortunately, I've set him a very poor example with this operation. Also madness,* he thought. Aloud he said: "Let's talk about silcoplast. What does it look like? Can we produce the parts?"

Clemmens passed scripto over the desk. "The first item is a production schedule," he said, keeping his tone cool and businesslike. It was not his role to discuss policy with Proctor; French would do that. When French returned. *If* French returned. "We've worked it out carefully and checked with all the producers. We had to get some plant managers out of bed, but it's hard information."

Proctor studied the sheet, looked up. "Four days? You can deliver in four days?"

"Yes, sir."

Proctor nodded. "And these other items?"

"Draft contracts and procurement orders. I didn't bring the specs and the drawings. I don't suppose you're interested."

Proctor shook his head. He took the production schedule off the pile and passed the other items back to Clemmens. "I'll keep the schedule; I don't need these things."

Clemmens made ready to rise.

"Stay a second," Proctor said. "What's your opinion, Fred? Are these really oscillation control devices?"

"I'm sure of it, sir."

"But French tells me that Fulbright disagrees."

"He does indeed, sir."

"Don't you respect Fulbright's judgment?"

"I'm not in a position to judge the professor's competence, Negotiator. I'm just a simple engineer. But even genius can sometimes be wrong."

"Very well, Fred." Proctor scratched behind his ear. Then he looked at Clemmens. "And suppose you're right. Can you defeat the device?"

"I don't know, sir. How can you defeat something unless you know how it works?"

"But you could try?"

"We can try, of course . . ."

"Then try," Proctor said, nodding. "Figure out some minor change that's difficult to detect and work it into the plans."

I only need a day, he thought. *One day.*

"Will do," Clemmens said, and this time he rose.

Proctor nodded to him. "Thanks, Fred. Do the

best you can. If we have to, we could deliver," he summed up, "in four days."

"Yes, sir."

"Very well, Fred. Your people did a good job."

Clemmens left and Proctor turned on the audio again. At the moment, the camera down in the stadium focused on another group of naked Flames. That picture suddenly triggered the memory, a long forgotten resentment, and Proctor knew why he had indulged himself with Hairy-Scary.

The memory molded Proctor's face into a mask of slightly cruel glee. He remembered it all, now. His mind returned to New Ivy League—"Nivylee," as the students called it. The school of schools. Cradle of leaders. Nivylee—the elite college that claimed uninterrupted descent from the best pre-structure universities. That school had accepted him on a scholarship for his uncontested brilliance, one of a dozen Mid-Level men admitted to the place. He studied with the fathers of the men who now screamed down there in the stadium—one after the other, each stupidly convinced that he would lose his manhood.

The rich boys had called him Narses Castratus after some obscure official of the Dimmest Ages, the Roman Time, which still inspired Very Big youths bent on the emulation of past decadence; it was a nickname which he'd refused to recall. When forced to disrobe with others for the weekly physical education class, compulsory in the first year, the fathers of these worthless Flames had chanted in the showers to spite him: "Not a dong, not a ding, not even a dingaling."

He had been a fat boy, his physical development retarded by gravitron, a not unusual phenomenon. In the second year his hormones began to flow. The butter of his moon face melted away, revealing the hard rock of his chin. The pillows of lard beneath his eyes disappeared, giving free range to his hard, cold stare. By the third year he manipulated tutors and men and virtually ran the college. He graduated with honors. But he came from Mid-Level and had to enter the civil service at the lowest rung of the ladder, while his classmates went right to the top of agencies and industries.

Proctor smiled and shook his head.

All that lay thirty years back. He had risen once more and now stood on the brink of another graduation. He could afford a slight indulgence, risk or no risk. If the greater scheme failed, at least he would have had *this* satisfaction. If it succeeded—why then he might think of other things to do with his erstwhile humiliators and their precious sons.

Now that he had found the memory, he lost interest in the activity below. He turned off sound and picture and fell to studying the production schedule.

Four days to produce the silco-parts, he mused. *Four days.* The basic schema he had turned this way and that all day began to crystallize in his mind. He would try it. He'd attempt to deal with Bono, an exchange of treasons. He would deliver the components, flawed components, to be sure. And Ecofreak, in turn, would deliver the illegal Interdiction that would catapult Proctor to ultimate power. And as soon as he was in power, the negotiations would take on another character altogether. He was not an Accommodationist, no bleeding heart, had no fear of using missiles; and Ecofreak would learn that. Perhaps he would explode a bomb or two just to show them that the sil parts didn't work.

He sighed tiredly. One last item and then he would try to snatch a few hours of genuine sleep. He reached for the dictation button laid into the surface of his desk.

"A letter to Mr. Mycal Bono, Chief of Mission, helium, the Ecofreak embassy, and so forth, the text is as follows."

He paused, thinking.

"Dear Mr. Bono," he began. "Union has analyzed Ecofreak's initial package, and we're pleased to give you the following reaction. Paragraph. Your demand for various products and components, including the communications switches made of welded silcoplast, appear acceptable." He hesitated.

"Comma," he continued, "provided that you immediately withdraw your demand for Miss Regina Unsler, the Unifer's daughter, and . . . enter with us into serious negotiations about various demands that we have. Paragraph."

He paused again, then went on. "Your demand for plastosteel is excessive in the extreme and cannot be honored. However, we shall be pleased to sit down and discuss a reasonable level of shipment. Paragraph. Technical analysis shows that the electronic components you desire can be delivered to the four staging stations—" He glanced down at the delivery schedule. "The *six* staging stations specified in your demand," he corrected, "soon after we sign an acceptable helium deal. Paragraph." Was that too direct? He decided to let it stand for the moment. "We look forward to a timely response and stand ready to resume talks immediately, provided that you can sincerely enter into the spirit of the points raised in this letter. Should you be unable to do so, I regret that we shall be forced to take appropriate measures to secure our well-being. Very truly yours, etc. etc."

Proctor replayed the tape and decided that some editing was required. The text was too obvious and had to be cast in a more subtle form. But he would do that in the morning. For the moment it would suffice. He'd sleep on it.

7

Prayer on the Pyramid

A leaden sky obscured the sun. Wind blew across the endless mutagrass, driving speckles of icy rain before it. The wide plain was almost completely empty except for a chain of uniform hills spaced one kilometer apart. The remains of an ancient highway could be seen in spots linking the hills. To the left of this chain, looking east, stood the Activist camp—a crowding of tents with horse corrals on one side and a formation of helicopters on the other.

On the flat top of one of the hills a group of tribesmen stood in clumps approximating a circle around Tack. He sat in the center in the classic meditation pose. The men were silent and endured the rain with stoic expressions.

Only Ted Fannin was out of the rain. He stood in the narrow observation room of a high wooden tower that had been erected here recently. He felt the cold as keenly as the others. He shook his arms and ran in place to warm himself. On the window sill before him lay binoculars through which, from time to time, he observed the distant camp, on the lookout for signals that might be sent to recall Tack from his morning prayers.

Fannin had a good idea why the meditation lasted longer than usual. The news of Bono's defection had spread from lip to lip the night before. That, combined with Jonny's other troubles, gave the chief lots of things to pray about.

Fannin wondered, at the moment, whether or not it might be time to head for home. He would have no trouble fixing it so that he'd make the mail run to Wellhead. Then he could become "sick" in Wellhead.

And then, a little later, he might send word that he had gone home to recuperate.

He ran in place, shaking his arms, feeling a little warmer now. His breath worked hard.

In the center of the circle, Tack wrestled with the Lord but made no progress.

He had awakened in a boiling rage, filled with hot, carnal desire. He had kicked his servant across the tent: the rascal had overslept and Tack had almost missed the dawn. Then he had come out here to commune with Him, seeking a clear nod, a firm assurance. Did He-Up-There care as much about the Plan as Jonny Tack?

The Lord wouldn't answer. Tack labored, worked. But he didn't hear the Lord. Snakes surrounded and encoiled him—writhing doubts, desires, and uncertainties.

Listen, Lord, hear me! Tack pleaded. *I'm surrounded by traitors. They violate Your law. They disobey Your servant.*

He felt the prayer in his guts, a strong emotion. But his face was stiff and masked his feelings. The wind drove particles of ice against his skin, where they turned into speckles of moisture.

Why did they do it? Tack wondered. Why the opposition? What had happened to the fervent commitments of a month ago?

Fear, selfish fear!

He recalled an elder Gulfrat's statement of the night before: "The venture is doomed to failure. Your own men betrayed you. It's a bad sign. The Lord won't smite all those millions. There must be righteous among them. Give up the plan, Jonny. Secure the parts, but give up the madness."

Then the man had come forward and spread out a map of Gulfrat's territories.

"Look at this, Jonny. Those are my people. What if Union betrays us? What if the parts don't work? A few missiles from Husten will destroy us."

Tack hit the table with a fist. "Why? Why have you changed your mind? You swore."

157

"We swore, but we've thought about it since."

Lord, he prayed, *give me a sign. Give me a sign so I can rally these people. Show me Your grace.*

In the tower Fannin stared out over the landscape. Yellow outcroppings of rock broke up the monotony of silvery mutagrass moving under windlash like the sea.

He wondered what the pyramids might have looked like in ancient days. He imagined them silvery, reflecting sunlight. And a constant traffic of tank trucks would have moved down below on the ancient highway, carrying toxic wastes for perpetual deposition in these structures now covered with dirt and overgrown with vegetation.

The ancients were gone, but the wastes were still here—drums of it, sacks of it, pools of hazard—liquids, solids, and hot stuff that would still be here when man had gone from the face of the earth.

Plutonium has a half-life of twenty-four thousand years, he mused.

For an instant he tried to calculate how much plutonium would be left a hundred thousand years from now if you started with a ton of the stuff at the time of LNW XIII. He gave up the effort as too tedious. Instead he mused about the enormities radiation had created. This area still produced mutants that lived a few generations before nature wiped them off the boards.

Near Santlu crater he had once seen a horse so tiny you could hold it in your hand. Around Liberal, in Mokan, people said lived a creature with a heart so big it squirted poisoned blood to catch its prey. Then there was a curious bird with one enormous right wing and an insignificant left that flap-flew backward. Near here he'd seen a feathered turtle that—

Motion from the direction of the camp drew his eye.

Straw-hatted Symbinuts marched toward helicopters.

Another group deserting the strict-constructionist paradise?

He watched the Symbies through his binoculars.

Several fems walked in the group, out in the open, un-abashed.

Fannin chuckled. He had guessed all along that Jonny's rules were not being observed. Some tribes had women in the camp. And those that didn't jutted fel-folk from mutie settlements in the rad belts. They came from all over in the night and sold themselves for salt and trinkets.

I should be so lucky, Fannin thought.

He imagined a wild fem scratching on the canvas of his tent. Well, Fannin had a ring or two ready for that eventuality. He too had sworn the Pact of Chastity, but on occasion you could close an eye. Best if you *did* close the eyes. Some of these fems were weird —eight nipples down each side of the belly, faces without noses, just little holes all covered with hair. But who gave a damn in the dark.

Mutant slaves loaded the Symby copters. Then Fannin saw blades begin to turn. Three big birds rose with a dull, whirring sound and curved away, away to Socal.

Tack also heard the faraway whirring chop of copters and almost opened his eyes. But he resisted the urge.

Is that Your answer, Lord? he asked with an undertone of bitterness. *Is that Your message? More defections?*

Five tribes had already deserted. If more left, who would mass around the structures to wipe out the remnants of structure life? It seemed to him as if fate conspired to ruin the glorious plan—the plan his father had formulated, for whose achievement he had sacrificed the family wealth. Herd after herd of Tack cattle had been sold to support those scientists in Kaysee.

For a second Tack yielded to an angry thought.

Damn. He *would* succeed without the other tribes. He'd march with his own army down the coasts of America, liquidating the remnants. And he'd subjugate these now-lost tribes as well, one by one.

The sound of copters faded.

Which ones this time? Planetfriends? Peacefreaks? Gulfrats? The word about Bono's defection had leaked out. He would find the man who had done the leaking and lock the bastard in this pyramid to eat of arsenate of lead and drink the milk of chlorinated hydrocarbons.

Tack stopped himself. This was no way to meditate. He would have to calm his mind.

In the tower, Fannin hopped around once more, beating his arms against his chest. Wind whistled in through the cracks of the tower. After a while he stopped and went back to the window. He saw that Tack had risen, stood now where he had sat. His blond horsetail of hair hung down dark yellow, wet with rain. Fannin gathered his binoculars and raced down the stairs, but when he got down, Tack still had not moved.

Tack tried hard not to see the delegates. He hated them for the doubts they held. How could they doubt him? How could they reject the prophecies!

He reached for the Crestmore bible on his belt. He would try one more time. He *had* to get guidance, one way or another. In meditation he had seen only conspiracies—and *her*. Regina's rutty voluptuousness had confused him with moist memories. He would open the bible at random and see what the book said.

From the shelter of the door, Fannin saw the gesture. Tack's fingers fanned the pages of the book. That was a bad sign. The delegates would see Jonny's indecision, his telltale reliance on the supernatural. Fannin wondered how soon he might head out for Wellhead and get sick.

Tack waited for the spirit's prompting as his fingers moved. He felt the impulse and let the book fall open. He lifted it and read the verse where his thumb had come to rest.

"Mercy is sweeter in the mouth than justice."

Tack slammed the book shut and let it drop down on its silver chain. *Goddamn,* he thought. *Goddamn!* That line offered no guidance. Of late he had gotten such verses by the score. He wanted to open the book to one of the many instructive stories—the Chicago Seven, say, or the Tale of Manson. Instead he got chapters loosely transferred from the Biblibooks.

He glanced up at the gray sky. *Lord, You're no help! I'll have to act without You.*

His errors would be the Lord's, not his. He had asked, so now he could not be blamed. Damnation. A man worked, busted his ass—but He didn't care. Sometimes Tack was sure that He wasn't there at all; everything up above and down below was nothing more than sky and rock and mutagrass. Tack wished it were so. But then, again, things did happen that he couldn't explain so well.

Disappointed, Tack started for the camp. Freckled Fannin came toward him with a grin, but he scowled at his aide, and the man fell back. Behind Fannin came the delegates.

They went down the steep slope of the pyramid in the involuntary quick-step forced by the gradient and then in long strides across the wet mutagrass toward flags flapping, moisture-laden, in the wind in the distance.

Tack was halfway to the camp when a figure slipped out between tents and ran toward them. The man held something yellow in his hand.

Tack grew alert, almost joyous. *Action! Something to read, something to do! Perhaps guidance will come from another source. The Lord's ways are strange.*

The man reached him, stopped, and gasped once or twice, out of breath. He handed Tack three sections of cable, said: "A message from Dart, Leader. Thought you'd want to see this right away."

Tack read the text of the letter Dart had just received from Union. His heavy mood gave way to buoyant elation as he read. He glanced up at the sky briefly—to show the Lord that he understood. Here was the answer. They had succeeded without even trying. Union stood ready to deliver the parts for an almost meaningless concession: drop the hostage demand. Tack felt like laughing. The strategy had

161

worked despite Regina's substitution for Sidney.

The second part of the report dealt with Bono's escape. Tack's face clouded, but this mishap couldn't obscure his relief. Bono would be caught—or else he'd die in the crash of Ricardo.

Tack turned to the waiting runner. "Is he standing by?"

"Yes, sir."

Tack came about and faced the delegates. His eyes swept the soaked figures, their hair matted down, leather tunics unevenly blackened by rain. Behind them towered the pyramid. Tack's lip curled.

"Gentlemen, the doubts that you all harbor about my competence are groundless. We've had a breakthrough. The sil parts might be in our hands within the week." He turned to Fannin and beckoned him near. "Fannin, I'll move my immediate headquarters north this morning. I want to be near when Ricardo falls. Make all the arrangements."

"Yes, *sir!*" Fannin cried. For the moment he would postpone getting sick. It looked as if Tack might win after all.

A Double Track of Desolation

Bono awoke to Regina's low moaning. A bright ray of sun pierced in through a crack and illuminated the dark hayloft. Speckles of dust played in the light.

He stirred and rose up to his knees, brushing dry hay from his leather tunic, beard. It was late or seemed so, judging by the brightness of the light. He felt a strong unease about that. Could they move in daylight? Could *she* move at all?

Regina lay next to him covered by two huge wire-bound bales of hay. He had placed them on top of her the night before as a substitute for the gravitron pressure her body demanded. He couldn't well imagine that it helped much, but maybe the illusion did.

He leaned over her and saw that she slept despite a constant movement of her head and a flow of pained expressions across her face. He watched her, touched by her face. Somehow it seemed so different and ordinary in this new setting, in the gloamy light of this simple, wooden barn. Just a girl. Dark shadows beneath her eyes hinted at the trauma she had undergone. It pained him to see it.

Bono had not imagined his first night in Hinterland with her as it had turned out. Their escape had come off smoothly. Dressed in the parka and wearing the oxygen mask, he had knocked a hole into the drilla-glass wall of her garden roof. She'd stood beside him, also masked, resembling some kind of alien creature. Air rushed out through the ragged hole. He enlarged it, listening to the scream of a siren set off somewhere by his breaking the structure seal. They passed out through the hole and then, sidejets blazing, put distance between themselves and the tower. Minutes later, dropping quickly through the darkness, Bono turned and took in Ricardo with a glance, now a random pattern of light. The unnatural exhilaration he felt, a consequence of gravitron pressure drop, should have told him that Regina was probably experiencing an adverse reaction to the outside. But he didn't discover just how badly she had been hit until they were nearly down and Regina ripped off her mask, turned to him, and gasped in a peculiar way. When they landed amid the loud abrasions of cricket legs, she stumbled from her tube and tried to vomit, but nothing came out. He held her by the waist as she heaved. Later still, many kilometers to the west—well beyond the staging station, which they had skirted to the north—and after they had found this lonesome barn, Regina had been in a state of great delirium, had suffered from frightful visions, had mumbled incoherently about serenity, being buried, oracles, ecology, and much more. At last, while he'd sat next to her stroking her hair, she had dropped off to sleep.

He reached out and gently stroked her hair again, now arranged in braids like those of a tribal maid. He was careful not to wake her. She was . . . just a girl. And in that realization, seeing her as she really was for the first time, without the distorting structure setting, Bono knew that he loved her more than ever.

How ridiculous to say that she was the Whore, that her seed could not mingle with his. People were people. She came from the same pod he did—in some misty past. They were alike. *Prejudice,* he thought. *Stupidity.* For a moment he thought of Myron Crestmore as a petty little man who had fancied that God spoke through his petty little mouth.

He moved from her and rose gingerly, recalling hard beams overhead. He had bumped into them during the night, arriving in total darkness, glad to have found a barn unguarded by loudly barking dogs. This barn was far from houses and people. They might be able to leave unobserved despite the advanced hour. If not, perhaps they could stay here until she passed through Adjustment.

He decided to go out and explore.

Bono climbed down the narrow ladder and ventured past rusty farm machinery to the small side door he had forced during the night. Outside the sun blazed high and bright. The barn sat in a valley whose rims were lined with pines. A dirt road snaked toward the barn. He had not seen that in the darkness. Instead they had descended into the valley from over there, from his left, across that meadow.

He glanced in that direction now, trying to establish the relative position of the barn, and he saw something that sent his heart into fierce throbbing. Across the meadow . . . !

The meadow was a mixture of silvery mutagrass and green fodder scrub. A tiny waterway crossed it diagonally marked by lush, reedy vegetation on its banks and small trees, probably wild apple, at random intervals. From the direction they had come, extending in a straight line right up to the apron of reddish dirt around the barn, he saw twin tracks of discoloration in the meadow. The green scrub was brown; the mutagrass was curled and blue; at the spot where they had crossed the creek, the reedy bushes had collapsed and died.

He ran to the edge of the apron and on a few steps into the grass. He bent down and fingered the vegetation. The grass had died. Each track was two meters wide, more or less. Bands of desolation . . . Desolation!

In a state of excitement, Bono ran across the valley, in the spoor left by the jumptubes. They had made it, no doubt about it. He only wondered how far the track extended. At this point they had been two or three meters above the ground. Earlier they had been higher. He ran, angry with himself. He should have guessed that, even without direct experience. He should have picked a course over rock, sand, dried-out stream beds. Or they should have traveled very high in the air.

He hoped they had been high enough for most of the night. He had kept the tubes ten meters in the air except in spots where they'd crossed over forests. Had that been enough? Well, he would soon know.

From the top of the rise, standing between fragrant pines on slippery, needle-covered forest floor, he looked down the way they had come. As far as his eye could reach, he saw the twin tracks, considerably narrower out there where they had been higher up, but visible. His heart sank. From some spot outside Ricardo, their trail led here in twists and turns, broken here and there, thin now and again—but a track any pilot could easily follow from airship or helicopter.

There was no time to lose.

He turned and ran toward the reddish, gabled barn as fast as his legs could carry him.

Poor Regina, he thought. However she felt, she would have to get up now and move—on foot. High up in the air they would be seen and reported. Near the ground they would leave a track. Time was of the essence.

Lasers

The official levi-limo dropped down from the airspace and settled in front of BTA.

Proctor gathered up his robes while the driver ran around to open the door. Then he climbed out and stood waiting for Gregory Korn. He had taken the bureau's lawyer along on this unprecedented visit to the Ecofreak embassy. Korn was also DA for Compliance and had supplied the technical language for the secret subagreement.

Korn clambered out, his narrow face pinched and blue. Korn was allergic to artisun, hence his expression of perpetual gloom. Once in power, Proctor intended to give Korn a Top Level cubohome where he could expose himself to natural sun through a drillaglass roof.

Together the men mounted the stairs and went inside.

In thirty years of official life, Proctor had never experienced anything like this. At ten o'clock, Ecofreak had called. They asked for an *immediate* meeting about the letter Proctor had sent earlier in the morning. Proctor had suggested that *he* come to the embassy this time—a gesture of goodwill. He had set out with mixed feelings. And now, forty minutes later, the subagreement was signed, sealed, and delivered. Korn carried it in a narrow attaché case. The Interdiction would start within the hour. The negotiations had gone nerve-rackingly smoothly.

At the elevator Proctor turned to Korn. "The moment we register the Interdiction, I want to be told. And alert Justin Todd at once. His people must be ready and in place. We must keep this absolutely secret, as prearranged."

Korn nodded and went off. His offices were on the first floor.

Proctor entered the elevator and punched a button. So French had been right after all. These men *were*

166

Activists. Dart had well-established Activist credentials. His sudden rise to power clinched it. Dart had accepted Proctor's conditions without a murmur. He cared nothing about the hostage demand, that much had been transparently obvious. He wanted only silcoparts. He hadn't even questioned the demand for an Interdiction. He had nodded his head impatiently, eager to put signatures on paper. Barney, Proctor reflected, would have understood the significance of that demand at once. He would have guessed that Proctor aimed for the supreme position. And once firmly in the saddle, he would be a very different force, very unlike Bernard Unsler. No more Accommodation then. But Barney had been absent. And so had Bono —reportedly suffering from a bout of malaria. Fat chance.

Proctor left the elevator and walked to his office. He knew that French had also been right about the oscillation-control properties of the components. That meant that they *had* to be made inoperative in some way. But there was a problem.

Earlier in the morning, Proctor had had an embarrassing discussion with Clemmens. Clemmens had evidently expected French to return, had expected French to tell Proctor what Clemmens did not want to tell him—namely, that the BTA technical staff was incompetent to defeat the Ecofreak device without some high-powered help. When French had been conspicuously absent, Clemmens had come to Proctor.

Probing questions revealed that Clemmens and Fulbright had had a huge spat the day before and that Fulbright was the only man even remotely qualified to do the job. If Proctor wanted parts that didn't work, he would have to negotiate a settlement between Clemmens and Fulbright. Always the negotiator.

He stopped before Mrs. Sedlig's desk. "Get me Carl Fulbright on the tel," he said and walked into his office.

Moments later Mrs. Sedlig buzzed. Proctor leaned

forward to activate his tel. Fulbright's goateed face appeared on the screen.

"Carl," Proctor said. "Thank you for taking my call. I understand you are in the midst of a conference. I apologize."

Proctor always said this—everybody was always "in conference."

"I forgive you, Res. I suppose this is about the sil components?"

"You are perceptive."

Fulbright made a deprecatory grimace. "Well, what pipe dreams has your staff related to you? Do they still think it's an oscillation-control device?"

Proctor recalled Fulbright from his days in Defense and chose his words carefully. Fulbright was tiny, dried out, but he owned the world's greatest ego.

Proctor had to be careful. "The staff opinion is ludicrous, but I wanted to talk to you about this personally. I owe you that at least for your trouble. I'd also like to get your gut reaction to this. Not your technical judgment, Carl, but your reaction as a citizen. Is it even remotely *possible*? My staff might be limited, but they have good hunches sometimes. If you were betting, giving odds, what would you say? What are the percentages?"

The tone had been right. Fulbright's face relaxed. His features softened. He thought about the question. Proctor remembered that Fulbright didn't like snap answers, liked to ponder. Proctor watched as one of Fulbright's hands appeared on the screen to caress the goatee.

"Well, Res, anything *is* possible, you know—speaking now not as a scientist with thirty years of polish in Vibration but as you suggest. As a citizen. But possible and probable are two different things. I don't think it's probable at all."

Proctor suppressed the urge to ask why. That would bring the wrong reaction. Instead he asked: "What conditions would you stipulate—as a man of science, now—that would make such a breakthrough probable?"

"Oh, I don't know," Fulbright said, thinking. He turned his head to one side and stared off into the distance. "I've been toying with this and that since my session with Clemmens on your staff . . . and it occurred to me that if you could concentrate a gravitron vibration as you can concentrate light—if you could straighten out that helical geometry . . ."

Fulbright looked back into the screen, raised his eyebrows, shrugged.

Proctor felt reassured both by Fulbright's answer and manner. No doubt Fulbright had rushed back to the drawing board, anxious to check out the situation. Proctor suspected that Fulbright had just now stared at some formulae on a blackboard.

"If you were to test that theory, Carl, what would you do?"

Fulbright gave a dry little snort. "Why, first of all I'd get myself a bunch of lasers and—"

"Lasers?"

"Why, of course," Fulbright said. "No need to re-invent the wheel. Not that the laser is a suitable device, but I'd start there."

Proctor looked interested. "Carl, five years ago Ecofreak requested five hundred lasers. We shipped them."

The little man stared out of the screen. "You don't say?"

"I do say," Proctor rumbled. "Carl, we need your help. Desperately. Could you, Clemmens, and I have lunch? The BTA executive dining room? Would you mind very much? We have some awfully tight deadlines to meet. The matter is extremely sensitive, and I don't want to discuss it over the tel. Could we meet? In half an hour? I'll send a limo for you."

Fulbright nodded. "This puts a very different complexion on the matter, Res. Yes, I'll be happy to join you. By the way, if your man Clemmens had told me about the lasers . . ." He shook his head. "Until later, then."

The face disappeared.

Proctor leaned back in his chair. He recalled the

long, acrimonious debate with French five years back. If French ever returned alive, Proctor would compliment him on his insight.

Not that French had much chance to receive that compliment, Proctor reflected. Belmonte had been told of French's exploit by Blottingham. French had gone off the deep end. His usefulness now lay entirely in the past. The laser insight had been one of his last signal achievements—disregarding the discovery of the silco-parts, of course, which anybody might have guessed. Dart had been so obviously, so single-mindedly interested in them . . .

The Ambassador

Dart had chosen Barney's prison personally. It was a windowless room in the very center of the embassy complex. Dart had assured himself from drawings that the room was not even *near* a service chasm. He had personally inspected the wall for soundness. Barney would not escape, like French had, like Bono had.

Bono's escape was *not* Dart's fault. The staff had blundered. They should have told him that Bono had left the embassy by a back door, as it were, instead of through the front, as Dart had assumed. Tack could not blame him for that. Not in the least. In the wake of Bono's escape, Dart had acted vigorously. Men had been sent out to search the landscape beyond the Desolation. Others had been dispatched to comb the chasm itself on the assumption that Bono had fallen to his death—a good likelihood. After all, he was a five-percenter. The pressure in the chasm was great. And it was easy to slip and fall in the darkness, on eroded walks.

At the moment Dart hurried to have a look at Barney. He walked up the narrow stairs from the communications room where he had transmitted the good news to Jonny. If it wasn't for Barney's troubling, haunting presence, Dart would have thoroughly enjoyed Jonny's exuberant congratulations. Twice in a day Jonny had praised him! First, for the letter Union had sent, essentially caving in on the silcoplast demand; second, for the subagreement itself, delivered within hours of the letter. But Barney troubled him, took all the fun out of it.

Dart stopped at the top of the stairs and waited until Dulsol had caught up. The man had a heavy, round head seated on a thick neck connected to a massive trunk. His arms were long and meaty. His legs filled the leather tunic to bursting. Short-cropped hair was a fashion on his district, Dallforth, something of an Activist stronghold. His red coloration was probably a sign of choleric temper. For these and other reasons —especially the courtesy Dulsol had shown him before he became Ambassador—Dart had elevated the man from his lowly post as maintenance chief to that of provisional First Secretary. Dart needed an enforcer who could make the rest of the embassy staff do his will.

Together they proceeded down corridors, turning several times, until Dart stopped before a peephole in a door. Dulsol had personally drilled the hole and had placed the glass before Barney had been incarcerated. Dart wiped one eye and fitted it to the hole.

At first he couldn't see anything, but then his focus adjusted and he spied Barney on the floor. The man was writing, writing on the floor of the empty cubicle. Dart's face wrinkled up in anger. Writing! *What* was Barney writing? The hand moved rapidly over the scriptoplast. Suddenly Barney looked up thinking. Then he bent down again and scribbled on. How had Barney obtained the scripto, the stylus?

Dart knew, knew what Barney was writing. It was an account of that dinner in the House of Eighty-Two Flavors. Barney was composing a falsified report of that evening. Dart had certainly not betrayed the negotiating strategy; at most his tongue had stumbled over a phrase or two. But Barney would know how to exploit that, would try to disgrace Dart with Jonny— now! Now that Dart had made a name for himself at last.

Who had helped Barney? Who had slipped him the scriptoplast?

Dart turned to Dulsol. "Who has keys to this room?"

Dulsol said: "It's an ordinary lock. Anybody could get in."

"Come along, Dulsol. Let's have a talk in my office."

He strode off, furious.

In his office—until recently Barney's and still filled with his things—Dart glanced about with distaste at the giant Harvey pelt on the wall, the collection of mutant skulls hung on little wooden plaques, the holograms of Barney's ranch in the foothills of the Sierra Petra. He sat down in Barney's huge leather chair, motioned to Dulsol to find himself a seat among the numerous hassocks. Peering down at his wrinkled hands laid on the shiny surface of the desk, he then looked up.

"Dulsol," he said, "as you know, Tack is coming north. He should have his camp set up by morning at the latest. I shall have to report to him, of course. I intend to leave tonight. While I am gone, you will be in charge. So far you have shown yourself an able, solid and loyal fellow. Now you'll have a chance to show what you can do. I don't expect you'll have any trouble. Everything is under control. But I am leaving you with one sort of messy chore. I mean Barney, of course. Just now I saw him writing. I don't know what he's been putting down, and I don't want to know. Probably some kind of seditionary message. Barney is a traitor. I have discovered that he had dinner with Rivera French the other night. He conspires with Union. As Jonny Tack told me yesterday on the cable, 'Franco, old buddy, I don't understand why Barney doesn't have the decency to commit suicide.' Or words to that effect, Dulsol. 'The man would be better off dead,' he said. I certainly agree, although needless to say, we'll probably have to go through with a long and dreary trial and all that. Of course, if he committed suicide, we'd all be spared that little formality. I am worried about that, Dulsol. I'm also worried about his friends. If anybody can get into that room, somebody might try to let Barney escape. Under no circumstances must he escape, do you understand?"

Dulsol nodded.

"Do whatever you must. He must be prevented from communicating with Union. At all cost. *All* cost, Dulsol. Is *that* understood?"

Dulsol nodded again.

"Very well. I'll be watching you, of course. If you do a good job, Dulsol, I'll put in a word for you. My recommendation should count for something now that I've pulled off the coup of the century. Well, that's that. Leave me now, Dulsol. I have to prepare my report to Jonny Tack."

Dulsol rose and left. Dart came to his feet as soon as the door closed on the man's hulking form. He walked over to the Harvey pelt, grabbed the fine fur, and jerked. The pelt tore a little as it came off. Systematically, Dart began to remove Barney's things from the wall. He tossed them into a heap in the center of the room. Then he walked to the pile and trampled on it, stamped on it with both feet, until the pictures, mutant skulls, and wooden plaques were nothing but a rubble of glass, fiber, and bone.

Blottingham

Blottingham sat in a genuine leather armchair at one end of a small gymnasium where Sidney worked out every afternoon with Roman sword and round shield to get his exercise. The weapons hung from the wall in racks together with horsetail helmets modified with screened masks in front. Blottingham had chosen this place for his interrogation because it was the least private of Sidney's rooms. He had no desire to trample about in the Fire's domain.

Circumstances had made Blottingham both the Unifier's agent and Sidney's. Sidney's disappearance and Meyer's withdrawal had left a vacuum in the Flame leadership. The ranks were decimated indeed. Proctor's ploy had been effective. Take Clafto. The man wouldn't budge from his father's palace, refused all calls. Fear was an effective weapon—but it could be used by anyone with a will.

Blottingham had been interrogating Sidney's body-guard, servants, and those Flames who had spent the entire evening with the Fire. Despite persistent prob-ing, he had heard the same incredible story from all who had witnessed the event.

A single man in a gas mask and armed with a chemgun had penetrated Sidney's domain. Alone and unaided, he had laid low one and all with chemgun blasts. His weapon had been turned to the maximal setting, and all those exposed to the gas had had an involuntary nap lasting between eight and twelve hours, depending on their metabolic rates.

Still another servant stepped in front of the leather chair. Blottingham knew that the man would add nothing new to the sorry tale. *This one and no more.* Blottingham intended to act.

Listening to these witnesses, he had formed a theory in his mind. Proctor had staged that Little Theater with the Flames as a diversionary exercise to mask Sidney's abduction by one of his best agents—French. The boldness of the act made Blottingham wary in the extreme. If Proctor had dared this much, something big might be brewing. Any direct action against Proc-tor could backfire miserably. Blottingham thought he knew a way to put pressure on Proctor and yet refrain from any overt conflict with the man. He had to be careful. What if Proctor acted in the name of other family members? They were known to be unhappy with Sidney.

He turned to a close aide. "Carmody, fetch me a tel," he ordered. Then he nodded to the waiting ser-vant. "Where were you when all this happened?"

The man was a butler or valet or table server. He didn't have the proud soldierly bearing of the palace guard—nor was he humiliated by having been over-come. He worked his hands in front of his chest in some embarrassment.

"Yes, sir," he began. "I was in the orgy room with

the Master and stood by his head pouring wine from
a flagon into his cup."

The man stopped short.

"And? Go on, man."

"And then, sir, the door burst open and there was
the man with a chemgun in his hand."

"What did he look like?"

Blottingham was bored by this tale. Servants were
stupid. He recalled the long and weary interrogation
in Regina's domain. All the servants there had sworn
that a meteor had hit the tower, knocking a hole in
Regina's garden roof. A meteor! The people were superstitious indeed.

"I don't recall seeing much of him, sir," the butler
said. "Being surprised, as you can guess. I sloshed
some wine on the Master's shoulder, and I was so
troubled by that, wiping his shoulder with a napkin I
always carry, that—"

"Get to the point, man."

"Yes, sir. Then it got me."

"What got you?"

"The gas, I guess."

"The gas got you?"

"I suppose, sir. The next thing I know, one of your
gentlemen was poking me awake, and I was laying
there in a pool of dried wine."

Blottingham wondered about that "pool of dried
wine," running a hand over his short hair.

"All right, you may go. But you didn't see the man?
You can't describe him?"

The servant shrugged. "Just a man, sir. I can't say
as I saw much detail. He wore a gray jump suit with
zippers in front and little zippers over the pockets.
He wore a gas mask, but underneath his chin was
visible. He had a cleft in his chin. And he was blond."

Blottingham nodded. He waved the servant away.
That man had been French, no doubt about it. He
turned to Carmody, who held the tel ready, took the
device on his lap, and punched out the numbers for
the garrison command.

"Please give me Roger Belmonte again," he said into the screen. "This is Blottingham from Top Level."

The formula always worked. He always got his man. Belmonte appeared in the screen, black face impassive.

"Roger," Blottingham said, "sorry to bother you so soon again, but the Unifier has just given me some new instructions. Meet me in front of the BTA with, oh, two or three plainclothes detectives. The Old Man is very concerned about Proctor's safety in light of the abductions. Can you meet me in . . . twenty minutes, say? See you there."

He signed to Carmody and told the others to return to Top Level. Then he walked through Sidney's domain to the front entrance, where he climbed into a waiting levi-limo and told the driver to take them to Old Top in Central Tower. After they were underway, Blottingham punched a button on his armrest and a soundproof pane of glass rose up to separate the two officials from the driver.

Blottingham explained his plan to Carmody, using his assistant as a sounding board. Under the guise of protecting him, Proctor would be confined to his cubohome. Blottingham intended to drop a strong hint that Proctor's release was contingent on the production of Sidney and Regina.

"That should work," he told Carmody, "unless, of course, Proctor is stronger than I think he is. Do you think there is something to the rumors? In light of what happened yesterday?"

Carmody shook his head. "I just can't believe that. The family might be restless, but Harvanth is solidly in the Old Man's camp. We've got the Army. Nothing can happen unless we lose the Army. If you want my guess, I think this has to do with French, not Proctor."

Blottingham brushed over his short red hair with a hand. Carmody was certain of the Army, but Blottingham wondered. Proctor and Harvanth would be a winning combination. Proctor was popular and Harvanth powerful. Harvanth had much to lose if Sidney took over, for Sidney had visions of military conquest. Blottingham turned to Carmody.

"Should we tell the Old Man? I'd hate to do it really. He's been very unstable lately. God knows what he'd do."

Carmody agreed with a nod. "Why don't we wait and see how Proctor reacts first. No sense in alarming the Old Man. If Proctor resists, however . . ."

"You're right," Blottingham said without conviction.

He knew in his guts that Unsler should be told. But then, again, what if Harvanth and Proctor plotted together? In that event he, Blottingham, could easily end up on the losing side. He decided it was best to keep the situation fluid, the options open, at least for a while.

The trip to Old Top took exactly twenty minutes, as Blottingham had guessed. Belmonte already waited before the glass-fronted BTA entrance flanked by detectives. For once Belmonte wore an ordinary blue robe rather than his ornate red uniform and feathered hat: he did not want to be conspicuous.

They went in together. A BTA security guard acted unusually officious. He insisted on seeing everyone's identity card, even Belmonte's, although the garrison commander was a well-known figure in Ricardo. Next he asked the gentlemen to "fill in these here logs." Then he laboriously prepared, and issued, visitor's passes to everyone. Only after all these preparations did he call Proctor's office on the tel to announce the guests. He had a long wait before Mrs. Sedlig came back on the screen and asked that the gentlemen come up. The guard then gave elaborate instructions on how to reach the Negotiator's office, although Blottingham knew the way. Finally the guard released them.

Halfway to the elevator, Blottingham took Belmonte by the sleeve, pulled him aside, and quickly explained the mission.

Belmonte was a thick-lipped black with a stony

face. He did not react to Blottingham's account of the Unifier's grave personal concern for Proctor's safety. He merely stared.

Blottingham stopped. "Can you handle that, Roger?" His tone betrayed a certain amount of exasperation.

Belmonte nodded gravely.

In Proctor's outer office, Mrs. Sedlig asked the gentlemen to rest for a moment. The Negotiator was on the tel. He would see them the moment he was off.

Blottingham sat down, feeling uneasy, and gave Carmody an oblique glance, but Carmody was staring at artificial bushes in large planters half masking a row of flagpoles in golden stands: tribal colors.

The patent tension in the room disturbed Blottingham. He glanced casually at the morose detectives, at Belmonte's noncommittal face, at Mrs. Sedlig's busy preoccupation with some sheets of scripto she pushed through a renewer. Some days ago this woman had conveyed a message from Proctor. Jump down a shaft!

For the second or third time this day, Blottingham regretted that he had shouldered so much of the day-to-day burden of running Union since the Unifier's last—and not much publicized—heart attack. In a rush to leave a record before death should claim him, Unsler had begun his memoirs during his recuperation period. That book had become his sole concern.

Power had never weighed heavily on Blottingham; he had enjoyed its exercise. In a pinch Unsler had signed papers or, more rarely, had made a telcall or two to back up his chief of staff's decisions. But now Blottingham sensed a yawning emptiness at his back. He wasn't at all sure that the government could pull together and defend itself against a strong attack.

Unsler had been protected too long from too many facts: Sidney's intense unpopularity, the Cabinet's neglect of business, the insolence of officials like Proctor, the carping of Media . . .

Blottingham was tempted to rise, leave, and burst into Unsler's study, interrupting all those literary labors, and say: "Mr. Unifier, I've botched it all up.

Sidney has been abducted. Regina has disappeared, might have been kidnapped. The family has turned against Sidney. They hate me because I really run things. Harvanth and Proctor are probably plotting a revolution. Help me."

No, no. That was inconceivable. Blottingham would have to tough this out. Another day or two at most. Besides, it was too late to leave.

Proctor's office door opened and out came three officials. One was balding, older; one had a bluish, pinched face; the third was black. Blottingham recognized the latter from reports: Dickens, the security chief.

Behind them came Proctor. He sported an uncharacteristic, beaming smile. His short, thick arms were extended in greeting.

"Paul," he rumbled. "How very, very good to see you. Quite an honor, I must say." He turned to Belmonte. "Roger! Are you with Paul, here? Gentlemen, do come in, come in."

Proctor ushered the men into his office, pointed at couches and armchairs. He rubbed his hands in seeming pleasure, but his forced cordiality served only to deepen Blottingham's anxieties. Blottingham sat down and brushed his hand over the short hair on the top of his head; more than ever, he urged himself to be cautious.

Proctor sat down, pleased with himself. In the last half-hour or so, when Belmonte's warning call had cut short the lunch with Clemmens and Fulbright—but not before they had reached an agreement—Proctor had made many rapid arrangements.

He had reached every member of the Group, had briefed them all about the arrangement with Ecofreak, had designated Korn as the intermediary should Top Level move against him. The helium pumping rate had begun to drop at noon. The Interdiction would be complete by evening. In four days, give or take a few hours, the change in power would be all set up.

For now Proctor had only one worry: French. Blottingham had come to demand that Sidney and Regina be returned—wherever in hell French had them. If only French had kept his cool last night.

"What can I do for you, Paul?"

Blottingham said: "Res, Sidney and Regina Unsler have been abducted." He stopped and took in Proctor's astonished expression. Did the man feign surprise? "Of course we are keeping it strictly under cover at the moment, but the Unifier has expressed grave concern for the safety of all prominent men in Union. Especially you. You are more popular than most. He has asked me to see personally to your safety."

"Are you serious, Paul? This is shocking news!"

"Strange things have been happening lately," Blottingham went on. "A large number of prominent youths were sexually molested last night by gangs of men—"

"You don't say," Proctor cried.

Blottingham peered at him. Proctor was acting, shamelessly acting.

"Yes. The Unifier doesn't want anything like that to happen to you, Res. As I said, he has asked me to make sure that you are protected."

"What have you got in mind, Paul? A special guard? These gentlemen here . . . ?" Proctor gestured toward the four detectives.

"These gentlemen will escort you to your cubohome and will guard it against abductors," Blottingham said. "We shall place a tap on your tel-line so that threatening calls may be traced at once. I know that this is inconvenient, but it should last less than a day. The moment Sidney and Regina are freed—"

Blottingham touched his hair and looked at Proctor, then away again.

"Until Sidney and Regina are found?" Proctor asked.

"Precisely," Blottingham answered. "The sooner they are freed, the sooner can we dispense with these precautions."

He looked up and met Proctor's eyes, but Proctor did not hold the glance. He turned his head toward the desk, toward the large hologram of Unsler that hung above it.

"I respect the Unifier's wishes," he said and rose. "Shall we go now? Or will you allow me to gather some scriptos?"

Awakening in Branco

Miri walked the streets of Branco with occasional glances back. Deep meditation in the aseptic BTA cubohome had brought forth the guidance she had sought. In the afternoon she had quietly slipped out of the building. Soon, wearing the new jump suit she had bought in a nearby arcade, she made her way to East Tower and down to Level 13. Her guidance had told her that Frenchy would be hiding in these domains of poverty, disease, and crime—back home, in territory he knew well.

Noise raged all around her—the noise of squabbling women, of music loud beyond sufferance, of quarrels in alleys, of bargainers at stands. Branco lived in the streets. As far away as she could see— the Ring curved gently out of sight—stalls lined the sidewalks, big, small, covered, open, screaming in a thousand colorful signs and with the cracked voices of hawkers.

She looked back again, troubled by a sense that someone was following her; but she saw no familiar face in the throng. People jostled and pushed. Teenagers ran past her, yelling. Wild, unreflecting people.

Odors bombarded her senses: the sweet smell of decaying garbage and food, of fecal matter, of air singed with ozone by escaping gravitron, of unwashed

bodies and clothing worn too often without launder-
ing.

Maintenance stopped around Level 30. In official
eyes these people did not properly belong to Union.

Yet how much more lively, racy, alive everything
here seemed. Just look at the walls, everywhere decorated by the strangely obscure paintings of the people. Initials, parts of words, numbers—they all glowed,
radiated. On the street, vendors sold fruits and vegetables—real fruit and vegetables—obviously obtained
by illegal barter with nearby tribes and smuggled into
Ricardo through subterranean routes below the Pit.

How, in this world, would she find Frenchy?

Then, up ahead, she saw a familiar sign. The Scuttlebutt, a coffeehouse where she had met her husband
years before on an artistic expedition to sketch "Bot-
toms" types.

A linkage point. Unconsciously she had been drawn
to this place, possibly the bridge between past and
present. Here she might meet Frenchy again.

She made for the place thinking of the Madonna,
who wove the psychic universe on her magic wheel.
On Madonna's spiderweb, The Scuttlebutt was a tiny
knot connecting two destinies—his and hers.

The place was large, with many tiny tables closely
packed together, awash in the murmur of voices. Jane-
weed smoke rose in walls and hung in clouds about
the place, its smell familiar to Miri from Cult sessions.
She sat down against a wall and ordered coffee. It
came, but she didn't drink it. She listened to conversation on her left watching the surface of her cup, the
swirl of steam on the back liquid.

A fuzzy-haired man spoke to another in a low, urgent monotone. He catalogued the sins of structure
culture, predicted its imminent doom. "A shitting jut,"
he said. Union was like a tired old man. It didn't want
to come up anymore. You had to read porn to make
it twitch. Education, art, religion, science, exploration
—all a shitting jut. Children floated in a vacuum. A
shitting jut. His voice hissed on breathlessly.

Familiar dirge. Miri had heard words like these
years ago. The speaker's aura touched her slightly. She

sensed his deep alienation and moved herself slightly to the right, out of his influence. As she did so, she looked up and saw a woman weaving her way between tables toward her.

Miri immediately recognized the cool, poised movements of a Cult sister. Thousands of hours of meditation, body and mind control, showed in the woman's face; the woman did not look at Miri. She came in Miri's direction in a brightly flowered sari. Passing the table, the woman slid an object toward Miri. It half rolled, half skidded toward her, silver and green. A ring. Miri picked it up with a quick glance toward the retreating, flowery back of the woman. She *had* been followed.

Miri looked down at the ring, turning it. The tarnished silver setting held an oblong, turquoise stone with black-and-white markings. For a second she stared at the pattern. Then she covered her face with her hands in an involuntary, abrupt motion.

The pattern in the stone had unlocked memories suppressed by hypnotic command, memories of meetings with Sister Serenita, the Cult Mother. The meetings extended over a period of seven years. Until this moment, Miri had not consciously realized that Serenita was the Cult Mother. Only the coven elders knew the identity of the Lady's living representative on Earth. Miri had also known it, but the knowledge had been kept from her conscious self.

The flood of recall caused an involuntary shudder. Now Miri understood the significance of her blemish and what it meant to "have a role in history." Against the backdrop of her memories, the events of the last few days suddenly seemed fraught with meaning. She sorted the memories in her mind.

Seven years ago, at the annual consultation of the Sybilline books, the fall of the oracodice had given Verse 39, Great Change. This fact had been kept from the Cult membership, because Verse 39 signified a momentous change in human consciousness, a dramatic transformation in culture. Each verse had nine lines. Three of the lines had been accented and therefore contributed to the meaning of the oracle. The first

line had said: "Ecosphere: flowers in the meadow."
The second had said: "A queen confuses the Male."
And the third: "The blemished artist leads the remnant."

A search through the ranks of the Cult had identified Miri as the blemished artist—she was a micromosaiker and had a birthspot on her cheek. At the time, she was a novice engaged in the acquisition of the most rudimentary of arts. The Cult Mother called for her, to look at her, to see if the oracle might have meant Miri rather than someone else. Satisfied for the moment, the Mother sent her on her way. From time to time thereafter, other meetings had been held to see how Miri progressed. Each meeting concluded with the hypnotic command of forgetfulness, given under the influence of this ring—Serenita's own ring, worn on the finger of Saturn on the nun's left hand. She had been commanded to forget, because only full adepts could know the inner mysteries, the Lady's visible representative.

There had been a meeting—she recalled now the relief she had experienced then—when the Cult Mother had concluded that Miri could not be the "blemished artist." She had just married Frenchy. He had entered the service academy, but he was nevertheless still very much a smuggler from Branco. In numerous other consultations of the oracle, the Cult had learned that "blemished artist" would marry a figure capable of delaying or impeding the Great Change, a figure of importance, prominence. Frenchy gave no such promise at the time, and no one bothered to ask the books about him. Later, when Frenchy rose with meteoric speed through the ranks of BTA, Serenita changed her mind, and Miri's sessions resumed once more,

Recalling this, Miri shuddered again. She did not want to be one of the so-called "queens of the change." She didn't want a "role in history."

What did it mean, "Great Change"?

Serenita said that the ways of the Male would yield to the way of the Lady. Great Change was a time of rejoicing. The oracle had spoken of the Ecosphere, of flowers in the meadow, of a healing. Change, Serenita insisted, was in the minds and hearts of people. But Miri had always understood that verse in more cataclysmic terms. As an ad-adept she had been permitted to study the ancient texts, and commentaries on the Change never failed to make the point that Verse 39 meant an ending, an upheaval, a disaster. If the blemished artist "lead a remnant," the clear implication was that some would *remain*. But what about the others? Would they be recycled, one and all, into the cosmic soul vats, to be born again into another age?

Miri did not want to live through anything like that. What would it all mean? The fall of the structures?

She had posed that question to Serenita as well, getting evasive replies. Structure or Hinterland—it didn't matter. The ways of the Male dominated both worlds. They would be swept away by a change in consciousness. That might or might not mean the end of structures. Structures didn't matter. They were merely shells.

Another question that had plagued Miri—and once more plagued her now that she remembered it all—was How? How would she lead a remnant? What remnant? From where to where?

Serenita's words still rang in her ear: "Miri, you think like the Male thinks. Causes, effects, motives. The Lady works by indirection. If you're the person chosen to do her will, you'll be led in the right paths. At the right moment, you'll know what to do."

"And the 'queen who confuses the Male'? Who is she?"

"That's not something you need to know."

Miri dropped the hands from her face. Her coffee was a dark, deep shining in front of her. The steam had disappeared from its surface. She pushed the cup aside and looked at the ring again. It was clearly Serenita's ring, the only one she wore on her pale hand. In the concluding hypnotic sequence of her meetings with the Mother, she had stared at the ring with utmost concentration. She recognized every detail. Now she held the ring. It meant that Serenita had reached a final conclusion: Miri was the person signified by the Sybilline books. It also meant that the time was nigh. The secret had been unlocked so that Miri could act with knowledge. And finally, disturbingly, it meant—or Miri sensed that it meant—that Serenita had passed on to her, to Miri, the symbol of her authority.

My God! Miri thought. *That means I am a full adept. It means I must be pregnant.* For to achieve the knowledge of completion, a woman had to have the final experience of womanhood, birth—or, at the least, conception.

She shuddered again, throwing off psychic tensions, and became aware of her surroundings. Next to her the fuzzy-haired man still hissed in a monotone. Doomed, finished, a shitting jut. The end, kaput, knockout . . .

Miri rose hastily and ran out of The Scuttlebutt. She wanted to get out of here, away, far away. She didn't like her inner feelings. She had to dissipate her anxieties in motion. She had to find her Frenchy, sanity, something familiar, something to hold on to.

After a while she calmed herself. The throng of people, the noise, the colors reassured her. The shadowy memories slowly settled down as part of her conscious awareness. Whatever happened, life would go on. The Lady wove fate. From her fingers issued the pulse of existence. Not Miri's place to question cosmic forces. Only, the Male pretended to rule over the world—a microbe on the skin of the legendary elephant. Whatever will be, will be.

She passed a clump of people from whose center a young boy's voice rose up with the scriptovendors' hawking cry.

"Getcher, getcher, getcher scrips. Getcher scrips and read abooot his Finkoo's kiddienap las nayte. Getcher, getcher, getcher scrips, Flame's been snufood aeught . . ."

It was the most distilled form of Branco dialect.

Caught by the urgency of the voices, whose broadcaster Miri could not see—the clump was a whirling of hands and arms from which people broke away, reading intently—she joined in, penetrated the clump, pressed a coin in a dirty urchin hand, and came away with a small, thin scrip.

She nearly stopped in her tracks when she read the bold headline across the front page of the thing.

SIDNEY KIDNAPPED BY BTA BIG.

She stopped to read the story. All around her people were doing the same, and there was a buzz of excited talk. People ran off; others arrived. In minutes the newsboy had sold out his supply.

The story itself was brief and factual. But much of the rest of the paper carried speculation about the meaning of the unusual event.

The story described how Rivera French, well known to the people of Branco, had penetrated Top Level North last night. He had immobilized the palace guard by chemgun and had abducted Sidney Unsler. His whereabouts were unknown. Sources within the Unsler household were cited as authority for the dramatic disclosure.

The speculation went far beyond that bare account. They identified Frenchy as a man close to Reston Proctor. They linked the mysterious roundup of Flames the night before to the abduction. They saw this move as the opening sally of the much rumored revolution—

Revolution?

Miri sucked in her breath. Blood pounded in her throat. For a moment she became oblivious of the scene around her, which began to clear rapidly of people. They ran, they disappeared into buildings. She read with total amazement, aware for the first time of Frenchy's probable involvement in some kind of surreptitious political movement.

So she, Miri, had already been associated unknowingly with Change—be it great or small. Her husband a conspirator? It seemed that he was.

Frenchy, oh Frenchy! she thought, overwhelmed in a delayed reaction by a crazy fear for her man. Abductor, revolutionary?

She bent over the scrip again, searching for additional clues. She stood reading when a small man grabbed her by the elbow.

"Lady," he said—it came out "leuydy"—"can't yer see the squeezoos? Ya better getcher rumpies uffa da belt, heay? Reading a scrips now, leuydy! Open yer eyes."

Miri opened her eyes and looked about. Far behind her on the movebelt she saw the blue of police uniforms. The man hustled her along toward a door; she followed him meekly. They entered the close, fetid atmosphere of a bar. Young men on stools and around tables looked up in unison as the two entered.

"An ufflevel chips I picks up reading the scrips in front of the squeezoos," the little man announced.

"Squeezoos?" the young man nearest to Miri asked. He had come erect on his stool. His tone was alert.

"Where you at?" the little man asked. "Don't yer read?" He waved his own copy of the scrips at the young man. "Frenchy stole the Finkoo las nayte; they's searching toyteen."

"Our Frenchy?"

"The sayme."

Young men crowded about them. Miri eyed them. These total strangers discussed *her* Frenchy in tones as if they were on the most intimate footing with him. They broke into exclamations now, crowding together over the articles the small man had spread out on the bar. One of their number read aloud. Miri gathered that only a few could read. Then they conferred. They concluded that Frenchy must be hiding in Branco, they listed possible hiding places only the Kayring would know about.

She watched them with apprehension and hope commingled—young men in hand-embroidered jump suits of various colors, some with faces pockmarked by gravitron blisters, some bearded like tribesmen, dark, light, black, white, chinoise. Beyond the group over the bar a slow-moving colormixer wove patterns on the glass screen. Drink spigots gleamed with curving necks. The stout bartender wiped a glass at the far end.

"Ya've yapped sufficient," the small man said. "Naw clear it uff, clear it uff. Squeezoos will be busting in heay. Move uff naw."

"What abooot the chips?"

Eyes focused on Miri.

"What abooot yer?" the small man asked. "Whatcher doing in Branco?"

Miri swallowed. "I'm Miri French," she said. "I'm looking for my husband."

Eyes searched her face, some with narrowed suspicion, some with an expression of pleasure. Then one man said: "It's er. I seen a pitch. That mark on er, see?"

Involuntarily Miri reached up to touch the birthmark on her cheek. Heads began to move up and down.

"Cum oon, then," the small man said. "Uff with yer and er, uff to Dachsy. Dachsy must be toold."

In a body the men made for the back of the bar. Miri moved in their center.

A Promise Satisfied

Up ahead Regina saw the dark lines of pines across the ridge, against the lighter darkness of the star-spangled sky. They made for the broken silhouette of some sort of ruined building up a steep, slippery gradient amidst a rustle of leaves.

She sobbed in Mycal's wake, sobbed with fatigue. And then she suddenly stopped because It stopped. She realized with a joyous feeling that she was herself again. But the feeling was more than that. She felt incredibly well, giddy with a kind of joy.

"Mycal, Mycal!"

Bono stopped and turned around, alerted by the change in her tone. Could she be over it? He put his hands beside her cheeks and tried to see her eyes in the darkness.

"Yes," she said. "It's over. I'm all right again."

He whispered: "Thank God, thank God!"

"Mycal, it feels so wonderful—I—I want to sing or something. Do you know what I mean? Did you . . . ?"

"Yes," he said, remembering the feeling. He had felt the same way on the morning of the ball and recalled that sense of miraculous healing, the loss of trauma.

Regina felt light and clean. Despite a very arduous day of hiking and the physical weariness she felt in arms, legs, and back, she was refreshed and rested as if she had just wakened after hours of sleep.

"Hungry?" he asked her.

"Ravenous," she cried.

"Come on, then. Let's go up to that hut. We'll hide there and rest for a spell—provided it isn't occupied by a bear. Then we'll head out again after a bit."

He felt thankful for her recovery but anxious about that trail of gravitron. It haunted him, it made him want to move on, ever farther. He would let her sleep for an hour or two. Then they would strike out again toward the dry bed of the old Ohio.

Inside the building they unloaded the clumsy packs he had fashioned out of oxygen canister straps. He inspected the place by the light of a torch and saw silver-gray wood of ancient vintage, the inside of some sort of park structure. He cleared an area of brush and leaves and handed her the torch.

"Open some cans," he said. "I'll try to find us some water."

Regina sat for a moment savoring the pleasure of being off her feet, the musty odor of vegetation, so different, so much more pungent than in her roof-top garden. At the same time she continued to feel giddy release. She ached with pleasure—and longed for pleasure. She was hungry and tired and lively all rolled into one. It was stimulation, she realized, nothing more. Nevertheless . . . Her body had been shriveled up under the assault of pain. Now her cells expanded all together and broke into a chorus of gladness.

She set to work unpacking blankets from the packs, finding canned food.

Wonderful, wonderful. I'm in Hinterland, she thought. *I'm feathering our little nest.*

She didn't think about the implications of her thoughts, feeling as close to Mycal as it was possible to feel. She recalled his anxious ministrations the night before, when she had lain under that huge bale of hay sobbing with terror. He was so sweet and kind to her. She was his and he was hers.

In the bottom of the pack, groping in the light thrown by the hand torch, she found golden spoons with the Unsler flower set into the handle in relief. She arranged the spoons next to the cans, removed the can lids. Mycal had insisted on taking only protein mush. The smell would have made her turn off under ordinary circumstances, but now she was so hungry that she took a nibble from the can. The taste was delicious.

This done, she unzipped her jump suit and climbed out of it. Involuntarily she ran her hands over her nipples, belly, and down the insides of her thighs. She trembled with an unaccustomed surge of desire, surprised by it. She inferred its cause as the readjustment of her body and a consequent euphoria; nevertheless, her mind swam with visions of copulation for a second before she controlled herself.

I hope I don't smell too bad, she mused. She had had no chance to bathe, nor any inclination. But her deodorant was a secret formula that released odor controllers long after application. Her hygienist had invented the cream expressly for her.

Outside Bono sniffed the air, searching for water. The air was moist here, but he knew the smell of a spring or brook. He had not been in the Acropolis long enough to lose his senses. He moved on.

After a while he sensed a deeper moistness in the air and soon found a trickle of water at the bottom of a rock face. Moist fingers touched his tongue, testing for pollution, but the spring seemed pure. He collected water in the bottle and went back to the building on the ridge.

When he entered the hut, he saw Regina on the floor draped in a blanket. In the dim light of the torch, which she had propped up so that its beam fell on the roof and reflected from the silvery redwood, he saw her eyes gleam. Yet there was a dull look on her face. She sprang up and ran toward him. She embraced and kissed him while her midriff pressed into his in an unmistakable way.

For a moment he experienced annoyance. Now that he was anxious, Regina was amorous. But his annoyance dissolved in passion. Tonight nothing would impede his groping hand. Their stumbling movement toward the blankets on the floor upset the propped-up torch and it went out. They made love in total darkness.

Bono rolled on his back, tired, a little sleepy, a little sad. The moment had come and fled too quickly. Her body had tasted much like those bodies on the other side of the refinery in Wellhead.

By his side Regina stirred, restless. The brief, clumsy encounter had left her stimulated but dissatisfied. She was sure she hadn't conceived. *Conceived?* She kept having that stray thought when in fact she meant something else. He had left her hanging. He had neither the experience nor the sophistication to match her appetite. She hesitated for a while, but then, impelled by hungry euphoria, she engaged his attention with tiny kisses on neck and chest and gently exploring fingers.

For Bono the ensuing time of sexual experience was like a mad dream of flesh, a wild tumbling and floating, a stormy trip through pleasure gardens by comparison with which the Wellhead night seemed a stumbling through a sickly cabbage patch . . . And then she fell asleep as soundly as a baby, leaving him bruised and cross-eyed, holding her form and breathing her perfume.

Ten minutes, Bono told himself.

An owl hooted mournfully, and yet it was a glad sound. They lay in an environment where animals thickened the Ecosphere again.

Ten minutes, then he would wake her and they would move on again. They *had* to move. Ten minutes, ten fingers, ten commandments, tents, tentacles of creeping sleep, of mountain fog, of owl hoots falling from the pines . . .

Caesar's Aborted Initiation

French was out there, far out, on the edge of sanity.

He ran down the narrow walk of the service chasm in the light of gravitron sparks. Sidney's heavy body went *bump, bump* on his shoulder with every step; and Sidney's right foot, encased in a heavy cast, hit French rhythmically on the buttock

The life of action, went through his mind. *The life of action,* he huffed. *Adventure,* he huffed. *Danger. Tests. Challenge. Battle.*

French often suspected that he was crazy. Now and then he *knew* he was. Why did a man choose a life that had such episodes in it? Times when all reasoning, deliberation, wonder, and examination were banished and a whole life hung on the instincts that guided feet over an eroded, dusty, treacherous path.

French had become one with his physical processes —the burning in his lungs and the pain in the limbs and shoulder, where Sidney now pressed down heavy and limp. Meanwhile French's brain drifted off like an uncaged beast into mischiefs of fantasy.

He exulted over visions of death.

He saw himself stumble forward, hit by bullets from behind. Cut loose from his grasp, Sidney fell against the flimsy railing beside the path and careened down silently, not aware enough to scream. The vision lacked drama, and French imagined other deaths in quick succession: a death fall through a shaft, holding his victim in an eternal embrace; death in the crush of a collapsing level; death in the radiation belt where he had once or twice thought of taking his prisoner; death at the hands of a maddened mob intent on lynching Sidney but mixing their identities.

Death appeared sweet and inviting. French had lost his will to live, although his body and brain disagreed; but he used his habits and training to keep on surviving anyway, just for the sheer damn hell of it.

French let it be.

He didn't mind living a little longer. He would pick his own style of death. He'd die with a bang, an explosion, a flash. The world would know that he had sacrificed himself to save his honor.

These thoughts arose from a dull conviction that Miri had died at the hand of the Flames. French fancied he sensed her absence telepathically. When the police had found his hiding place—something he would never have thought possible—he'd seen that as an omen, a sign.

Gasping wildly, he stopped and turned. Sidney's cast-heavy foot hit a wall.

It seemed to French that he had gained on his pursuers. He had left them behind around the turn. For an instant he listened, holding his breath. He heard gravitron pulsing, a kind of silence. But then he could distinguish the far-off rustling of steps.

They were still coming and they had no need to hurry. With every step French had left behind a clearly visible trail in the plastosteel dust of the walkway. It would appear sharply outlined in the blaze of their torches.

He caught his breath, chest heaving.

Momentarily he wondered—still half in fantasy—if he should go on like this, weighed down by Sidney. What if he just dropped the vile flesh-sack into the chasm? Union would owe him an eternal debt. Then, free of this burden, he could swiftly escape his pursuers and wander through Ricardo, a dangerous seeker after Miri; a vengeful seeker, alone, unimpeded, slipping from disguise to disguise; a hunter after the ultimate prize of life, the love of Another; a stalker after those who had done her harm; a gardener with a scythe in hand; a reaper of chaff.

Or should he, instead, do what he had determined to do in saner moments—use Sidney as a hostage to force her release? But what if it was too late? Still, there might be hope . . .

But he couldn't stand here any longer, gasping. He turned and ran on. Sidney went *bump, bump, bump* on his shoulder; the cast spurred him forward with blows on his rump.

The whole mad, undeliberated sequence of events went by in his mind as he ran: the violent entry into Top Level North; the furtive trip through Ricardo, guiding what seemed an empty jumptube alongside his own; the choice of a hiding place, an excellent, secret spot only a few members of the Kayring Gang could know about (and yet the police had found the spot nevertheless: a poor omen!); the wait; then the proposition and Sidney's disbelief; troubled sleep; discovery; and now his flight.

The pattern was one of madness and disorientation conceived by a man stupefied by anxiety and grief. The life of action fell to pieces without a little bit of thought.

French had chosen as his hiding place an ancient crane operator's booth made of silcoplast (silcoplast, alas!) to resist gravitron, and left up inadvertently after construction of East Tower's southern quadrant. Over the years the booth had been surrounded and obscured by other constructs. It was totally private. French knew about it only because some boys he had run with had found it on forbidden explorations of the service chasm.

He had dumped Sidney on the floor of that booth toward early morning. The Fire sprawled out, unconscious, still under the spell of chemgun gas administered to him as he had dined. French sat down beside him. He set up the small visi-recording device he had taken from Sidney's domain. Then he waited and waited and waited for Sidney to sleep off the effect of a full-force chemblast. As he waited, resisting the urge to fall asleep, French had spun schemes of extortion and escape.

He didn't plan, exactly: he ran after feverish imaginings. The time of planning was behind him. He had broken with his past. Sidney's abduction would almost certainly derail the Secret Agenda. And if the revolution went forward successfully, Proctor would no longer want him on his team, not after this treachery. But the Secret Agenda could not succeed. How would Proctor get his Interdiction unless he gave up the silco-parts? And what if he did?

It must have been nine or ten in the morning when French started up from a doze. Sidney had begun to stir. He came awake, his long face uncomprehending and disoriented, his eyes blinking in the beam of French's torchlight.

A face of dissolution and arrogance: a long face with thick, sensuous lips, red even in the harsh brightness of the torch. The lips contained Sidney's total character. They were mobile and changed shape with his thoughts, while his eyes were cold, malignant, and fixed in a stare.

His voice husky after long silence, French explained the situation to the celebrated Ignis. Sidney did not understand him immediately, so French had to repeat himself several times. At last Sidney's lips curled contemptuously; then he laughed without much humor.

"I understand, I understand. This is a practical joke, eh, Tanti? That's you, Tanti, isn't it? Your makeup and wig don't fool me. Well, I see through it. Is this my *initiatio*? Did you boys decide to test the mettle of your Caesar? You will find me tough and unyielding on the test. How can the Fire be burned, my dear Tanti?"

"I am Rivera French, as I said, lately an official of BTA. You really *are* my prisoner, Unsler, and I mean to get my way." French pointed his torch at the small visirecorder set up next to one of the jumptubes. "I want you to tape a message to your friends. Here's what you say."

Again Sidney laughed. "Slowly, Tanti. Your Caesar can't be made to yield. He is a man of courage. *Vir Fortitudo.* I'll say nothing, nothing at all."

French stepped in front of Sidney, who sat on the floor leaning against the wire-backed silcoplast booth.

"Snap out of it, Unsler. This isn't any kind of game. This is for real."

Sidney guffawed, and in exasperation French hit him across that sneering mouth with the back of his hand.

A bitter thought flashed. *There is no reality. There are only games. His game is as real as mine.*

But French wanted Sidney to play French's game.

The Underunifier wiped blood from the corner of his mouth. His expression had hardened, but French had not got through to the man. The cold eyes stared. The red lips worked.

"You can't fool me," Sidney said after a moment. "You're Tanti, no matter how you disguise your voice. Caesar can't be broken, not by a slap, not by anything. I have passed through greater crises. Go ahead, Tanti, hit me again. I can stand initiation. And I will be generous with you, after the ordeal. You and I, we shall be brothers. You'll be my godfather, my initiator, the witness of my fortitude . . ."

Sidney went on. In the midst of this, French turned away from him and looked around for a suitable gag. He found an old towel, soiled and torn. He himself might have used it for some purpose as a boy. The cloth was dusted with age. He gagged Sidney and then tied his arms behind his back. Finally, he placed the man head first into one of the jumptubes.

Sidney struggled for a while, his legs extending beyond the tube's rim, one foot in a cast. Then his motion subsided.

French sat down.

He decided to give Sidney an hour in the tube. That would sufficiently soften the man. French had his doubts about Caesar's courage in a real situation of acute discomfort.

Finally, exhausted beyond measure and lulled by the song of gravitron, French fell asleep despite his best intentions.

He awoke to a furious metallic noise. Someone approaching the silcoplast booth had stumbled across the trip wire French had rigged during the night and had caused a pyramid of empty lubricant drums to fall.

Blood beat in French's throat. He ran to the tube and hauled Sidney out. His long face was gorged with an accumulation of blood. Sidney's eyes were dull with pain or terror. The dirty gag obscured his expressive lips. French had slept long. He felt the pulse of restored energies. Therefore Sidney must have been confined for hours.

French checked his chemgun. He pulled the gas mask over his head and pressed the trigger, releasing the last of the gas left in the ammunition cartridge. Sidney slumped and French threw the gun aside. He ripped the gag from Sidney's mouth, placed the body on his shoulder, and left the booth by way of a manhole and rickety stairs. Above him he heard the police bang on the door. When they entered, chemgas would incapacitate them for a while.

Sidney went *bump, bump, bump* on his shoulder.

Where to go now? What to do?

In his hasty flight, French had left behind the visirecorder. The police had found his hiding place. He had lost his base of operations.

He would go down, he decided, down into the abandoned tunnels of the ancient undercrust. The police would not search for him down there. The tunnels were not well known except to gangs operating smuggling rings. Even if they followed him, he could easily elude them.

He would think about next steps once he was safe.

French stopped again, unable to continue at this pace with such a load. Now, far behind him, he saw the jerky motion of torches and running figures.

Somewhere up ahead there had to be a stairway or slide bar that would allow him to descend.

He gave himself a moment of breathing time, watching the lights jerk in the hands of his pursuers as they ran. Then he turned to continue and saw with shock another group of men coming toward him, very close, from the other side. They must have entered the service chasm seconds before, through a door.

French stepped to the railing, and when the men drew up before him, their torches a blinding wall of light, he cried: "Not another step, people, or Sidney Unsler goes right down the chasm!"

Loud laughter answered his command. Then a voice said in the thick Branco brogue: "Go ahead, Mr. French, dump the bastard. We don give a shit."

A short figure detached itself from the lights and came toward him, backlighted and therefore obscure. Nevertheless, French recognized Dachshund Jones and saw that the man smiled.

"Dachsy!"

"The same," Dachsy answered. "Before you say anything else, sir, let me tell you this. Miri is safe. She's with us."

Gang Council

Young men from the Kayring Gang had arranged empty crates in an oval in the center of a well-lighted area of the murky warehouse. The councilors sat around the circle and listened to Frenchy with troubled expressions but with a forward-leaning concentration as great as Miri's own.

His words mesmerized her for several reasons. First, she had lived with this man skin-to-skin, as it were. She was an accomplished psychic. Yet she had never suspected that he had plotted revolution. Second, what he said slowly filled in an empty matrix in her mind, cell by cell; and she gained an insight into the crude mechanics that underlay the Great Change. Finally, she realized that Frenchy had made a momentous decision in the last several . . . days? Hours? He had decided to cut the cord that bound him to BTA and upstriving ambition. So he told these people, who were total strangers to her but to him members of his larger family in Branco days. They appreciated him, considered him a hero, and Dachsy

Jones' introduction had been warmly admiring. He revealed to these people the entire intricate schematic underlying something he called the Secret Agenda. But to what end did he say all this? What conclusion would he reach? Why had he pleaded with Dachsy to call the council?

Half her mind retraced the immediate past, seeking clues, lingering over the glorious reunion, the tears—the hungry, cramped, repeated embraces—the long and tender looks they had exchanged, so happy to be together again. But after a time Frenchy had sobered. A look of distraction had come over him. He had excused himself to find a tel.

Outside, police were searching every centimeter of Level 13. They had already rummaged through the warehouses and had sealed all the doors. The gang had known how to enter here without disturbing the seals. Nevertheless Frenchy had gone off on tiptoe. She watched him talking on the tel in a brightly lit supervisor's booth in the center of the warehouse, surrounded by small, yellow, forklift trucks parked in orderly rows before ceiling-high, gleaming stacks of reddish plastosteel rolls.

He had come back to her after a while, his face darker even than it had been when she'd first seen him, even more weary and fatigued.

"It's no use," he sighed. "Proctor has gone mad. I checked with Clemmens, who wouldn't talk but who gave me enough of a hint so I can piece it all together. I reached Proctor in his cubohome. The man seems to be under house arrest but not a bit bothered by that. I asked him to level, but he lied to me."

He stared at her, through her.

"I don't know what you're talking about," she said.

He glanced at her, as if awakening. "Of course you don't, girl. But you'll hear it all soon enough. Now what I need is your help. Stick with me, baby. For me, at least, there is no place but out."

Miri looked across at Frenchy with affection. She would stick with him, through thick and thin. She loved him, after all. Wherever he went, she went.

Across the circle, French sensed Miri's emotion. He

addressed much of what he said to her. His eyes swept the faces of the councilors, many of whom he had known well as a boy. But his glance returned to Miri's face. Her eyes gleamed with a strange kind of brightness. She sat leaning forward, lips slightly parted, hands folded in her lap, very still. She wore a green ring he didn't recognize.

He went on inexorably, step by step recounting the history of the past few years. He knew himself a traitor, revealing secrets not his to reveal. Or was he, perhaps, merely an unconscious agent of the Kayring Gang sent out years ago by a pulse of collective will to secure gang survival now?

He felt no real guilt doing what he did. His heart belonged to Branco, always had.

The cells of Miri's matrix slowly filled in, and at one point she began to experience the wild flash of insights. From the matrix—a pattern. From the pattern —a forecast of events to come.

This was a story of two parts, she realized; and Frenchy only knew half of it. But someone knew the other half, and that would be . . . Regina! Miri wondered if Regina really knew her role. Or was she also, like Miri herself until hours ago, a willing but unconscious agent of Madonna's spinning hand?

And had she, Miri, also played into the hands of fate? If she had listened to Frenchy's pleadings and stayed away from the ball, would there have been an Operation Hairy-Scary then? She would not have been in the embassy and French wouldn't have gone berserk. He would still be up there arguing for sanity with Proctor. Didn't the oracle say that she would marry a man who could delay, prevent the Change —if permitted? Had she, unknowingly, derailed the rational unfolding of events? Would Regina confuse the Male in turn? Which male? Bono? How?

Her excitement increased.

She marveled.

Her Lady of Indirection. The subtle Female's dark, healing work . . . In Cult lore they likened Madonna to the long-legged stork picking puffed-up, croaking frogs from a rotting log with a sharp beak. She was

the docile cow dispensing milk with her watery eyes
staring stupidly into the green, her jaws working
slowly on the cud. Or yet again they likened her to a
carry bird shamelessly feeding on the dead. Or yet
again to the phoenix who burned in consuming psychic fire, who fell down in ashes that fertilized. She
was the cunning snake and meek dove of Jesus Christ.
Somewhere she had seen Madonna with a hundred
arms, festooned with skulls, and also as the Ocean
Maid dispensing nourishment.

Nature red in tooth and claw. Nature green with
bud and seed.

Slow and subtle. Cunning and indirect.

She insinuated herself into the cracks of the Male's
concrete. She abided and waited for the coincidence of
events . . .

And at the end she prevailed.

She could be yoked, but not enslaved. She was a
whore you never used, a sea you could not drain, a
song you couldn't break by singing, a time you
couldn't hold in your hand . . .

Around Miri the warehouse, with pyramids of
plastosteel coils, straight corridors, neat yellow forklift trucks, the blaze of lumiglobes set in a girdered
ceiling, seemed like a mausoleum—the geometricities
of logic. While in her now burned an intuition of a
world burgeoning in utter silence. The Lady was helium, and if she refused to flow there would be still-
ness.

Soon Miri heard French winding up. He predicted
structure collapse at worst, great turmoil and destruction at the least. He called upon the council to reach
a great decision. He asked them to leave Ricardo using the ancient tunnels of the undercrust for a new
life in Hinterland.

The words nearly paralyzed her. Not she, *he* would
lead the remnant. Something had been amiss in the
oracle.

French sat down and looked at the faces in the circle. The council stirred uneasily, frightened by the proposal, embarrassed, perhaps, that he had made it.
French might be the "best-loved son" of the Kayring

Gang, as Dachsy had said, but for that reason, also, he was an outsider.

French sought support in Miri's eyes, but she was still away in some contemplation of her own. Yet . . . how oddly her face shone! Could she be meditating in the midst of this company? Was that brightness the nimbus he sometimes saw about her head and shoulders? Could others see it too?

There were nine councilors, and Dachsy now turned to Number Two for comment.

The man rose, cleared his throat. "Dachsy, I don't know. These are strange times. The Fink lies over there unconscious." His hand gestured toward a group of young men against a wall. "Frenchy tells us we should abandon our turn, but I don't know. We worked eight years to reach one ton of vegetables a month, and in two years we're up to ten tons. We're all rich now. I just can't see us abandoning the routes just like that. On the other hand, there's the Fink, and who am I to argue with Frenchy. I don't know, Dachsy. I just don't know."

Dachshund turned to an ancient, shriveled man. "Phil?"

The ancient rose. "I've been on the council forty-five years and twenty as your Number Three, the gravitron having spared me. Dachsy, you tell me I hark back too much, and I guess I do. I remember when we were four small clans and I went out there to catch cricks for a living back in the days when up-level folk thought that crick pincers kept men from going sterile. When that went flat we hunted rat for a while, in the chasm, and we sold rat meat pretending it was mutachick. Then we won the apple route, and I was there, Dachsy, that night we outbid the Ayring at the Peace-freak village they used to have east of what's now the staging station, and I broke my ankle in the fight on the way home that night when the Aycats fell on us just after you went down into that narrow part of the oceanside foundation break BTA closed in '22. Most of you younger ones don't even know that route. And slowly we expanded, Dachsy. I saw us grow. At first it was ten clans, and then it was fifteen. We grew and we gained turf, humble and deferential like. And then we started using muscle, and now we have the ring as ours and going beyond."

The old man paused, as if to stop, but he merely caught his breath.

"If you think those times were peaceful, you're wrong. I was a kid in '98 when mercury in a wellbreak poisoned the anaerobics and the tanks were down for eighteen weeks. A million starved then, and all of them below Level 20. Oh, I can name them all for you—repair riots in 1002, wallbreak in Branco when I started in school, the 'lectrostorm of 1008 when the power failed although the grav-drums held and people went berserk and ran like mad sheep and fell into the shafts. And the Helium War of 1011. I remember that like it was yesterday. People said the world would end, but it blew over . . ."

The old man went on reminiscing for a long time. Finally he sat down, and Dachsy called on the others, one by one. French could sense the mood shifting. They rose and sat down in turn, one after the other, echoing the old man, discounting the dangers, stressing the positive of the current situation.

Gyrations toward inertia, French thought, recalling a hundred similar meetings, scores of committees, working groups. His heart sank as he listened, all too aware of the dynamics.

The final man finished his speech at last, and now all eyes turned to Dachsy. In that moment, French glimpsed motion. Miri had come to her feet. He started at her appearance. The faint glow he had seen about her head had intensified. *God!* The girl radiated as if on fire. Her eyes were brilliant, and she drew the attention to herself, away from Dachsy.

She stood with hands extended, her face entranced. French saw awe in the councilors' faces. They stared at her with parted lips.

Slowly Miri looked around. Then, in a voice oddly vibrant, she said: "Listen to me, people. There is a prophecy . . ."

The Pact

It was dawn.

With a small retinue, Tack returned from the pine-covered ridge just above the temporary campsite next to the barn where Bono's jumptubes had been found, charred heaps of metal and burned gear. From there, the night before, Fannin had set out with a group of men and hounds to hunt down the traitor. No word had come during the night, and this morning Tack had combined his meditation with a bit of looking out toward the west; but in the deep mists he had seen no sign of Fannin nor had he heard the yelp of dogs.

The meditation had gone well this time, and Tack experienced a stir of pleasure heightened now by what he saw below. A copter had just landed. Its blades still turned, churning dust. He made toward it down a slippery slope. That could be his harem, at last. The *moment* Ricardo fell, the *moment* he knew the Plan had succeeded, he would plunge into a great festival of love to dissolve the Pact of Chastity.

He had been right! Through settling dust, fems jumped from the aircraft, unsupported breasts deliciously a-bobbing. Tack abruptly changed his course and headed for his own tent. He didn't dare talk to the fems. The temptation might be too great. Tack would not endanger his great achievement now by a false step that might anger Him-Up-There.

Despite these resolutions, Tack sat down to breakfast woefully aware of his many weeks of deprivation. It was worst when he was rested and full of energy. His mind played tricks. The soft-boiled eggs, the grass-seed gruel, the thick molasses he mixed into it, the pink of Harvey ham, and even the rolls he broke to smear with honey reminded him of fem flesh. It was as if his harem sent out vibes. Come to think of it, a couple of the girls were mutants, and they did emit a rut smell quite strong and compelling once a month. Henrietta . . . As soon as Ricardo crumbled,

205

he'd scoop out Henrietta like he scooped out this egg, but he wouldn't use a spoon to do so, by God . . .

To some extent he felt relieved when Robartus announced Dart's arrival. Dart moved into the tent. Tack asked for a second table setting. His eyes gleamed mischievously. He would tease the old skunk a bit. During the night Barney had committed suicide back in Ricardo.

Chewing mightily, leaning back in his chair, Tack wagged a finger at Dart, chided him. Couldn't stand to have rivals around, could he, the sly little ferret.

Dart opened his eyes wide, raised his hands in surprise, and asked what Jonny meant. Dart was dusty from his long ride through the night. His eyes were reddened from fatigue.

Tack laughed uproariously. He leaned even farther back in his chair and reached out for a cable on a table at his back.

"Listen to this, Franco," he said, looking at the cable. "It comes from your deputy, Dulsol. 'Barney committed suicide, 0300, 7/7/1056, as per instructions.' It's addressed to you personally, my friend, but we read it anyway. That's good—'per your instructions.'" Tack chuckled. "I'll keep my eyes on you, Franco," he cried, gesturing with the cable. "You're a sly one, you are. Deep, but sly."

At these words Dart went white in the face. He heard an echo of Barney's words from Tack's mouth. He stared in fright at Tack's face, half expecting to encounter Barney's eyes. During that eerie ride in the night, he had had hallucinations. He turned to the side now, seeing motion. Not a ghost. Robartus had entered and announced that Fannin was on the radio.

"Come on, Franco," Tack cried, jumping up, "let's see what our Teddy has found."

In the com-tent Fannin reported over the crackling frequency.

He had them. He had them both.

"Them?" Tack asked.

"Yes, sir. Bono and Regina. We came upon them in a ruined hut," Fannin elaborated. "They were fast asleep. Naked. I'll let you guess what they'd been doing. All worn out, the pair. Now we need to get some transportation back. I'm not about to trek all day after trekking all night."

Dart observed a transformation in Jonny's features. Tack had been in a funning mood. Now he'd turned purple—a deep purple the more accentuated because Jonny had a light complexion and blond hair. Tack screwed up his face into a grimace whose character Dart could not decipher—some sort of mix between pain and pleasure and anger and a kind of nasty joy. Tack's voice was choked when he replied. Transportation would be sent. Tack signaled a man and told him to get the coordinates and to dispatch a ship at once. Then he turned abruptly and walked off, leaving Dart standing by himself.

Back in his tent, Tack again sat down before the breakfast table and stared at the food for a second. Then he raised a boot and kicked the table with such force that the flimsy portable affair buckled under the impact, spilling its contents all over the tent.

"ROBARTUS!" Tack bellowed.

His manservant appeared at the tent flap; he knew his master well and stayed out of kicking range.

"Clean up this goddamned mess, goddammit! But do it quietly. I have to think."

The servant whisked and crawled about as quickly as a mouse, keeping close to the edge of the tent, while Tack sat in his chair. Tack laid his face into his hands and remained some time in the attitude of a thinker. He thought about vengeance. His blood beat at his throat and in his temples. His breath came very hot. Nevertheless, his reasoning powers functioned perfectly. He argued with himself about the Pact of Chastity.

In strict-constructionist terms, mutants and structure dwellers were not really people but actually a kind of lesser breed. Right? Right. When a man said fem-folk, he meant *tribal* girls, *tribal fems*. Right? Absolutely right. Therefore Regina Unsler couldn't be said to be a fem, not by a strict construction of the meaning of the term. Right? Right, precisely because Book Nine, Chapter Seven, Verse 28 forbade all intercourse with the Whore, and in the greater context of Book Nine the reasoning was clear: they weren't people! Verse 14 also forbade all striving with beasts. Right, right! But what about Verse 28? Wouldn't that be a violation . . . ? No, Tack decided. Verse 28 applied only when a man sought structure flesh for itself, for the pleasure of it. Tack didn't propose that. Not at all. He proposed to visit vengeance on Bono; and Regina Unsler was merely a tool, merely an instrument to carry that out. Therefore Tack would violate neither the Pact nor the Crestmore bible if he went ahead with his plan.

"Robartus! Where in the hell are you?"

"Here, sir." Robartus stuck his head through the flap.

"I want a tape recorder."

"A tape recorder?"

"Yes, dammit. Your ears dirty or something? A tape recorder. Move!"

The servant disappeared and Tack stood up. He stretched and yawned. His good humor had returned again.

The Second Queen

The copter flew high over pine-covered ridges. It was a spacious craft with rows of seats in the cabin facing the pilot: two on one side and one on the other, a small aisle between them. Regina sat in one of the single seats, staring rigidly down at thick white mists in valleys, with here and there a treetop visible faintly in the mist.

She did not want to look inside, still humiliated by her capture. She could not help the feeling that she was as much a prisoner as Mycal. The shame of that awakening! She had opened her eyes and had stared up at a man bent down over her naked form with a corner of the blanket in his hand. The hounds had indecently sniffed her rear. And then had come a certain amount of harsh verbiage. The tribesmen had watched her dress with strange looks in their eyes. They had separated her from Mycal; and later, when the craft had arrived, she had been hustled into the copter roughly.

She could still hear the hounds. They had been loaded into the ship and now cowered between seats on the other side, their tongues extended, their lean, rib-marked bodies heaving. Near them sat some of the men, and she could feel their observing eyes.

For the first time since setting foot in Hinterland, Regina experienced with clear consciousness an intuition, a premonition she had had moments after landing in the darkness outside Ricardo. It had hit her then, an odd sort of awareness that her life would soon undergo a radical change, a great change.

Under the tortures of Adjustment pressure, she hadn't thought about it. Nor had she later, during that glorious night of striving, which had dissolved in sleep.

But now she felt it very strongly, and it was more than just the usual culture shock any structure dweller might have on the outside. It was . . . She couldn't put her finger on it. A feeling, a forgetfulness? *"Great change,"* she thought; the words kept echoing.

Perhaps it's simply that I'm in love.

She no longer tried to conceal the feeling from herself. From the start she had loved Mycal—perhaps as far back as the ball, certainly after their long night of chaste conversation. She had tried to tell herself it wasn't so, still thinking of Jonny, who had been so very different. But now she knew she had found the one man for her future.

She turned her head despite the staring tribesmen and looked tenderly toward the archangel.

He sat up front, apart from the others, next to the leader of the group that had hunted and found them. From the facial expressions and behavior of the men, Regina inferred that the leader was prying and her lover uncommunicative. Mycal sat with a morose expression, occasionally nodding, answering in curt phrases. The other man spoke with rapid gestures of his hand.

She was determined to save Mycal, confident that she could do so. During their long cross-country trek, he had told her enough about Jonny so that she understood why Mycal was fearful. But she also relied on her own powers of persuasion. Jonny owed her a favor, for old time's sake.

A change in the pitch of the blades signaled the start of descent. The copter began to drop, and Regina felt the surge in the stomach so familiar to jumptube users. It signified "down."

She pressed her nose against the pane again. Trees rushed by on one side. Red clay ground blurred. Then she saw a circle of tents with an odd metal construct in the center, a kind of tower supporting machinery on a platform. A loaf-shaped device reminded her of a miniature grav-drum. The copter dropped toward a large circle of flattened mutagrass. Clouds of dust rose in greeting and obscured the view.

Nudged by tribesmen, she moved forward, following Mycal. She picked her way down the narrow metal stairs, eyes on her lover as he was being led away toward the . . . yes! It was the same barn where they had spent a night. Men ran toward the copter with bent backs as they passed beneath the still whirling blades. One of them grabbed her roughly.

"Just a minute," she cried, "let go of me!"

"Shut your yap, fem-stuff," the man growled. "Out here you're nobody, understand? Nobody."

They moved her at forced quick-step toward the camp. She looked ahead, saw an ornate complex of tents connected by low, covered walkways. The ecology flag flapped from the highest peaks. The hands on her arm were hard, relentless.

The men led her into the complex and stopped in a kind of outer room. A man seated on a canvas chair in the attitude of a guard rose and went through a flap into an inner chamber. He reappeared and gestured. Her captors led her to the flap and shoved her through.

Regina caught herself, then looked up.

She looked at the back of a man, the back of a head adorned with a horsetail of hair. He stood next to a bed, the covers pulled back to reveal a triangle of white. A tray with a bottle of wine and two glasses stood on a stand. The man turned and moved toward her with an odd expression on his face.

"Jonny Tack!" she cried, breathless with astonishment.

Regina's surprise was not occasioned by seeing Tack, whom she had recognized easily from the back. She was caught off guard by an internal shock of such force that she clutched her head and bent double as if hit by a sudden attack of migraine.

Great Change! Great Change!

Memories assaulted her, a shock of surprise. She was a member of the Madonna Cult going back many years—yet she had been made to forget it.

Tack's face had released the hypnotically held memories. She had been commanded to forget everything until she faced him again. Now she realized in a flash that nothing, nothing in the last few weeks had been pure chance—not her meeting with Mycal, not her longing to escape to Hinterland, no, not even her ravenous sexual hunger last night. All this had been predicted, vaguely at first, then in greater and greater detail as Serenita had sought more and more information from the oracles, the crystal, the visions.

Regina knew herself a full adept now, and that meant she was pregnant with Mycal's child.

But, shockingly enough, she also knew what her role would now be—to confuse the Male, to shatter his powers of judgment, so that an era could end at last, so that the last remnant of a dead age could be buried.

Jonny's intentions were revealed by the bed and its pulled-back cover, the wine, the glasses. But she no longer loved him; she loved another.

Do I want to do that? Do I want to do it?

Who was she? Was she flighty, irresponsible Regina, the playgirl, forever concerned with the excellence of her articles of consumption and use? Or was she that other Regina—the one schooled in all the psychic arts?

She realized now that she was both, that the many long conversations she had had with Serenita—several each week, forgotten but now remembered as clearly as anything else—were *her* conversations. That she believed in the oracles and knew that she would do what had been predicted, would *have* to do them, one way or another, voluntarily or by force. Not *she* confused the Male—he confused himself. She was but the Lady's instrument.

More than ever she hoped against hope that Mycal would understand and forgive—if he, if she, survived the Great Change which stood immediately before them.

Her odd motion had stopped Tack in his tracks, his eyes puzzled as he stared at her bent-over form. She forced herself to smile as she looked up again. Many years of secret practice had taught her how to command her body and emotions. So she knew how to do it once more. Imperceptibly she took a deep breath and exhaled it gradually, gathering energies from the ether. Slowly her smile turned salacious and her lips curled, her cheeks dimpled.

"Jonny-boy," she warbled. She held out her arms as he came toward her, a glazed expression in his eyes. He was the Male, stupid and destructive, but ultimately in her power.

9

The Consort

French pulled in the reins of his pony, and the horse came to a stop. He nudged the animal forward. In no time his mount walked half submerged in water, groping toward the other side of this depression filled with water seepage. French let the animal find its own way.

Lumiglobes strapped to his arms gave more the illusion than the reality of light. The tunnel was very wide at this point, its ancient walls caved in, and darkness reached out hungrily for the faint gleam of his lamps.

He heard the splash of other horses as the two explorers he had brought along followed behind.

The cold water brought French out of half-sleep —lately the most common state of his mind unless some new crisis or decision demanded his attention. In the four days since the council meeting, he had yet to see a bed. Organizing an exodus had taken all his time.

The horse strained up the sloping bank of the underground lake and continued on, dripping. Once more French saw rails to the side. The tunnel walls became visible as they left the area of the cave-in. Then, in another ten minutes or so, French saw moving lights in the distance. That must be the lead column of the exodus they had passed some time ago on the way out to explore the tunnel.

He spurred his horse into a trot, eager to get back now that home was near.

As he came abreast of the column, the people cheered. Those who had lamps lifted them high into

the air and swung them back and forth. French
waved his arm and smiled tiredly. He had yet to
accept, deep down, that he was now a Very Big
chief in the eyes of these people. No, much more
than that—he was the consort of a goddess.

He wondered with an undertone of gallows humor
whether simple, ordinary Rivera French would become a mythical figure someday. At the moment,
thank God, he was still considered human. Unlike
Miri. Miri had already assumed the mantle of divin-
ity.

More likely, he thought, *I'll be remembered, if I
am remembered, as one of the great crackpots of the
eleventh century, conned into playing Moses by a
small and nutty religious cult. They'll laugh and joke
about me. "French? Oh, French was that slum kid
who made it big in the upper world. One day he
dreamt that the structures would crumble. And so he
talked these people into leaving Ricardo, see; but
when they got out of the tunnel, Ricardo was still
there, same as ever."*

On the other hand, he thought, *there is Serenita*.
To think of the Cult Mother was to deepen the ambivalence he still felt about this—all this.

The tall, severe figure of the nun appeared before
his eyes as she had stood in the darkness of an ancient
parking lot, face shadowed by a cowl. Serenita had
come down to visit Miri in the temporary headquarters French established next to an enormous hall, an-
ciently a station of the undercrust. He had followed
her back up when she left again, after tearful farewells
with those sisters of the Cult who had joined the exodus. He'd confronted her in the darkness and had ac-
cused her of creating crisis, of deliberately fostering
disaster.

Snatches of that conversation floated through his
mind as he rode past the column, waving to the people.

"I do nothing," the nun had said. "I serve the
Queen of Heaven, the sweet Jesus, God the Father,
the Holy Ghost, the Trinity, the Great Unknown, the

Cosmic One, Buddha, Krishna, Shiva, Aphrodite—name your god, Mr. French. I don't make the Great Change, Mr. French. It comes of itself when the time is ripe. You and I and all the rest—we're witnesses of a drama we don't direct. There is no one in charge, Mr. French. No one. *She* is in charge."

He insisted that she had rigged the confusions surrounding the helium round, had had her agents—like Miri and Regina—interfere.

The nun shook her head inside the cave of her cowl. "How can I cause war between Union and the tribes? War must be there in the heart first. We are a tiny cult, Mr. French. We merely predicted the Great Change. We don't pretend to rule—only to know."

The future cannot be known, he had insisted.

"You're half right," she said. "The future is murky. But sometimes quite inevitable. When a seed is planted, it may or may not germinate. But once a flower has sprung up, it will surely wilt again? Eh?"

She went on to liken culture to a plant that grows, flowers, gives fruit, and dies. The plant was Western Christendom and the world today its final manifestation. In the scheme of things, she said, the culture had died long ago—long before LNW XIII. Real life had left the dead trunk of the tree. Great Change meant a new beginning rather than an ending. The end lay centuries back.

A hundred million people dead, he protested. That's what Great Change meant. He thought it was terrible.

"Why?" she asked. "Life will go on. Cells may die, individuals may die, but life goes on. You are mesmerized by numbers, Mr. French, and you're dishonest and sentimental on top of that. You agonize over the death of millions. But you killed two men yourself in the past week or so, and you never gave them a second thought."

The words shocked him with their truth. How did she know, he asked, had Miri—?

She shook her head ever so slightly. "I *know* you, Mr. French. I'm standing in your aura, you know, and

I'm a psychic. I know all about you. The life of action. Adventure, danger, tests." She smiled. "The mind," she continued, and pointed a slender index finger toward her temple. "The human brain cannot encompass these cosmic events. But, as we say: the Male pretends to rule. Give it up, Mr. French. It doesn't become you. You're a man of the future. Action, eh? Life, movement, love. Not dark, puzzling thoughts and reckonings. You can't make sense of it, so why pretend? You've done well so far. You've followed the Lady—your heart. Not the Male—your head. Your future is bright. 'Flowers in the meadow,' Mr. French. 'Flowers in the meadow . . .' "

Flowers in the meadow . . .

Her words echoed in his mind as he rode past the people in the tunnel, smiling, waving automatically. Miri said that Serenita spoke obscurely, that being the Lady's way, indirection. The old woman had made him think, had convinced him, had left him doubtful. He was not sure at all about his future, didn't know if he had bet on the right color at all.

The human mass he passed came from the very dregs of structure life, crackpots like himself. But of another sort. In the dim light of lumiglobes, their faces were bluish and sallow, gravitron-burned; their forms were stunted. They had nothing to lose.

Maybe they will inherit the Earth, flashed in his mind.

At last count ten thousand had joined the exodus. They had come down by hundred of paths, following smuggling routes. They had lain on the floor of the undercrust station in areas marked out by luminous paint, writhing and spasming from pressure loss. Then, later, supplied with food and lights by foragers, they were formed into companies and launched on their way to ancient Chicago by several westbound tunnels. Ten thousand superstitious slum dwellers, these, who had believed the rumors leaking out of Branco that the world would end and that a woman would lead the chosen to safety.

French thought of the other Ricardo millions—

those who were more sensible. They too sought salvation, but in another way. Pent-up frustrations had exploded into riots all over the city.

French left the first and reached the second group. The cheering and light waving began all over again. He figured he had to pass ten more companies before he would get some food and drink. It was early afternoon, although you couldn't tell it in the tunnel's perpetual night. He hadn't eaten since morning.

French wondered who would be more disappointed: those who had stayed above and were now being systematically pacified by the troops Harvanth had flown in from several neighboring structures . . . or those who had thrown in their lot with the Goddess Miri and Her nearly divine consort, Rivera French.

It would all depend on the Secret Agendas—Union's and Ecofreak's.

And God help us all, no matter what!

An hour later he and his explorers arrived at the station and handed the horses to attendants at a kind of livery stable where exodus leaders and explorer teams could get animals for tunnel travel. The animals had been obtained from tribesmen in the foothills of the Allagains.

French mounted a makeshift ramp to the platform where people had long ago waited for trains. This portion of Eastcoast had been abandoned following LNW XIII. The bunker complex where survivors had lived, experimenting with gravitron, lay farther north. Explosions above had trapped large numbers of people down here. Their skeletal remains had been gathered and piled up by explorer teams to make way for the exodus. French passed such a pile on his way through a darkish structure to the station hall.

He surveyed the busy scene for a second.

On his right a disorderly littering of humanity spasmed on the ground in the grip of Adjustment. Only children were up and about. They appeared immune to the effects of gravitron deprivation. Members of the Cult moved about between prone figures. Ministering, they called it, although all they really had to

217

offer was an encouraging word—that plus the magic aura of the Cult itself.

On the left a group of foragers piled boxes and canned mush into a pyramid as they unloaded a transport jumper. French wondered how they had gotten the jumper down here. But the foragers were ingenious and their job had been made easy by the riots. They'd hauled down into the catacombs an incredible tonnage of loot: food, textiles, lights, fuels, medicines tools—everything that might be needed for a new start in life out there.

French set himself in motion across the hall. He had reached the center, the point where the luminous lines of demarcation came together, when he heard the dreadful thundercrack.

It seemed that he'd be known as a consort after all, rather than as a crackpot.

Dynamite the Refineries

Dart scurried out of Tack's sleeping chamber as fast as his short legs would carry him. His face revealed fear, disgust, and unnatural excitement.

The Leader had satisfied his lust at last, from all appearances, Dart decided. The Whore was nowhere in evidence, although the rush of water from the shower stall adjacent to the chamber had hinted that she was cleaning up after the four-day orgy—and she had much to clean off, that Unclean Thing. The stench in that chamber still gagged Dart. Oh! They'd sweated and drank and jutted up a fearful storm of sin and damnation in there, and the place looked a mess. Dart had barely found a spot to put his feet on the floor inside, cluttered as it was with empty trays and bottles. The linen had looked positively gray with wear. And Tack himself, a pale shade of his past magnificence, had lain darkly amid the creased and mangled sheets with an iced towel wrapped about his shaved skull like a dirty turban of misery.

In the outer chamber Dart turned jerkily at a

fancied motion. His eyes were terrified. But he saw nothing in the murk. *Damn you,* he thought. *Damn you, Barney. Don't you dare stalk me in the shadows!* He dashed out. The ghost wouldn't follow him into the bright sunshine.

Six or seven members of Tack's guard idled outside, drawing circles in the red clay of the ground, joking with fems from Jonny's harem. The fems spent much time around the Leader's tent, either spying on their rival from·Union or else trying to seduce the men.

Dart could almost smell the rutting fetor of one or two of them—especially that Henrietta, the mutie with the deep red eyes. He reckoned that nothing remained of the sacred Pact of Chastity. Alongside Barney's hallow whispers, Dart had heard lascivious laughter in the woods at night. Jonny's own sported with the jealous fems among the pines while their master groaned inside the tent, completely captured by that abomination from Union. First Bono, now Tack. In his grave, Old Tack—

No, not that! Dart hurriedly thought. He shivered again, only too aware that Barney's ghost had come out into the sunlight after him and must be standing right next to him now. No thoughts about graves. An idea came to Dart. Barney must somehow be buried. Yes. He probably still dangled from a rope in the embassy, the last Ecofreak in Union. He had to be put underground with a heavy stone to weigh him down.

Across the empty circle of the camp, past the metal tower on top of which the shielding mechanism, equipped now with its critical silco-switch, gave forth an invisible but potent oscillation, Dart could see Ecofreak elders and leaders from other tribes stand outside the council tent waiting too hear what he had accomplished. They had come north in copter after copter, determined to persuade Jonny to hold off, to countermand his orders. But Tack refused, despite the disturbing speculations that Sonder, the physicist from Kaysee, had offered. They wanted change, these gentlemen, but none dared to confront the Leader. They insisted that Dart do it. "You're the only man he trusts," they had argued. And they forced him to go in.

Well, he had gone—but he had not pressed Tack hard. Dart had no intention of ending up like that damn-fool Gulfrat leader who had barged in there two days ago. That night his body had been found bruised black and blue by the boot heels of the guards. Dart had said "Yes, sir" and "No, sir" to Tack's curt commands. Yessir! "Yes, *sir,* I'll bring you copies of the transmission to Wellhead. As soon as we get through." *And I'll do it, too, by God!*

Dart set out across the empty circle toward the council tent. It might have been so nice, triumphant. Union had delivered the parts. Jets and copters had moved the precious components all over Hinterland. They had been snapped into place. Hinterland was safe and secure. Or *was* it?

Sonder wasn't sure. Dart had been present when Sonder looked patiently at one of the ear-shaped components. His thick fingers with square nails had scratched at the fine, thin lines of reddish copper print laid down into the ear by microwelders. Sonder had shaken his head. The color. He didn't like the color. Some other kind of metal might be alloyed with the copper, just enough to destroy its effectiveness. He wasn't sure that all the parts had defects, not even that any had them. The parts behaved correctly enough in the small test device Sonder carried about with him. But he claimed that Union would try to avoid an obvious defect. The parts had to have thorough testing, and that meant a testing program in Kaysee, perhaps taking three weeks or so. Dart had been sent in to convince Tack to give them time. Dart had one of the ears in his pocket, and Sonder had shown him how to explain the problem to the Leader. But Dart did not even take the ear out. Tack had not been in a funning mood, not at all; and he had darkly muttered about trouble-makers who might get some attention from the boys.

Dart avoided the eyes of the people as he walked past them into the council tent. Barney had a trick he liked to play: he possessed now this man and now that and stared at Dart accusingly through the man's eyes. Inside, Dart took up a central position and waited until the men had filed in again.

Among the men who entered was Fannin. He kept to the back, shadowed by the sloping canvas, his eyes alert. He looked at Dart and knew that Dart had failed. Fannin could have predicted that. The bad news was in. Sonder had thrown up all these clouds of suspicion, but Tack would never admit that he had failed. Better to go down in a blaze of glory, eh? Back home he wouldn't stand a chance, but here he could still lord it over the tribes, surrounded by his goons.

So what if Union bombs the tribal settlements, Fannin thought. *This camp won't be hit. It's too small a target. The Great Leader might survive the holocaust. Then, gathering the remnants about him, he'll try to play king of kings. Only, of course, I won't let him do that. Its frightfully uncomfortable around Jonny-boy, now that he has let himself go.*

Dart held up a hand and the murmurs stopped.

"Tack is adamant. Dynamite the refineries. Cut the pipeline. It's still the same order, and he wants to see the cable transmitting the command. In fact he wants a console moved into his tent so he can monitor everything we say."

The people groaned.

Dart held up a hand, asking for silence. "He said that Ricardo will fall tonight by his reckoning, and he plans to watch it. We've been asked to organize a column to move up to the edge of the Desolation. We move in two hours."

"Wait a *minute!*"

Fannin glanced to the side where burly Sonder stood. The physicist was one of the most patient men alive, but now even Sonder seemed to have lost his composure. He moved forward through the tribesmen, stocky, angry. His red beard blazed up like fire when he passed through a sun beam falling from the skylight. He stopped directly in front of Dart, fists balled.

"Did you *tell* him? Did you tell him we need time? Did you show him? Well, speak up, Franco!"

"Get away from me, get away from me!"

Dart threw up his hands and backed away from Sonder as if he had seen an apparition. Then he controlled himself and glanced abashedly at the people.

"Don't you rush at me like that again," he growled at Sonder in a changed tone.

Fannin was puzzled by Dart's manner. The old man had become even more paranoid since his return from Ricardo.

"Yes, I told him, but he wouldn't listen. He nearly threw me out."

"Did you *show* him? The color?"

Dart hesitated.

"Well?"

Dart looked away from Sonder and still refused to answer.

"You didn't show him, did you? You were too cowardly, like all the rest of you so-called leaders." Sonder turned and swept the people with a glance. His blue eyes, usually so placid, burned with anger. "Well, gentlemen, *I* will tell him. In no uncertain terms. Give it to me. Give me the part."

He wants to die, Fannin thought, watching Dart hand Sonder the part.

Next to Fannin, Sonder's friends moved nervously toward the entrance. They intercepted the out-rushing scientist, but he shook loose the restraining arms and disregarded the pleading of his friends.

High time to mosey on along, Fannin decided. *Better to be out of the way. Tack might order a general carnage.*

Fannin made for the entrance slowly and inconspicuously, while up front Dart squirmed under questions. Outside at last, Fannin slipped off between tents and then, in the obscurity of some pines, headed into the valley toward that distant barn.

Bono had been right, more or less, he reflected, recalling the conversation he had had with Bono in the copter. Tack would blow it, Bono had asserted. Now Fannin knew that it was so. He would head out, up into the Allagains. He knew an isolated hut up there where a man could hole up until the mess was over. Meanwhile, he would just open Bono's cage a crack. After what Bono had been through, he would take care of the king of kings without much urging.

Fannin walked carefully, wanting to catch the guard by surprise. He had almost reached the barn when he spied, in the distance, the silvery gleam of a Union airship also headed toward the camp. He understood instantly. They had also found the trail of desolation at last and came in search of Regina.

Fannin decided to seek safety on the other side of the ridge. But before he could carry out this intention, the airship suddenly described a graceful turn and headed back the way it had come.

Number One

The airship rushed back to Ricardo. The chilling message over the radio had caused the pilot to lose all color. The soldiers in the back became unnaturally still. Blottingham understood their silence. Gravitron failure made you *think*.

From the distance, Ricardo looked safe and sound —five silvery stalks of urban life swaying almost visibly with the motion of air masses heading out over the Atlantic. Blottingham didn't expect to *see* anything, of course. Grav failure did not mean immediate structure collapse. That would follow in some hours unless the problem was quickly corrected. At worst, the highest levels would begin to sag a little by nightfall, metal pressing on metal, molecules cozying up to one another.

Blottingham reached for the radio speaker and gave a string of instructions to Carmody; but when he stopped and Carmody had a chance to speak, he learned that his aide was more or less on top of things. Blottingham hung the radio speaker back on the dash, sat back in his chair next to the pilot, and ran a hand over the red brush on top of his head. His face was tense.

Lately he had learned to hate the exercise of power. The burden of responsibility rested too heavily now that Unsler had had a stroke and was paralyzed and struck dumb by a failure of his nervous system. Blottingham could see him: one eye frozen open, filled with terrorized pleading, a strange noise in his throat as he tried to speak past a paralyzed tongue. The stroke had come while the Old Man had watched the riots on the Media. Even if he had wanted to, Blottingham could not draw on support from Sidney who, though he was back again, had returned an imbecile, a raving maniac, calling every man Tanti and blabbering incoherently about his initiation. Blottingham had ordered him locked up in a spare cubo right next door to his stroke-struck father. As for the Cabinet and the rest of the family, Blottingham had kept the information from them. Had that been a good decision?

Yes, he decided, *it was a good decision*. In times like these it was best to hold down panic, even if it meant that Blottingham had to endure the weight of power.

He fell into a reverie, and it occurred to him that he could continue as Unifier-in-all-but-name indefinitely if he wished. Hypnosis and drugs might be used to prepare Unsler for rare public appearances. Tapes of his voice might be used for speeches. A blurry picture on Media . . . Then it occurred to Blottingham that he did not really want the power. It nauseated him.

The airship docked at last. Blottingham hurried to a waiting limo. Outside the airport he noticed at once that the troubles were greater than he had anticipated. He could hear a cacophony of sirens near and far: the rarely used public address system syruped with soothomuse. What damn fool had ordered that? Nothing panicked people more than hearing soothomuse on the PA. Blottingham got in and angrily slammed the door.

"What's happening?" he asked the driver.

The man shook his head. He activated the gravitron and lifted the jumper above the movebelt. "God help us all," he said. "We're heard it twice already."

"Heard what?" Blottingham asked.

"The clap," the man said.

"*What?!*" Blottingham cried.

The driver nodded. "Somebody really screwed up. No warning. It's just like '44. It's East Tower. Mobs are pouring out. This is big, Mr. Blottingham, big!"

Almost as if to underline what Sanchez had just said, came the sickening, sharp, ear-ringing report. Blottingham jerked involuntarily.

Sanchez looked at him, cocked his head, made a face.

God! Grav failure must have been underway for hours, unreported. It must have begun even before he had left to follow Regina's telltale track into Hinterland.

They crossed from West toward Central Tower through the beltway. From the mixing bowl in Central Tower, Blottingham observed a mass of humanity moving onto the beltway from East. A dark ooze of people. Blottingham shuddered. People trampled people in a kind of frenzied, animal panic.

Sanchez lifted the vehicle up into Central's shaft.

Arrived at Top Level, the Staff Chief ran through the lobby, where Union's thirty-nine structures hung about the wall around a centrally placed map of the helium pipeline. He saw no one as he ran. The place was deserted, swept clean by panic. He took an elevator to the office wing.

Not everyone had fled. A handful of his closest aides were still on the job. They had gathered in an open area usually occupied by visitors; their faces were ashen. They formed a clump around a visiset, turned when Blottingham came into the room.

Carmody disengaged himself from the others, neat as usual, his black hair almost blue of sheen and meticulously combed. "Paul, things are in a terrible shape. Communications are down. Belmonte can't be located. The people in Media laugh when we call and disconnect us. We're trying to raise Defense, but no one responds."

"Defense?" Blottingham asked. "Why Defense?"

"Haven't you been told?" Carmody asked. "There is no helium."

Blottingham gave Carmody an uncomprehending stare. The man repeated his message slowly and with emphasis. *"There . . . is . . . no . . . helium!"*

"Are you mad?" Carmody must have discovered this recently, since their discussion on the radio.

"No, Paul, it's the God's truth. The storage tanks are empty. No people in the Pits. The expanders are shut down. And there's nothing in the pipeline, not one molecule. We finally got Engineering to check it out." Carmody paused. Then he went on. "There's been an Interdiction, Paul, lasting more than four days. But nobody reported it. The records have been falsified. All the gauge watchers are gone. It's some kind of conspiracy."

Blottingham sank down into a chair. He rested his flat palm on top of his brush of hair.

We'll be mobbed. That was his first thought. Once the other towers began to crack, the mobs would make for Central Tower. It was the only one that had a chance. Its drums could be operated with helium from the stand-by air liquefaction units anchored out at sea. But Central Tower could not hold all the millions. If they came here . . .

He looked up and asked: "What about the other structures?"

"Interdictions have just been reported—but they just started."

"Oh, God!" Blottingham rose abruptly. "Gentlemen, I'm afraid we'll have to come out into the open. I mean about the Unifier and Sidney. This is big trouble. We'll have to call the Cabinet."

Wry smiles greeted this announcement.

"Too late," Carmody said.

He beckoned with a hand. Blottingham followed Carmody out to the lip of the glass-enclosed terrace.

Carmody pointed to a large fleet of ships—jumpers, limos, and individual jumptubes could be seen heading away from Ricardo.

"There's your Cabinet, Paul. And everybody else. Gone to save number one."

"Harvanth?"

"I suspect he was the first to go. I told you. We can't get anyone at Defense."

Blottingham stared out the window, chin in hand. His elbow rested on an arm he had folded across his chest.

An unreported Interdiction . . . That could mean only one thing—the tribes and Proctor were colluding. Only men completely loyal to Proctor could have hidden an Interdiction, which meant that Proctor controlled the BTA even from the prison to which he had been transferred. And that meant—Belmonte was part of the plot!

Suddenly Blottingham giggled. It tickled and amused him that Proctor and Belmonte and all manner of men from BTA and other agencies had deliberately created chaos. He felt the chaos. What he saw was peaceful enough—the glint of silver from the airships, a few thin clouds, the dark Atlantic. But throughout Ricardo raged a maddened mob. Those thundercracks would drive people crazy. He felt it also. He was human. And Proctor thought he could control this phenomenon? Proctor was crazier than Blottingham had imagined.

He chuckled to himself, then turned to the men just as another crack sounded—from the direction of West Tower this time. It was physical, tangible. It caused involuntary physiological response. Blottingham noticed that he was on hands and knees on the floor. He stared at tiles marked by the Unsler flower. He laughed.

"Do it again," he cried, turning to the west. He pointed an index finger in imitation of a pistol. "Do it again. Bang, bang, bang. Gotchya!"

The staff, also on the floor, stared at him with terrorized eyes. Blottingham didn't care. Stupid of him to pretend to be in charge. Insane of them to look at him with those childlike eyes. Who did they think he was? God?

His mind snapped back to reality.

"The Ecofreaks," he said in a cool tone. "Did anyone talk with the embassy?"

Carmody scrambled up. "None of the embassies answered our calls. We think that . . ."

Carmody's voice trailed out. His eyes stared past Blottingham and out through the drilla-glass. All the others on the floor did the same. Blottingham turned to see what mesmerized them.

The air outside visibly trembled as if heated by a gigantic fire below. Blottingham knew the cause: compressing plastosteel generated heat. In East, in West, the upper levels would be heating up. The drilla-glass would melt. The seals would break. Then escaping air would create a fantastic updraft in the shafts, powerful enough to lift men—an internal typhoon. They could not stay here. They had to leave.

In quick succession came a series of sharp reports. *Crack, crack, crack, crack-crack-crack!* Fireworks exploding against the roof of your mouth. Everything swayed and shook. Things fell on the tiles, shattered and slid. Blottingham, like the others, ran across the room crazed with fear. His bowels and bladder released their contents, but he was unaware of it. When the sound stopped, he stood embracing a door. Around him men lay on the ground in fetal postures, rocking. One man had three fingers in his mouth and sucked violently.

"Bang, bang," Blottingham mimicked. Then, in the continuing silence, he found control again. He cried: "Let's get out of here!"

His mind latched on to a simple plan and held tenaciously. In the hall outside, as in all halls, hung cabinets with emergency gear, insurance against surface ruptures: oxygen masks and canisters, sensitized gravitron webbing, medical kits, the like. He ran out toward the cabinets, aware now that his robe was soiled, that waste moistened his legs. He tore open doors and threw gear toward his staff. Some had followed on foot. Others had crawled after him on hands and knees.

"Check your seal," he cried. "It should be blue. If it isn't, take another. Don't pull the rip cord until we're outside."

Another series of thundercracks made them all curl into terrorized balls on the floor. One man had inadvertently pulled the rip cord on his gravitron gear and now floated in mid-air. Blottingham pulled him down and made him exchange the webbing. Then he ran down the hall followed by the staff.

On the way he passed an office where a visiset glowed. He thought he heard Proctor's voice exhorting the public, but it might have been illusion. Carmody puffed behind him and now called: "What about the Unifier?" Blottingham shook his head and waved a hand dismissing the Unifier. He had a simple plan: escape. He couldn't be bothered.

They reached the emergency exit, a small chamber. Pushing the men into the room, he carefully closed the seal door. He had never used such an exit, and he looked about, undecided. Glowing dials on the wall drew his attention. In a second he understood the mechanism.

"Put on your masks," he called.

He donned his own and tested it. Then, glancing about, he assured himself that all had done the same.

"All right," he called. His voice was muffled by the mask. "Grab your rip cords. When the door opens, out you go. *Run* out. You've got to get well away from the building. Once you're out there, pull."

He turned dials.

In seconds a hissing sound indicated that internal and external pressures were being equalized. Then the door swung open, and they felt the intense heat of the air outside.

"Run!" Blottingham yelled. "Go on, somebody. Carmody! *Go!*"

Carmody took a run and leaped out into the void. His head disappeared in a second. Blottingham walked to the door and peered out. Carmody had pulled his cord. The activated webbing had broken his fall. He floated downward gently, his body weight overcoming the gravitron. He would have a soft landing.

Blottingham turned back to the men.

"Easy," he said. "Nothing to it."

At that moment the dreadful sound came again. This time it was not cushioned by plastosteel, drilla-glass. The air pulse threw Blottingham back into the chamber. He fell on top of others at the back of the room. When the sound died out at last, they scrambled up. One by one Blottingham launched the men out. They floated down in an uneven string—men in the bright robes of the nobility.

Alone at last, Blottingham went to the back of the room so that he would get a good start for his jump. Then he hesitated, brushed his hair. His efforts to help the staff escape had banked his terror somewhat. Now rationality asserted itself. He recalled Carmody's words in the hall: "What about the Unifier?" Unsler could not be abandoned. Simple humanity demanded that he should be saved—if not from the collapse of Central Tower, then from the mobs Proctor would launch. Blottingham, for one, had more of a sense of responsibility than to save himself and let the world go hang.

He turned dials again. The outer door of the chamber closed. Blottingham heard a hissing sound and felt the rise of pressure. He opened the inner door. Once more he hesitated. He had a hunch he shouldn't do this. He had a simple plan. Why change it now? But he put the feeling down and ran, drawn by years of loyalty to the Old Man.

Moments later he burst into one of Unsler's sitting rooms carrying grav-webbing and oxygen gear. The sight of men in police uniforms made him recoil, but he was too late. The men had turned toward him. As they did so, the Staff Chief recognized Belmonte kneeling on the floor next to an armchair. His dark, inscrutable face was turned toward Blottingham, but his hands continued to press down on a pillow. The pillow lay on the Unifier's face.

"Get him!" Belmonte said evenly to no one in particular.

Blottingham turned abruptly and ran down the hall. He heard a series of explosions. They were not thundercracks this time. He fell down, torn by a force; but he felt no pain, only a kind of giddiness. His head was full of fireflies, his throat full of blood. He laughed inwardly. He rolled away into laughter.

No Cause for Panic

Proctor sweated under the bright lights. He could see almost nothing. He spoke to the cameras before him and to the microphones—those mounted on the lectern as well as the one that floated in the air just in front of his head.

He exhorted the people to calm down. The helium already flowed again, he told them. The thundercracks would continue for a while longer, but the danger was past. He urged the invisible masses to get off the beltways. He told them to return to their cubohomes. "All is well. Calm down." He repeated this message over and over again.

His voice resounded over millions of visisets, thousands of loudspeakers.

Proctor hoped that his forcibly calm tone would reassure them at last. He had been before the cameras for more than an hour now, interrupted only by infernal blasts of sound. Yet he persisted, despite a growing hoarseness and fatigue. From time to time Hondo Weinberger had appeared to stand between the cameras. Weinberger monitored the activities outside through banks of cameras. At each approach, Weinberger had turned his head from side to side to indicate that panic still persisted, that Proctor should continue to talk.

From the corner of his eye, Proctor now saw another figure between the cameras: Korn. Korn made an urgent gesture, repeated it twice.

Something had gone wrong, Proctor realized, but it didn't bother him too much. In such an operation something was bound to go wrong. Nevertheless, he brought his remarks to a close. He repeated his assertion that helium flowed. He called for calm.

Away from the circle of light, he mopped his face with a handkerchief.

"Ecofreak isn't responding," Korn said. "We have sent the message five times. With the code signal."

"Are you sure?"

A string of thundercracks cut off Korn's answer. Proctor looked at the people in the studio, pleased at their discipline. Of course they knew that the danger would pass. Unlike the mob. Proctor had not expected quite so much panic. Much time had also been lost in his very slow progress from the police confinement to Media Central. The beltway had been impassable, filled with trampled corpses.

The noise subsided. "I have bad news, Res," Korn said. "Helium Interdictions have been reported from *all* structures. It all started about an hour ago."

"Damn fools," Proctor said grimly.

He meant the Ecofreaks. He imagined the tribal yokels dancing and grinning in stupid glee, thinking they had outwitted him. They were even more careless than Proctor had assumed they were. He had expected them to do the obvious—test the parts carefully before making a move, a matter of a week or two. They had not done so. They had to be led by a madman or fool.

In a corner of the studio, BTA had installed a communications center. Proctor made for that area now, stepping over cables. He stopped before a keyboard console manned by a young man. From a corner of his eye, Proctor glanced toward a set of gauges mounted on wheeled consoles. BTA staff and a clump of studio people stood about and stared at the gauges.

Proctor didn't like that clump. He knew that the gauges showed zero gas flow. He lowered his voice as he spoke to the operator.

"Send this message to Ecofreak: 'This is Reston Proctor. You must immediately restore helium flow. The silcoplast components . . .'" He waited until the operator caught up. "'The silcoplast components are deliberately faulty and will not protect you from nuclear attack.'" He waited again. "'I shall order an attack on your settlements within fifteen minutes unless helium flow is restored to Ricardo and the Interdiction to the other structures is terminated. Acknowledge immediately.'"

Proctor turned questioningly to Korn. Korn nodded as if to say: Good. You have no other choice.

Proctor said to the operator: "Give them the pre-arranged code."

The man typed numbers.

The machine clacked rhythmically in readiness. There was no acknowledgment, only the noise.

"While you were speaking," Korn said, "Belmonte called to say: 'Mission accomplished.' They also got Blottingham. But most of the family had already fled."

"Sidney?" Proctor asked.

"Dead," Korn said.

Proctor nodded, then turned back to the machine. He noticed the clump of men near the gauges again. They looked expectantly at him. Proctor forced himself to smile, gave them an encouraging nod, only too aware that his face was a grimace of strain.

He allowed himself to think the unthinkable. What if there had been a communications failure? That could be disastrous. A simple breakdown in a component, unnoticed at their end. The fate of Union would then be decided by an electronic wafer. He turned to Korn.

"How do we communicate with General Martinez?"

"By radio," Korn answered.

"I have to have a talk with him," Proctor said. "But could you . . . ?" He gestured toward the people around the gauges. "I don't want half the world to listen in."

Korn moved toward the group.

Soon a series of thundercracks much longer and

much more intense than any before exploded the air in the studio. The entire place trembled and moved. The lights dimmed, went out, came on, dimmed, flickered. A camera broke loose from its moorings and sailed across the open space in the center. It careened as its small wheels hit loose cable on the floor and crashed against a wall, emitting sparks. Weinberger, his hands to his ears, stumbled toward Proctor, who half hung by the communications console. Korn had gone down on his knees. His head was just above the floor as he waited for the noise to stop.

Proctor thought: *We're safe. We're safe. Central Tower still has helium. It's nothing. Nothing at all.*

Beneath this conscious incantation, he perceived for the first time a kind of dark doubt. Could the plan misfire? Could the game be up? Could all the plans, deeds, acts of his life have led to a strange end in a visi studio? To die in a man-made storm of his own devising? The final practical joke?

The noise stopped at last and Proctor gratefully submerged his thoughts in action. He moved to a radio and gestured to the operator. The man had lain on the floor, trying to hide from the thunder. Korn no longer had to disperse the observing group. The people had scattered all about the studio.

"Get me Martinez," Proctor said.

The operator's voice quavered, his face was white, sweat stood on his brow.

". . . Martinez here." The voice had a cheerful sound.

Proctor took the microphone. "This is Proctor. Are you all right, Richard? *Where* are you?"

"I'm fine, Res. I'm in a command ship. We are about ten klicks off shore."

"Are you up on the latest developments?"

"Are you kidding?" Martinez cried. "I'm up to my ears in messages from the area commands. Helium Interdictions. The people in the regions are agitated but not panicked yet, of course. Was this part of the plan?"

Proctor ignored the question. "Richard, can you explode a bomb some kilometers from Wellhead? In a

safe area? By safe I mean away from the pipeline facilities. Quickly? I have to send these birds a message
they'll understand."

There was silence from the other side. Only static
hissed. Then Martinez came on. "It can be done, Res,
but it'll take time."

"Why? Why time?"

"We overlooked something, Res. The bloody heat.
Our automatic equipment is ruined, fused. We have
to go to manual firing, which means time. I'm out here
supervising the diving operations. We're sending people down to the undersea bunkers."

God! Proctor said: "Why don't you order a firing
from Husten?"

"That'll take time too. This is a missile launch,
Res, but Husten won't do it on my orders alone. They
think I'm just a duty officer. They'll want verifaxed orders from Harvanth, countersigned by Unsler."

Who'll never sign anything ever again, Proctor
thought. "How *much* time?" he asked.

"Two hours, three hours, maybe longer."

Silence. *Oh, God!* Proctor thought. Aloud he said:
"The towers will be down by then."

"I'm sorry," Martinez said. "I just can't act any
faster."

The long narrow face, the white sunburst of hair,
and gold-rimmed glasses of Weinberger approached.
Weinberger started to speak, but Proctor silenced
him with a raised hand.

"Richard, get ready to fire as soon as you are able.
I don't know what'll happen. I have to evacuate Ri-
cardo. You get ready and wait for orders. But if a
tower goes, you are on your own. Obliterate the swine.
Try to get help from the regions. Tell them everything.
It's too late for anything else."

Proctor handed the speaker to the operator and
turned to Weinberger.

Weinberger burst out: "Res, my God, the intertower beltway broke in two places. More than a million must have fallen. Sucked out by the vacuum. Oh,

Jesus, Res. You've *got* to get back on again. Will this never stop? Have we got the gas yet?"

Proctor slowly shook his head. No gas. No helium.

"I'll speak to them," he said.

He took a path toward the podium up ahead. He formulated words as he went.

People of Ricardo. Mechanical difficulties make it look as if there will be a short delay before helium flow can be restored to normal. In the interests of safety . . . evacuate in an orderly . . . No cause for panic . . . no cause for panic . . .

Hunting the Other

Bono had been in the darkness of his tunnel so long, he did not realize that day had fled and that darkness had descended outside. Down there, hypnotized by the rhythm of his digging, he'd lost track of time.

He crawled out of the tunnel slowly with a wiggling motion, feet first, scooching up with the action of his elbows and knees. The smell of clay was strong about him. At first he had liked the smell. But after three days, four days, five days of digging—he had no real sense of time—he had learned to hate it. It was thick, hard, red clay. It clung to his hands, clothing, beard, hair. He was a red man, red all over, a clay man, a man afire with the earth.

His slow motion brought him to the surface. His feet hit the bale of hay he had placed over the opening to hide it. He pushed it aside and immediately heard the hateful sounds coming over the loudspeaker mounted high in the gable of the barn that was his prison—so high that he could not reach it to destroy it.

Bono climbed all the way out and stood up. It was dark in the barn. The sun had still been up the last time he had taken a rest. He took strips of clay-soiled cloth from his pockets, torn from his underwear, and he stuffed them slowly, methodically into his ears.

236

The plugs diminished the sound somewhat, but not entirely. He knew that the air about him vibrated with the tape recording of Regina's treachery. The noises of their fornication penetrated the cloth and touched his eardrums ever so slightly. He heard the grunts and groans and the rhythmic beat of bodies on the bed. He heard the smacks and slaps and the agonized breathing. He heard Tack mumble incoherently as he reached out for peaks of passion; and he heard Regina cry out when the dam of her resistance broke and she stumbled into orgasm. And he heard their breathing subside again. Over and over. The tape was spliced so that a series of strivings followed each other, and when the string was completed, it started all over again. The tape ran and ran. Day and night. Bono heard it in his sleep. Only in the tunnel could he find peace.

He stood for a moment in the middle of the barn. He had no idea of the mad picture he made: a red apparition with crazed eyes; a beard matted with matter, its forks fused into a single clump of hair and mud; ears extruding strips of cloth that had been white; arms slackly suspended; fingers half curled; nails broken and black. He was alone and knew himself unobserved. He was a soul, now, his physical being immaterial. But his soul too was on fire with a red burning.

He undid his fly and urinated where he stood. The pure physical act almost brought him back to sanity, but the touch of his genitals reminded him of a wondrous night in a cabin high in the Allagains—and its ruin, heard now muted but for that reason so much more intensely.

An overwhelming rage gripped Bono.

"God damn you, bitch!" he yelled with total abandon. "God damn you, God damn you to hell. God damn you, God damn you."

Screaming this at the top of his lungs, he went down on his knees and pounded the hay-littered ground with a balled fist, putting all of his strength into the act.

Then he sagged down into a sitting position, his fury momentarily spent.

God, he was tired. His back, legs, arms—they all ached from the endless labor of digging. He longed to sleep but knew that he would go back to digging again after a brief respite. By morning, if his calculations were correct, he would be far enough from the barn, on the side which the guard avoided in the morning sun, to emerge unobserved. And then!

And then he would be the incarnation of vengeance. He would be pure hatred stalking. He would be Evil with legs and arms and trunk and head and hands—hands that would seek her neck, hands that would castrate her lover as if he were a sheep.

Bono brooded over fantasies of revenge so vivid that he momentarily forgot the tape recording. He sat for a while. Then, groaning shamelessly, he rose. He glanced with longing up to the hayloft where, behind the sound-cushioning bales, he had snatched what little sleep he allowed himself. But not tonight. He didn't even dare to lay down. He might go off and not awaken until morning. A drink of water. A bit of bread left him from his single meal. Then he would go down again.

He walked wearily toward the door where the empty bowl and the pitcher stood. He bent down for the pitcher, aware of muscles in his back he hadn't known he had. Near the pitcher he noticed something he did not remember seeing before. Something white. He picked it up. A piece of scriptoplast? Huh? He unfolded it and dimly saw writing, but it was too dark to read.

Bono moved closer to the barn door, to a spot where through a crack between door and wall a little of the moonlit night came into the interior. As he did so he touched the door. With a painful screech of unoiled hinges, the door opened.

Bono stared in surprise. He expected to hear the cry of the guard. Instead there was only silence out there: the silence of nature, filled with a rasp of cricks. He stepped out and immediately saw the guard. The man appeared dead. Strangled?

In the moonlight Bono read the note. It said: "Remember who helped you. F."

F? Fannin. Yes. Had to be Fannin.

Bono puzzled over the slip. In three days, four days, whatever the time had been, he had almost forgotten that the world had people other than himself, Regina, and Tack. Fannin. His mind went back to that conversation in the helicopter. Something must have happened. Fannin had decided to secure himself a friend.

Far away Bono heard thunderclaps. He looked up at the sky. Odd. The night was unusually clear. He could see a trillion stars. Yes, there it was, the dusty wash of the Milky Way. He had thought to gather it up for Her once—long ago. Thunder? Strange.

Then Bono suddenly ducked and sought the shadow of the barn wall. He had not seen anything. He simply remembered that he was an escaped prisoner; another guard might be on his way now to relieve this fellow. Bono glanced to the side and examined the guard closely. Here was another odd thing: This man should have been relieved some time ago. He lay there stiffly, his balled fists high up, tugging at something around his neck. Strangled. Marks in the mud showed struggle. A groove in the clay revealed the final spasms of the man as he had kicked out helplessly, trying to free himself. Fannin's handiwork?

Bono pulled his earplugs out. He heard the tape again. He went in search of the transmitting source and found the recorder on a crate against the side of the barn. He kicked the crate. The sound died.

So shall THEY *die!*

Thunder in the distance, direction Ricardo. Storm over the Atlantic?

To Bono's left, high on the ridge, pine trees offered the shelter of deeper darkness. He ran across the clearing and up into the trees, and in their shadow half walked, half ran toward the camp. When he arrived on a level with the place, he crouched and looked down. The camp was dark, deserted.

He was puzzling over this state of affairs when he heard thunder again and this time clearly saw what appeared to be fireworks against the eastern sky. In a flash he understood everything. Why Fannin had acted, why the guard had not been relieved, why the camp lay so dark and empty, why it thundered without clouds.

The Great Change had come.

As it was written, so it was. The Bastions of the Whore were crumbling.

He ran down into the camp.

Bono sought two things: a weapon and a means of transport. He knew where Tack was. Tack would want a ringside seat at the spectacle. And where Tack was, there would be his structure whore.

Like a man possessed, Bono ran from tent to tent. He picked up a hunting knife but threw it away when he found an ax. He searched further, wishing for a pistol or rifle, something that could kill at a distance. He would have to get through Tack's guards before he could use this ax on Tack, a crude but effective emasculator.

In the communications tent he saw coils of plast on the floor, exuded by one of the machines. Stopping, he found a light. In its gleam he read the messages—a monotonous string of demands and threats from Proctor, who promised to launch hydrogen through the air.

Bono laughed. Death, destruction, obliteration, mayhem, pandemonium, oblivion, doom.

Yes, sir. Let the world go up with a bang.

He ran on.

At last, in a tent, hung on a pole, he saw a crossbow and stopped dead in his tracks. The weapon seemed to invite him to take it. It hung there, dark, oiled, menacing—as if placed by the Evil One for His obedient servant Bono. Bono took it down lovingly. He cranked back the bowstring. The weapon was in excellent shape. The wire was taut. It gleamed. He twanged it with a finger. It sang. He had what he wanted; no weapon suited his fancy better. A full belt of murderous, blunt bolts hung next to the bow. Bono girded himself with it.

Outside he soon found a clump of ponies, two or three animals. He had a long ride ahead, and he wanted spares. He didn't bother to saddle the beasts. His fierce will alone would guide them without bridles. Moments later he was off.

After an hour, the rhythm of motion became hypnotic. The ponies steamed. Sweat lather penetrated Bono's tunic, dissolved the red clay, and discolored the horses' flanks. The beasts snorted. Up ahead light flashed and thunder sounded.

Ricardo appeared over the horizon. It was a brightness. It threw off showers of sparks, each spark a giant piece of plastosteel brought to brilliant incandescence by pressure—but at this distance only a firefly.

Bono recalled another ride, an evening ride; he had been gloomy then and oppressed by a childhood memory. Then, later, he had thrown off all that and had stepped out, a free man, in love with an indescribable dream of an unapproachable girl who had let him approach after all and then treacherously left him for the bed of another until the story would end with her body entombed. He meant to dig her in with hands already used to tearing clay. Yes.

He exulted with a joy of despair.

Oh, God! Oh wonderful, oh beautiful, oh tremendous, passionate Hate! How he longed to destroy, tear, rend, demolish, crush, sever, rip!

Yes, yes. He would bathe himself in gushes of blood. He'd breathe in the hot, steaming smell. He would smear himself with blood. He'd wash in life destroyed.

Crack! Fireworks! *Crack, crack, crack!* A flower of fire. Higher, higher! Explode! Disintegrate!

Bono stopped his pony, rolled off, then mounted another.

"Heeeey" he cried, and they were off again.

In the third hour he saw Ricardo clearly. Two of the five towers were mere stumps of blazing fire and smoke. Central Tower had begun to sag as well, and the others were in states of disintegration. The thunder was now a continuous noise and the fireworks a permanent feature of the sky—one burst renewed by another before it could die.

In the brightness and noise, Bono did not notice another, much less spectacular but, from his perspective, much more interesting phenomenon until he was nearly upon it. Several small Union airships maneuvered directly ahead of him. Bono saw the broken light lines of tracer bullets aimed at the ground. Tiny explosions threw up dirt. But in contrast to the overwhelming noise of Ricardo's break-up, these lesser sounds were inaudible.

When he noticed the action, Bono froze. He realized that he had reached Tack's temporary camp. He realized also that the airships, no doubt bound outward to hit Hinterland targets, had surprised Tack and now wrought destruction.

Bono shook an impotent fist toward the ships. *"They're mine!"* he screamed. He could barely hear his own voice. He spurred his pony ahead.

Then the airships formed up and came his way, their work done.

Bono rolled off his pony and sought cover in the high mutagrass. The ships went over him—long, lighted cylindrical tubes.

He let them get away before he rose. The ponies had fled. The noise, the lights, the grav-vibes of the ships had chased them off now that Bono's iron will no longer imposed itself on them. He continued on foot. He cranked back his bowstring again and put a bolt into the oiled slot. But he was sure he didn't need a weapon anymore.

The temporary campsite was a place of carnage. Bodies lay all around, dead, dying. He moved from man to man. They lay in a rough circle. They had run out from a center to escape the ships. One by one Bono examined their faces. He knew most of the men. Some he did not recognize because they no longer had heads or faces. Among those still alive was Franco Dart. He lay on his face, and when Bono turned him with a boot, the old man's eyes stared up in terror.

"I didn't mean it, I didn't want to do it, Barney. I swear. I meant no harm. Don't! Don't you dare. Go away. I swear it—"

His voice abruptly ceased.

Bono went on.

He found Tack. Dead. For a long moment Bono stood over the blond giant. Tack was unmarked, but from his posture Bono inferred that Tack had broken his neck in a fall caused by an explosion. Or perhaps his spine had been cracked by shrapnel. The eyes were open and stared up. Empty eyes. They showed no emotion. Bono let the ax slip out of his fingers and went on.

After some searching he found the harem girls. He inspected each one carefully by the light of Ricardo's disintegration. He did not find Regina, but he knew that she was here, somewhere. He sensed it. The deep conviction excited him. Inadvertently he experienced something akin to lust: the certainty of satisfaction, the breathlessness of approaching passion.

He carried out his search with bent head. All the people lay on the ground, and so his eyes were on the ground, seeking depressions in the tall mutagrass. At one point, however, he raised his head, thinking he saw a carry bird land, attracted by death. But his attention had been attracted by another kind of motion, a motion on the periphery of the ring of bodies—in fact beyond the ring. A figure. It came toward the ring. It was a white figure. He knew it was she.

Bono let out a murderous yell and ran toward her, holding the crossbow at the ready. He was a hunter. She was his prey. This was the Plain of Baez. And a memory of a dream in a tub, a dream of hares and stinking gel.

She ran in fright at his approach. He changed direction to intercept her. She zigged, like a hare. He zagged to prevent her escape.

Bono knew he was near enough to kill her with a well-placed bolt, but he meant to confront her first. He meant to tell her who it was that stalked her, why it was that she must die and bathe his face and hands with blood.

She wore a dress of some sort, a harem gown. Light blue or white. Maoling silk. The sparks of exploding Ricardo were caught in its sheen. The dress made it difficult for her to run, and she stumbled and fell. He stopped before her. She half crouched, half kneeled; her eyes looked at him. They were calm, open, strange. Then he saw recognition.

"Mycal," she cried, and she rose up—tall like a she-hare.

Any second she would leap to the side. Oh, yes. Now was the moment to steel the heart against that onslaught of cloying pity. He raised the bow and took her in his sight. He aimed for her left nipple, a visible target even in the dark.

"Mycal," she cried, "for God's sake, I love you." She held out a hand toward him.

He knew the rules of the hunt. No hesitation. Let the index finger firmly curl around the trigger like a man's arm around a woman's waist. Let it squeeze calmly, without undue hurry. But though he knew the rules, Bono hesitated. Her tone stopped him. She had cried out her lie with total sincerity— and in a voice so changed and strange it did not sound like the Regina he knew. He took his eyes from the sight, from her nipple, and glanced up at her face. No harm in that. After all, she was a woman, not a hare. She couldn't leap out of his reach.

Her face.

It had a spot of sooty dirt beneath one eye. Her

face was calm, serene, yet filled with a touching fondness. Bono felt a weakness in his stomach. No! He jerked his eye back to the sight, but it was too late. A question had formed in his mind, and he knew he would have to ask it.

He looked up again.

"But why?" he cried. They were close to each other, but he had to shout in the constant noise. "Why did you do it?"

"I had to," she called back. "There was no other way. It was an assignment."

Bono stared at her. Slowly the bow dropped down. Should he ask her another question?

He still struggled inwardly when the world suddenly filled with light brighter than midday. It was a flash so intense that it blinded him. *Staging station,* came the unsolicited thought. Hydrogen. Then the blast sounded. A fierce air whistled past, sharp enough to cut. He dropped the bow and groped forward. Her seeking fingers encountered his. They rushed together and clung to each other as the shock wave picked them up and swept them away.

Encounter

The wind blew relentlessly, laden with dust.

Sometimes it let up a little, and then particles of matter glinted in the atmosphere and the landscape could be glimpsed—rolling country, lines of trees. At such times the column stopped with a collective sigh. People shook dust from their garments and scraped dust from their faces, rubbed dust from their hands.

Miri did as the others. She walked in the center of the spearhead group, surrounded by women, children, and old men. Up front and bringing up the rear were young men, a kind of protective guard. They were laughing and joking, happy to be freed for some hours from the burden of carrying gear. Horses! If only they had horses.

Miri removed the cloth that protected her mouth

and nose, wondering about the wind and what it carried. Dusted earth, yes. And tiny seeds of mutagrass. Maybe that. And broken structures? Surely that too. And particles of radioactive stuff? Yes, a little. Flower seeds? Certainly. The books had foretold that.

You're strong and resistant, she thought, addressing her child. *The radiation can't harm you, baby. You're safe and sound in Mami. Don't you worry, little one. You'll grow up healthy. The world will be full of flowers. The wind will settle. The dust will rain out of the sky. You just sleep and smile.*

A man on horseback approached from the distance, and though his face was obscured by cloth, she recognized Frenchy. He came near, embraced her lightly. By now she had accustomed herself to his strong odor. Ah, for a bath!

"Everything all right?"

She nodded, smiling. "We're fine," she said, meaning the baby and herself, but he didn't catch her meaning.

Excitement danced in his eyes. "I'm going on ahead," he said. "One of our explorers has sighted another column. A large one, from what he reports."

She blew him a kiss as he remounted, happy with him. Frenchy forever sought more people, delighted each time he found some little pocket, be it tribal or structure. She watched him ride up a rise, the horse kicking dust. Then the wind began to gust again, and she covered her face. The column slowly got into motion again, going deeper into the interior.

French rode forward at a trot. Mounted on the pony, his head was above the heavy sand and silt carried by the wind, but the finer particles were just as bad.

That wind! It was the perennial subject of thought and conversation. He pondered its causes again and concluded, as he always did, that it must have been caused by the explosion of Union's total arsenal over Hinterland. Shock waves, in combination, still traveled around the globe with undiminished fury. There seemed nothing much left of either structure or Hinterland, and if this dust kept obscuring the sun, there would be desert here in a few years.

He rode on, trying to spy ahead through narrowed eyes.

After a while, just above the shoulder-high rush of silt, he saw figures moving. This was what the explorer had glimpsed, a long line of people, bundled up much like the folk of the exodus. And animals! By God, French thought he saw a herd of animals revealed and then veiled again by a windgust. And the animals had not been loaded.

He yelled out, but in the wind noise he couldn't have been heard. He dug heels into the horse's flanks and made toward the tip of the column.

As he came nearer, he noticed that a large group of people—yes, real people!—had settled down in the shelter of a small, low building. Others were still coming, and behind the first herd of horses he saw another.

French yelled again, excited by the horses as much as the people. Two people detached themselves from the squatting clumps and came forward a ways—a man and a woman, faces thickly banded. French slid from his saddle and ran toward them.

"Hello," he cried. "More survivors. Am I happy to see you people. Where—?"

He stopped abruptly, shocked by recognition. The man was Bono, the woman Regina. French saw that Bono also recognized him.

And then, impelled by some kind of elemental gladness, the two men embraced like long-lost friends. They disengaged and laughed, slapped each other on the shoulders, laughed again.

"You!" they cried, pointing at each other, and they laughed again.

Later all four were settled in the shelter of the little hut, which turned out to be a compressor station. Once it had pumped helium toward Ricardo. Miri and Regina sat to one side, discussing the problems of maternity, Cult business, and the burdens of being divine.

The men sat on the other side and compared plans. Bono and his column were headed south; French and the exodus, west. Both had gathered fifty or sixty thousand. A census in this wind was impossible. Stragglers kept joining. After a long set of preliminaries, Bono finally broached the subject very delicately, inquiring gently about the stores the exodus carried, and what items were in surplus and which in short supply. French replied evasively and turned the question around. "Oh, this and that," Bono said. Knives were in short supply, and now that the column lived on cricks, knives were important, but they were doing well enough without them. "Hmmm," French said. Exodus just happened to have a goodly supply of cutting tools of all kinds. Matter of fact, he had almost abandoned several tons of tools because of a shortage of transport. Of course the exodus managed well enough without horses, but . . .

"Perhaps we could do some business," Bono said.

"Perhaps we could," French answered.